RED CITY REAPER

Book 0 - Dead in Red City*
Book 1 - A Shot For Death - March 26, 2024
Book 1.5 - Death Uncaged - March 21, 2024
Book 2 - Death Orders a Double - July 23, 2024
Book 3 - Death With A Twist* - October 8, 2024
Book 4 - Death On The Rocks* - February 25, 2025
Book 5 - A Fifth Of Death*
Book 6 - A Dash Of Death*
Book 7 - A Chaser of Death*
Book 8 - A Nightcap of Death *

*Forthcoming
Titles and release dates may be subject to change.

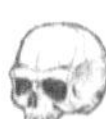

DEATH ORDERS A DOUBLE

AN EXILED GRIM REAPER URBAN FANTASY NOVEL

RED CITY REAPER
BOOK 2

C. THOMAS LAFOLLETTE

DEATH ORDERS A DOUBLE
C. Thomas Lafollette

A Broken World Publication
13820 NE Airport Way
Suite #K395495
Portland, OR 97251-1158
Death Orders A Double
Copyright © 2024 by C. Thomas Lafollette
ISBN 978-1-960766-14-4
(ebook);
ISBN 978-1-960766-15-1
(paperback)

Cover Design: Ravven
Editing & Proofreading: Amy Cissell

CONTENTS

AUTHOR'S NOTE

This story contains words and phrases in Louisiana Creole and Haitian Kreyòl. They are spelled according to Creole and Kreyòl standards.

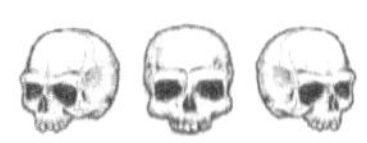

PROLOGUE
IVAR

Ivar peered out from behind the steel bars meant to block the tunnel entrance into the underworld of Red City. Things like locks and social mores meant nothing to a man with bolt cutters. They meant even less to a man who had keys obtained from corrupt officials. He checked the time. Still early.

He'd returned to Red City the evening before, crashing in one of the Black Sun Motorcycle Club's safe houses. Other than the dust, no one had used the place since before the fire at Valhalla. Every time he thought about the ashes of their bar and clubhouse, he was forced to tamp down his burning rage, banking it away to use against those who'd nearly destroyed his club. When he found the girl, he wouldn't hold back.

He'd urged Ulf to hire someone to take out the mark, preferably one of the high-end killers for hire the club liked to use when they didn't want to expend their own blood and sweat to get a job done. But Ulf had gotten greedy and wanted to kill two birds with one stone.

But the stone had betrayed them, and the mark had killed most of the club and burned down their clubhouse. Fortunately for him, the regional bosses rightly blamed Ulf for the events leading to the destruction of the club. Though they'd tasked Ivar with fixing the problem. If he did, he'd get to reform the local club as the new president. There was a lot of money to be made in a city like Red City, assuming he could reestablish the club's contacts after such a boneheaded failure to complete their contract. That was one of the reasons he'd decided to lie low and keep out of sight. He didn't want his contacts seeing him until he was ready to present himself from a position of power.

Gritting his teeth, he dropped the spent cigarette and snuffed it out under the sole of his motorcycle boot. A shift in the wind brought a whiff of putrid garbage to his sensitive nose. He couldn't decide if it was better than the occasional stench of sewage drifting through the tunnels toward the gate where he now stood.

He pinched his nose briefly. "This fucking city stinks."

Pulling out the pack, he tapped it several times against the palm of his hand, then shot out a single stick on the upswing, clamping down on the pack before it flew out completely. He grasped it with his lips and returned the mostly spent pack of unfiltered cigarettes to his pocket. He'd have to find a place in this part of town that sold his brand. The unfiltereds were getting harder to find. Sighing, he shook his head. He didn't want to have to start rolling his own. With the flick of his thumb, his Zippo sparked to life as he moved the flame to the tip of the cigarette.

He'd kill for a couple belts of whiskey to help settle his nerves, but he didn't want to be seen in some random bar. He'd have to find a liquor store that stayed open late and pick up a bottle after his meeting.

Checking the time again on his wristwatch, he took a long drag and narrowed his eyes as he listened into the distance.

Like clockwork—assuming it was who he was meeting with—a car stopped nearby and someone stepped out, the whump of their closing door announcing their approach. Ivar took the cigarette between his thumb and forefinger and flicked it away with his middle finger, sending it tumbling into the darkness as little glowing pieces fell away from the cherry like dying stars.

He pushed open the steel-barred door and stepped into the

shadows of the underside of the overpass. He liked Kondor. She always arrived on time and had never failed to complete her assigned task. Normally, he wouldn't trust something this important to a woman, but Kondor had come to the club with a well-earned reputation. If you paid her to kill someone, they died.

An average-looking woman—both height and weight—strode confidently toward him. Her shoulder-length blonde hair swayed around her pale white face. About her, there was always a whiff of magic. It was said that no client or victim had ever seen her true face.

She stopped about ten feet away and nodded shallowly, briefly revealing her face, her lips drawn into a neutral line. "Ivar. It's been a while."

"Kondor."

"So…" She patted her pockets briefly. "Can I have one of those unfiltereds?"

Stepping forward, he pulled out the pack and slipped one out of the opening.

She took it and stepped back, quickly lighting it before releasing a puff of smoke. "I hear you're out of a home."

He ground his teeth together before forcing his mouth open to answer. "Yup."

"My condolences on Ulf's death." Her expression remained neutral, almost disdainfully so.

A growl rumbled from this throat. "If it wasn't for Ulf, we wouldn't be in this mess. If he'd hired you in the first place, he'd still be alive." He spat onto the ground. "Stupid fucker."

"I guess that makes you the president now." Kondor smirked, raising an eyebrow.

He scoffed. "President of what? Piles of bones and swirling ashes?"

She gave a half-hearted shrug—the sign she had reached the end of her interest in the small talk.

He inhaled sharply through his nose. "I have a job for you."

"I'd assumed as much. You want me to take out the people who burned your club down?"

"I only need one person killed. I can handle the little stoolie myself." He'd enjoy it, too.

The girl would pay for betraying them. As soon as he found her. It wasn't easy to find someone without feet on the street, and it was even harder when the someone was a no-one without much of a trackable presence.

He pulled out an envelope with the details and a picture of the mother fucker who'd murdered his brothers and burned down his clubhouse. "This is the piece of shit I want you to kill."

She popped open the envelope and pulled out the picture. "This the guy that torched it?"

He nodded tersely.

"Double the rate."

His eyebrows shot up. He was normally better at controlling his expression, but… "What? We have an agreed upon rate."

"If this guy took all you guys out and came out alive, this requires hazard pay. And you better tell me anything important I need to know now, or the price will go up. Or I'll keep the money and put the bullet in your brain."

He growled but stepped back, forcing himself to calm down. He knew her practices. He knew her procedures. With a sigh, he ran a hand through his greasy, unwashed hair and told her how the mark had burned down the club. "And one other thing. The bullets I made don't seem to work on him."

Her eyes widened. He wasn't sure he'd ever seen her display that much emotion before.

"The ones that we've both tested and used many times? The ones that always work on supes?"

He nodded.

A clench of the jaw was her only reaction. "You're lucky I don't triple the rate, but your club has sent a lot of business my way. Consider the deal struck as soon as you wire the money into my offshore account."

ONE

DAX

Dax peered at his watch surreptitiously for the third time in an hour. Normally, Tomi would be working the night shift with Little Suzie, but he'd asked for it off. In truth, Dax didn't need to even be there. The rough rain had kept even the regulars home. Usually it didn't rain this hard in the middle of the spring.

He was glad he'd taken the bus this morning. The ride would have been very unpleasant on his motorcycle. Plus the check he'd made upstairs on the roof had proved it was keeping out the weather well enough to hold them until they could get someone in to give it an in-depth look-see. Overall, it wasn't too bad of a day. Now if only Tomi was having a similarly good evening…

"Don't worry about Tomi," Little Suzie said, stopping to lean up against the bar. "He'll be fine."

Today, the short Black woman had her natural hair in two puffs. She wore holey black jeans and a black band T-shirt with the collar cut out and the waist hem removed to reveal her midriff. Her thick-soled Docs elevated her a couple inches, though she was still a few short of average.

"I know. It's just been a while since he's had a date." It had been a couple months since the night Dax'd burned down the biker bar, and he was glad things seemed to be returning to normal. Though, the extra work of getting the restaurant ready for Adele to open filled a lot of the spare time he used to have. Soon, they'd be able to at least open for to-go business while they finished the more decor-oriented work.

Little Suzie snorted. "You're not kidding." Tipping her head toward the can of beer in front of him, she asked, "Need another?"

He lifted the can and threw back the last warm swallow. "Gack. Yeah."

Laughing, Suzie cleared the empty and grabbed a full one from the undercounter cooler, popping the top and setting it in front of him.

A skinny white man in ratty, faded black jeans and a matching denim jacket sauntered a bit unsteadily to the bar. "Suzie, my love, when will you agree to go out on a date with me?"

Suzie glanced toward Dax, rolling her eyes. "When you stop being a straight white man, Chet."

"Alas, our love will go unrequited then…"

" 'Our'? You got a mouse in your pocket or something?"

Straightening up on his bar stool, Dax swiveled around and put on his grumpy face, which in all fairness was almost always his normal expression. "Chet. You know you're not supposed to hit on the bartenders. If I have to warn you again, I'll eighty-six you."

Chet leaned toward Dax. "But—"

"Unless the next words out of your mouth are an apology and a promise to remember the rules, I'll add you to the wall of assholes right now."

Chet, head hanging, turned toward Suzie and mumbled something.

"I'm sorry. I didn't hear you." Suzie leaned closer, her hand cupped around her ear and an eyebrow raised.

"I apologize, Suzie. I won't let it happen again."

Narrowing her eyes, Suzie nodded once, her shoulders relaxing a little. "What can I get you?"

"A shot of whiskey." He set a ten-dollar bill on the bar.

Pulling a rocks glass from the stack, she plunked it down on the bar top a bit more forcefully than was necessary and grabbed the whiskey from the trough where the other well liquors were stored. She kept a careful eye on the pour, making sure Chet didn't get a drop more than what was considered a shot.

Chet almost made like he was going to complain then caught the thunder in Suzie's eyes and thought better of it, slamming the shot back.

Suzie snatched the ten. "Thanks for the tip."

Sighing, Chet wound his way through the bar and left.

"Thanks for having my back, Dax," Suzie said, clearing the glass from the bar.

Dax shrugged. "Everyone deserves a harassment free work environment. If he does it again, take his picture and add it to the wall of assholes."

Tomi had found an old polaroid for the purpose not long after they opened the bar. When it broke, they replaced it with one of the new versions that were becoming popular. Once a patron made the wall of assholes, they rarely got off of it. It was a far more reliable justice system than the courts of Red City.

"If he argues or tries to give you shit, bring out the judge." Dax smirked and winked at Suzie before taking a deep drink of the cold, cheap beer.

The judge was a two-thirds sized wooden baseball bat they kept behind the bar to handle anyone who decided they'd had more booze and balls than brains. They'd never had to use it in earnest—usually a mere appearance was enough to get the idea across.

The door to the bar opened, and Dax swiveled on the bar stool, sagging in disappointment when a white man in his late twenties or early thirties wearing a gray suit walked into the bar. The few regulars who had ventured out looked up from their conversations to check out the stranger. With the talk fading, the Pixies track on the jukebox sounded louder.

Men in suits, in Dax's experience, meant trouble. But city officials and inspectors rarely were out and about at this time of night. If it was a liquor agent running an ID sting, they typically sent someone who looked barely legal and tried to dress appropriately to the venue. Dax narrowed his eyes as the man approached the bar, calmly weaving his way through the tables.

They still hadn't seen hide nor hair from the bikers. He expected retaliation at some point; too many had escaped. Though sending a man in undercover in a business suit seemed a bit out of character.

The man stepped up to the bar, staring at the wall of liquor bottles on the back bar. Absentmindedly, he hoisted himself onto a stool. "Damn, you've got a good whiskey selection. I'd like some of the Dickel Bottled in Bond, please."

"I'm going to need to see your ID first," Suzie asked.

She must have been getting the same vibe Dax had. The man raised an eyebrow but grinned politely, pulling his wallet out of the inside breast pocket of his suit jacket, and handed it to Suzie. She looked at it thoroughly under the light of the small lamp they kept behind the bar, even going so far as to take out the UV flashlight they kept for checking seals and larger denomination bills to make sure someone wasn't trying to float a counterfeit by them.

Making a small noise to indicate it surprisingly checked out, she handed the ID back to the man. "Dickel Bottled in Bond it is. Rocks?"

"Neat, please."

She reached for one of the scratched-up rocks glasses, like the one she'd just served Chet in. The man winced, his eyes flicking to the nice dram glasses they kept for higher quality whiskeys. She snickered and grabbed a dram glass for him.

He pulled a credit card from his wallet and set it on the bar. "Can you leave it open?"

Suzie nodded and grabbed the card, clipping it up by the register. The man took a sip and sighed happily, going back for another drink.

"Rough day?" Suzie leaned against the bar, propping herself up on one elbow.

"I just finished work."

"Yikes. I'm guessing you weren't working the swing shift at the old suit factory."

The man chuckled. "No. Accounting. Quarterly taxes are due

soon. Didn't want to go home to unpacked boxes, so I thought I'd see what this place was about."

Dax eyed the man. He seemed to check out, though he wasn't sure why a man in a suit would pick their dive for his drinking needs. He thought about taking a peek at his life thread to see if he could glean anything from it but decided against it. The man appeared to be just a whiskey lover in a suit looking for a drink.

The only suspicious thing about him was Dax's heightened paranoia after the recent shootings. Unless the man did something more questionable than existing in a suit, there was no reason to elevate him to the level of a potential danger and snoop in his thread.

"Well, welcome to the House of the Rising Sun Pub and Teahouse. I'm Little Suzie."

He nodded and extended a hand. "I'm Geoffrey." He leaned a little closer after Suzie shook his hand. "Is this really a tearoom?"

Suzie snorted, her eyes flicking toward Dax. "In the back room, though it's not open this time of night."

"Hmm," Geoffrey sat back on his bar stool and contemplated his whiskey, the conversation apparently exhausted.

Everyone was welcome at the Rising Sun, but they didn't often get someone in a suit who chose to stay as a patron. Geoffrey seemed comfortable, ordered a good whiskey, and was polite. They could do far worse than a regular customer of his type. But Dax would keep an eye on him until they were certain he wasn't affiliated with anyone that wanted Dax dead.

The sound of the door opening drew Dax's attention away from the new customer, but before he could swivel around to see who it might be, Suzie called out, "Hey, Cuz!"

Dax relaxed. Tomi had arrived—Dax checked his watch—at a time that meant nothing to him. He didn't know if this time indicated a good date or a bad date. He'd never even been on one. It seemed a silly human pursuit and meant nothing to him.

"So... How'd it go?" Suzie waggled her eyebrows at her cousin.

Tomi, a heavy Black guy, wore his customary black T-shirt and jeans, though they were new and in good condition. He had a black beanie pulled over his short, black, curly hair. Saying nothing, he pulled his large bulk up onto the barstool between Dax and Geoffrey, resting his elbows on the wooden bar top. With a groan, his head sank onto his hands.

"Not well, I take it?" Dax asked quietly.

"I don't know," Tomi replied, leaving his head in his hands.

Suzie reached out and patted his forearm. "Sorry, Cuz. Can I get you a little liquid condolence?"

"Give me a tallboy of Rainier." Tomi lifted his head when she slid the beer in front of him.

Dax spun to face Tomi, resting his elbow on the bar. "What happened?"

"I'm not sure. We seemed to be doing good. The conversation was flowing. I made her laugh a few times. I thought I was a shoo-in for at least a second date. Then…" He huffed and shook his head. "Then she asked me my star sign."

Suzie snorted. "Seriously? 'Hey, baby, what's your sign?'"

Tomi nodded, taking a deep drink from the can. "I didn't think anything of it, so I told her. Then it was like Antarctica in there. I could see her interest waning until she called the date, saying she had a meeting in the morning she needed to get rest for."

"Did she say why?" Suzie asked.

"No. I was so thrown off by the sudden change, I couldn't get my mind working fast enough. All I know is she asked me my sign, then couldn't get out of there fast enough."

"That sucks, Cuz. If that's all it took, then she wasn't a good fit for you." Suzie patted his hand then walked to the end of the bar to help a customer.

"She's right." Dax reached over and squeezed his friend's shoulder. "You're the best guy I know. If she couldn't see that, then she's a fool."

"Thanks, boss."

Dax felt bad for his friend, but at least it had only been a first date. It'd been a while, but the last time Tomi dated anyone, he'd gotten attached after a few dates and been sad for a while when it didn't work out. He'd probably get over this quickly. But what did he know?

Tomi shoved the empty can toward Suzie.

"Want another?" she asked.

"No, I'm going to head out. I have to help Mama in the morning." He shoved the heels of his palms into his eyes and sighed.

Dax signaled to put the beer on his tab, not that any of his employees ever paid full price.

Standing up, Tomi waved then headed out the door without saying anything.

"I hope he's not too upset," Dax said.

Suzie shrugged. "He's always been a bit of a romantic, so he can take it a hard when things don't go as well as he wants them to. But he's resilient."

Finishing his beer, Dax threw down a few dollars to cover Suzie's tip. "Since it's not likely to pick up, I'm going to head home and make sure the Morty hasn't burned down the apartment." He paused before stalking toward the door, finding the nerve to step outside.

"Later, Dax." Suzie turned to Geoffrey. "Another?"

Geoffrey leaned onto the bar. "Sure. Uh, who's Morty?"

Suzie laughed. "His kitten."

TWO

DAX

Dax cast a flick of his wrist wave over his shoulder by means of a goodbye, then pushed the door open, hesitating again. Apparently getting shot a couple times when leaving his bar made a guy jumpy. He didn't feel anything sinister waiting for him, but his human body seemed to want to respond, anyway. He huffed and shook his head. It was OK to be cautious when several someones wanted him dead.

Stepping out into the rainy night, he ducked his head and popped the collar on his leather coat as he walked toward the bus stop. He might have preferred having a car, but Boudreaux still hadn't finished working on the 1965 Lincoln Continental sedan he'd recently "acquired." But a bus was better than his motorcycle in this kind of weather until his car was ready.

His eyes narrowed as a shadow emerged from across the street and darted across the dark pavement. Nearby, a lamppost flickered irregularly as adrenaline seeped into his bloodstream. The street was dark enough without another one going out. If it did, who knew when city maintenance would get to it.

Focusing on what looked like the shape of a woman, he tried to avoid making it obvious so he didn't look like a creep, but he also didn't want to be politely shot. He slipped back into the shadow of the bus stop, letting it partially block him from view and the rain. The woman stepped up onto the sidewalk and strode purposefully in his direction. If she didn't step into one of the buildings, she'd pass right by him. As she passed under the flickering streetlight, it illuminated the face of Minh—the daughter of the convenience store's owner, Thuc. Her long black hair cascaded around her shoulders and fluttered in the breeze. Behind her, the bus stopped a few blocks away. She looked over her shoulder and slowed.

Reaching out, he tried to find the impending threads linking himself and Minh to the world, looking to see if there was any fraying as they extended forward. Both lines appeared solid with little of interest in the immediate future beyond the closer linkage they'd gained when he and Tomi had freed her from a kidnapper a couple weeks ago.

As the bus approached, it back lit Minh. Reaching into her coat, she grabbed something. Dax tensed, preparing to shift out of his human flesh and into the skeleton and robe of the Grim Reaper—the form he'd been forced into because of his banishment. It didn't render him impervious to damage, but it made it a lot harder to sustain injuries.

"Psst, Dax." She looked over her shoulder. The bus was nearly upon them, blocking them from the view of the other side of the street. "Here." Something plastic in her hand caught the light and flashed as she held it out. "Take it."

He reached out and snagged it as she walked by. At no point did she make eye contact or even look at him as she passed by. Behind him, the bus's hydraulics hissed as it lowered itself to let him board. With a shake of his head, he stepped out of the shelter and onto the bus, flashing his pass as he moved by the driver.

He stuffed the flat piece of plastic into his coat, wanting to wait until the bus was moving. As it pulled into traffic, he looked for Minh but she'd disappeared from view, crossing in front of the bus to return to the other side of the street or turning onto the side street by the bar. They'd never spoken more than a handful of words to each other at her dad's convenience store. He had no idea why she'd been captured and caged by someone who collected supernatural creatures and beings. But she was a mystery for later. The disc she'd handed him was the more immediate curiosity.

After a couple blocks, he pulled out a plastic CD case from his pocket. Inside was a DVD with the date of the first shooting written in sharpie on it—the day he'd found Morty.

He stashed it in the lockable pocket inside his jacket and zipped it, securing the disc. As they wound through the neighborhood, he looked out the window, staring off into the middle distance as streetlights and neon signs flashed through the raindrop covered window. There was always something churning under the surface of Red City. Unfortunately, Red City seemed to have too little surface and too much churn. This time, it had caught him in it.

Since he'd been exiled to the mortal plane by Earth's death gods, he'd tried to keep a low profile. He didn't have the juice to mix it up with the heavy hitters in Red City. He just wanted to run his bar and disappear into a city full of supernaturals where his quirks might go unnoticed. But someone had finally noticed him and decided he needed a lead injection. He didn't like the paranoia that seemed to be taking over his life. But multiple murder attempts could do that.

After he pulled the cord for the next stop, he stepped off and stopped at Ciudad Roja Taqueria to pick up a burrito and a horchata before heading home. Morty greeted him at the door by pouncing on the chains of his motorcycle boots. Taking the straw from his bag, he ripped the tip off the paper wrapper and blew into the straw, sending the sheath flying deeper into the living room. Morty flew after it, rearing up before attacking it. With the kitten out of the way, he grabbed a plate and set it on the coffee table.

He dropped the disc Minh had given him into his DVD player and sat down to his dinner. A grainy black-and-white image of the front of the convenience store and a bit of the bar's sidewalk flicked onto the screen.

"Ah, scintillating viewing."

Morty looked up briefly from his straw wrapper to see what his person might want, then backed up to make a running charge at his new treasure. It had been too much to hope she'd edited it down to the time in question, but he'd have to be grateful for even getting the DVD. Thuc hadn't seemed interested in providing the video even after Dax'd checked back when there weren't any cops around.

After he finished his burrito, he sat back with his horchata to watch people wander in and out of the store with the occasional car parking out front. When the sucking sound announced his beverage was empty, he paused the video and fetched a beer from the fridge.

The first hour redefined tedium, then he found the button to speed it up. Then it was double speed tedium. Nothing looked suspicious—just customers entering and exiting. Every car disgorged a driver or passenger to head inside and back out again before pulling away from the curb.

Yawning, he paused the DVD and turned on the sound system, playing a metal mix he'd been working on. If he didn't have something to keep him awake, he'd never make it through the security video. Two hours of watching the video had seemed like so many more, and now it was after midnight, and he had to open the bar in the morning.

The kitten, tuckered out from his new toy, had passed out on his back, his plump white belly pointing up. With food and shelter, Morty had thrived in the short time he'd lived with Dax. And in return, he found the aggressive little ball of black and white fuzz to be amusing. Something he rarely found anything to be. Other than Tomi and his family, he'd tried to avoid making the sort of attachments that would sink him deeper into humanity. Mostly, he just skimmed quietly along the surface, hoping not to be seen.

Bending down, he scooped up the kitten and carried him back to the couch, setting him next to his leg. The animal barely stirred. With music and a kitten to keep him occupied, he returned his attention to the DVD.

He nearly missed it, but when a car pulled up and didn't drive away, he rewound and slowed it down. There. Someone had exited from the passenger side and ducked into the store. The man acted as if he knew where the camera was and kept his head pointed down, except when something must have drawn his attention. The man looked up for the briefest of seconds before hiding his face again.

Rewinding, Dax put it in slow motion, going nearly frame by frame until he caught the face and paused.

He jolted, startling the kitten. "Son of a..."

Detective Ryan said there'd been a witness who'd seen Dax get shot. He just didn't mention that the cop himself was the witness. And possibly the shooter. Other than when he'd first arrived in Red City and claimed the body of the biker he now wore, he'd never killed anyone in cold blood—only in self-defense. For Ryan, he might make an exception.

THREE

DAX

"Fuck, man." Tomi stood up and paced the length of the long table in the tearoom. "I knew Detective Ryan didn't like you, but I didn't realize he'd be willing to kill you."

Dax snorted, folding his arms. "He's a Red City cop through and through—a petty schemer and a corrupt bastard."

"But to kill you because you won't pay for his protection racket?"

"Tomi. You're not thinking big enough." Dax paused as the timer went off. He picked up the small clay teapot and filled his and Tomi's cups. "There's no profit in killing your mark. And that biker gang didn't sic a kid on me randomly out of the blue."

"You sure about that, boss? You sure they didn't finally figure out where you got the money when you first"—he rolled his hand, looking for a word or phrase—"appeared and took over that body. I realize you blasted off the tattoos and got a haircut and shaved the beard, but you still look like the gang's enforcer."

"It's possible. But why now? Why so many years later? What it's been? Over five years? Other than when they first came sniffing around, it's been quiet for a long time."

Tomi opened his mouth to speak but closed it with a clack of teeth when Dax held up his hand.

"Also, think of the timing. It seems like entirely too big of a coincidence that Randal Ryan, who is fundamentally a petty coward, would take a pop at me at the same time as that kid. And we still don't know who killed Jason."

Tomi scowled. "Yeah."

Dax held up his hand with three fingers raised. "That's three bullets likely intended for me, but we only can account for two of them. Jamie and Ryan"—he folded down two of the fingers—"or whatever lackey he had pull the actual trigger if someone was in that car with him. But that third bullet. The one that killed my employee and your friend, it was meant for me. Was it Ryan again? I'm certain it wasn't the kid. Or was it the biker gang mistaking Jason for me?"

Tomi pursed his lips and nodded. "I agree. It's so rare to run into honesty in this city, when you see it, it leaps out at you. She put one in you, but she didn't clip Jason."

"So, we can remove her from the list on Jason, but we can't assign the guilt to Ryan yet. It's entirely possible the bikers had another gun in play."

"Are you sure?" Tomi took a deep breath and exhaled noisily before sitting down to his teacup. "Saying they're linked means someone with a whole lot of pull wants you dead. Who have you offended that badly?"

"Besides the bikers? No one that I'm aware of. At least in this city. I thought I'd been doing a decent job of being a nobody. At least in Red City…" Dax let the steam from his tea waft into his nose and relax him with its complex, earthy aroma.

"Yeah, but what about…you know, before?"

"They're supposed to leave me alone. That was the deal."

Tomi raised an eyebrow. "What deal?"

Shaking his head, Dax held up his hand. "Let's just say that's a bit out of your league and leave it at that."

He'd never told Tomi why he'd been exiled to earth and forced to live as a mostly human, nor had he mentioned the visit from Baron Samedi after they'd celebrated their victory over the bikers. Tomi, as far as he could tell, was pure human—death and trickster gods weren't something he was capable of handling.

Sighing, he shook his head. "Let's just say, I was given a tip by an unreliable source that I may not have gone as unnoticed as I wanted." He wobbled his head side to side as he debated what to say next. "Well, it would be more accurate to say someone is keeping more than just a passing interest in me."

Tomi narrowed his eyes. "What? When did this happen?"

"Right after we celebrated our victory."

"And you took all this time to tell me?" Anger crept into his voice. "Dax, you've got to keep me informed of shit like this, especially when I'm putting my life on the line. I can't have your back if you keep me in the dark."

Dax clenched his jaw, the muscles in his cheeks twitching. With a sigh, he shook his head and took another drink of his tea. Seeing he was nearly out, he hit the button on the kettle so he could steep the leaves again.

"I'm sorry, Tomi."

"Look, Dax. I've known you for more than five years now. I know you're not quite human, in more ways than just your...origin. But I'd like to think we've become friends in that time."

Dax nodded. "I consider you my closest friend."

"Good. Then don't keep me in the fucking dark!" Tomi's anger rose as did the volume of his voice. Calming down, he added, "You're a weird motherfucker. Both times getting shot only emphasized that. And the morgue..."

The morgue had been particularly harrowing. He'd been confronted with dozens of angry spirits tied to the earth in ways that felt unnatural compared to normal spirits. That was something he didn't want to deal with now, especially with more immediate dangers to his physical well-being.

He didn't even want to think about what would happen if he started messing with the spirits of the dead, not with the Baron's warning. He'd been banned from escorting the souls of the dead as part of his deal. If he suddenly wiped out a whole morgue of trapped spirits, it might invite more scrutiny than he could deal with under the present circumstances. He'd just been happy to free the spirit of Jason.

"Fair enough. I was told that I was being watched and that I had been since my arrival."

"When we first met?" Tomi asked.

Dax nodded. "Yeah. I replied that I knew I was being watched. It had been strongly intimated that I would be. My source then told me that not everyone watches with their eyes."

"Implying that someone was doing something active to you?"

"That was the gist."

Tomi rubbed his hand over his jaw as he thought. "And that's it? Do you have any idea who specifically is out to get you? From your old days?"

Shaking his head, Dax sighed. "No. Not really. There were a sizable number of psychopomps—death gods and soul guides—allied against me. But things could have changed since then and it could be someone with a new axe to grind or with an old one that chose not to grind it then. There are just too many options."

"Psychopomps? Well, fuck."

"That's pretty much what I thought." Dax turned the kettle off and filled the small clay teapot.

"Do you think someone…not human…could be putting out a hit on you?"

"There are lots of nonhumans in this city."

"You know what I mean. It's not some werewolf who has a bone to pick with you." Tomi smirked.

"I see what you did there. No. It's not a werewolf or a vampire or some witch."

Dax didn't actually know if that statement was true. He knew that the death gods were watching him. And Baron Samedi's warning, if he could be trusted, would back up the assumption that it was likely one of those entities behind a conspiracy to kill him. In this body and in this time and place, he was uniquely vulnerable to harm. They would never have a better opportunity to remove him from the cosmic chessboard. But that didn't mean some supernatural being couldn't also have a beef with him, though he doubted few if any knew his true identity.

Well, the manbo knew his true identity or strongly suspected it.

She was a sharp one and wise. But he trusted her. Partially because Tomi's mama trusted her but also because of the aura she put out into the world. She wasn't particularly tied to the prevailing morals of her fellow humans, but she did right by her community and sought to bring goodness and balance into the world.

"This is someone with a lot more juice than a werewolf or a mage. Unfortunately, there's not a lot we can do about it at this time. The best we can do is ferret out their contact point and get them to stop hiring out to kill me."

"Cut off the head of the snake just below the neck?" Tomi turned off the tea timer and poured the liquid into their glasses.

"Exactly."

"How are we going to do that?"

"It's not my favorite idea, just my only one at the moment…"

Both of Tomi's eyebrows shot up. "The Rat?"

"The Rat."

FOUR

JAMIE

It was another shitty day at school. It had at least been something of a sanctuary away from her family life, but even that had been stripped away because of her father. Not even the familiar and comforting scents of the school library could soothe her.

She hadn't thought her life could get much worse after being forced to shoot a man to pay off her father's gambling debts to a gang of Nazi wolf shifter bikers, but she was wrong. The relief that had come after escaping with her life and the life of her parents had quickly faded after she and her mom Sharon briefly moved in with her bestie Cory and his mom Linda.

For the first couple of days, she'd felt lighter than she could remember. Then Linda turned cold.

"Hey, Jamie." Cory—a tall, handsome white kid with shaggy brown hair—stopped next to their favorite library table and looked down at her. Even weeks later, he seemed hesitant to approach her, as if afraid she blamed him for his mother's actions. And that lack of previous closeness hurt the most, adding to her general misery.

She shoved out the other chair with her foot so he would take the invitation to sit. "Hey, Cory. How you doing?"

He sighed and shrugged. "Shitty. Mom took my car keys away."

Jamie's brown eyes shot open wide as she blinked quickly. "What? I just thought it was a regular old grounding."

"Me too. I wanted to run and get a soda at the corner store, but when I went to get my keys, I couldn't find them. I asked her if she'd seen them, but she said she'd taken them, and I wouldn't be getting them back anytime soon. Now, it'll be forever before we'll be able to go for a run and burgers again."

A tiny pit opened in her stomach. She'd already guessed this would be the result, but Cory seemed optimistic that he could sneak away once he got ungrounded as long he didn't expressly say he was going to hang out with her. He was naïve to think that would happen, but some small part of her had kept hold of that dream. Even though they'd probably never run together as their wolves again, the idea had been a small modicum of hope.

She sighed in frustration, rubbing her eyes to stop the threat of tears. "That sucks, Cory. I'm so sorry. It's —"

Cory reached out and covered her mouth with his hand. "It's not your fault. I'm eighteen. I made my own decisions, and these are the consequences. They suck, though. I never thought my mom would do this to me, but…"

"Yeah."

Linda'd always been sympathetic and kind to Jamie, doing her best to look out for her because of the failings of her father. But this time, her son Cory had been dragged in. In truth, he'd shoved his way in, refusing to let Jamie proceed on her own.

But no matter how many times he told his mother that he'd just tried to help his best friend, it didn't matter to Linda. Cory's friendship with Jamie had gotten the shit beaten out of him by bikers. He'd gotten off lucky. And Linda seemed to recognize that more than he did.

"Has your mom found a permanent apartment yet?"

Jamie shook her head, then put her wavy black hair up in a messy bun when it got in her face. "I don't think so." She shrugged. "I don't know. I don't think I've spoken more than a handful of words to her in a couple weeks. We're still in that shitty weekly motel place, so I'm gonna say no."

"I'm sorry."

Why? Because your mom said she cared about me then kicked me out onto the streets? That's what she wanted to say. That's what she felt. But no matter how much anger she had churning under the surface, she didn't want to burn the last bridge she had, especially as fragile as it felt. It wasn't Cory's fault for how Linda had reacted.

Though she'd been cordial, it became very clear that her house was only a very temporary waystation for Jamie and her mother. Sharon had quickly found them a medium-term-stay motel to move into. Her mom didn't like asking anyone for help, especially if it meant revealing anything about the failures of their little family unit. And no doubt, she'd picked up on Linda's frostiness.

"I'm alive. I guess I'm supposed to be celebrating that." She rolled her eyes and huffed at the idiocy of the sentiment.

Once they were out Linda's house, she'd grounded Cory and forbade him to spend any free time with Jamie. They'd both hoped it would be temporary. But with nothing to fill her after school time, she was either forced to go home to a tiny studio, where she slept on the couch, or somewhere else. She opted for the nearest Redemption City Public Library branch, coming home late to eat whatever cold leftovers her mother had left in the fridge.

She and her mother rarely spoke more than a few words to each other in passing. After the brief fiery moment of kicking out her husband, Sharon sank into a deep funk. Jamie just focused on doing what she had to do to graduate from high school.

Though she couldn't hang out with Cory, Linda couldn't control their time in school. Even after all this time and all the disasters, Cory was still a loyal friend. And that might have been what stung the most. If Cory was mad at her or hated her or blamed her, it would have been a cleaner break. A quick severing of their relationship then nothing.

Now, though, it was a festering wound that wouldn't close. Always painful, always raw. It seemed like she was constantly having to bite off sharp comments so she didn't drive him off, though she was of a split mind there. If she drove him away, then maybe the wounds would scab over.

He sighed again. "We should head to class before we're late and get in big trouble and someone writes us up." He winked at her and attempted a silly smirk, mostly achieving it.

After getting the shit kicked out of him by bikers, being given detention by an overly officious hall monitor didn't seem like a real punishment. She'd nearly died and almost had been killed. The school didn't even use corporal punishment. Her grades were mostly in. They had very little power over her anymore. Though she wasn't into being hassled, neither of them seemed ready to move yet.

"Which library you heading to tonight?" He tapped his finger on the table. "Maybe I can talk my mom into letting me take the bus there."

"Maybe. It'd be worth a try. We have that A.P. U.S. history final next week." She paused, thinking about which branch she wanted to hit tonight. "I don't feel like lots of walking today, so the closest branch. Up on Shelby."

"Excuse me, have you seen Jamie Rodriguez?" a woman asked from near the front of the library.

"She's back that way with her friend," the librarian replied.

Jamie turned around as Mrs. Orville from the front office approached them. The woman's brow was furrowed as she stalked across the library.

"Jamie, honey, we're going to need you to come to the office." Mrs. Orville twisted her hands together.

Saliva filled Jamie's mouth as she slowly reached out to picked up the book she'd set on the table, her light brown hand trembling slightly at the sudden injection of nerves. Stuffing the book into her backpack and standing up, she cast a last glance to Cory then followed Mrs. Orville out of the library.

She couldn't think of anything she'd done at school to get in trouble, and Mrs. Orville's tone didn't sound like she was in trouble. She sounded almost solicitous. Had something happened to her mother? Her stomach dropped further.

Mrs. Orville bustled ahead of Jamie, clearing the path as people moved out of the way at the sight of the administrator. It seemed like it took forever to traverse the hallway she'd traveled hundreds, thousands of times over her four years attending Gus Atlas High School. As they finally neared the office, she saw blue and red lights flashing off in the distance in the parking lot. She swallowed a mouthful of saliva, hoping her light lunch would stay down.

She bumped into Mrs. Orville's back. She hadn't noticed that the older white lady had stopped.

"Sorry," she mumbled.

"It's OK, honey. Your mom is here."

"OK."

That meant her mom was OK. Why else were they here? Her eyes flicked around, looking for an escape route. After all these weeks, the cops had shown up for her. Her breaths came in shallow gasps.

Mrs. Orville pulled the door open and gently ushered Jamie inside. Her mother, who'd been sitting in a chair near the door stood up. She'd been crying. When Jamie stepped close enough, her mom pulled her into a hug. Jamie stood there motionless, her arms hanging at her sides.

Jamie, in a daze, had no idea what was going on. Her mom hadn't hugged her like that in years.

"Sweetie, we need to go. Alright?" Sharon said.

Jamie nodded numbly, letting her mom guide her out the door and to their waiting car which was parked in the no parking section behind a police car. After her mother shoved her into the passenger seat of the ancient Ford Taurus, she stared at the Redemption City police cruiser, the steady pulse of its rotating lights almost hypnotic.

Her mother didn't say anything until they'd pulled away from the school and were on the streets, following the cop car. "I'm sorry, sweetie. It's…um…it's your father."

That jerked Jamie back into the car. "What did that idiot do now?"

Sharon raised a hand to her face and made a sound like a choked sob, following it with a few sniffles. "The police"—she sobbed again —"the police want us to identify"—she paused and cleared her throat—"his body."

FIVE

DAX

They parked Tomi's car a few blocks away from their meeting point. It had taken Boudreaux almost a week to get The Rat to agree to a meeting with them after they decided he'd be a solid next step. He'd been a good ally on their last venture.

If a city like Redemption City could be said to have a sketchy section of town—Red City was almost all sketchy and no nice—this was definitely on the sketchier side of the spectrum. Tomi's old beat-up Toyota looked like one of the nicest cars parked along the street in front of derelict apartments and empty warehouses and industrial blocks. It was also probably the only vehicle that was both legal and functional.

Tomi had volunteered to drive since Dax still hadn't received the finished car from Boudreaux. They wouldn't have brought it anyway since Tomi's car was less flashy than the classic Lincoln Continental Dax had recently acquired somewhat surreptitiously—though illegally would probably be more accurate. But the previous owner wasn't going to be missing it.

They slipped out of the car, and Tomi left the windows down and the doors unlocked. Last, he popped the trunk. He'd cleaned it out before they'd left so there was no temptation for someone to smash in the windows.

Tomi stared at his car for a moment, sighed, then followed Dax down the alley toward the address Boudreaux had given them. "I just hope someone doesn't use it as a toilet while we're gone."

"Me too." Dax didn't fancy riding home in a bathroom, nor did he want his friend forced to clean up that kind of mess. The toilets at the bar were bad enough.

"Hey, bro!" a tall, muscular, handsome, bald Black man called from the other end of the block. He wore a tight black T-shirt and a pair of nearly worn-out jeans—the perfect nondescript outfit for a neighborhood like this.

"Boudreaux!" Tomi approached him, and they exchanged an elaborate handshake.

"I see you can't keep your boy here out of trouble," Boudreaux said to Tomi, while extending a hand to Dax for a simple handshake.

"Seems like trouble keeps looking for him," Tomi replied.

"Good to see you too, Boudreaux." Dax crossed his arms, a sardonic smile crooking up one side of his lips. "How goes the car?"

"Almost done. We've just about got it 'legal,' and then I'll take it to the paint shop and make it pretty."

The manbo had hooked them up with Boudreaux when they'd needed a way to sneak into the city morgue. He'd also helped them out a bit when Dax raided the bikers' bar, making a killing on all the choppers they'd stolen in the process. The Rat was his contact and insisted he be there if there were going to be any strangers, even though The Rat had helped them out a couple weeks ago. Dax and Tomi meeting him once before still qualified them as strangers.

"The Rat waits for no one," Boudreaux said, turning to head into the darkness of a series of closed off overpasses and other tunnels leading to the underside of Red City industrial westside.

The sound of cars and trucks passing over head drowned out everything else, though their exhaust only served as a top note for the stench of rotting garbage and sewage. A few makeshift cardboard abodes had been set up in the nearly abandoned alleyway. This neighborhood tended to be popular with the city's homeless population. Though, most preferred the abandoned buildings to the streets.

Tomi breathed shallowly, making occasional faces. But Boudreaux looked as cool as ever. Nothing seemed to bother the man who'd been an army medic before becoming an EMT in his civilian life.

Once they passed entirely into the tunnels, the drone of traffic, along with the light, faded into the background. Reaching into his pocket, Boudreaux pulled out three small but powerful flashlights, handing two of them to Tomi and Dax.

Sure and confident, Boudreaux led them through a series of tunnels—just tall and wide enough to stave off the worst of the potential claustrophobia—and switchbacks until he found a marking on the wall he'd been checking for. Whoever had made the mark had used chalk so it could easily be wiped away and likely missed if you weren't looking for it. Dax didn't recognize it. Of course, that meant little since he barely had access to any of the knowledge he used to have prior to his banishment.

Cities built both up and out, sometimes over the corpses of their former selves. Red City was no exception in that regard. He'd have to look into the history of Red City and these tunnels. A city this big had a hidden underworld of sewer systems, maintenance tunnels, and other access points. While these tunnels had the aroma of sewage, they were too dry and clean—in the sense of a lack of sewage—to be part of the sewer system. If he was going to have to keep dodging assassins, a bit more knowledge about the place he lived might come in handy.

"Alright, you two turn off your flashlights. Three is too bright for him. We'll hold up here and wait for our host."

Dax and Tomi turned off their lights. Last time, only Boudreaux had one. If they had to keep meeting with The Rat, they'd need to get themselves something better than the dim affairs they used to check IDs behind the bar.

A steady drip accompanied the even rhythm of three men breathing, but little else imposed on the sepulcher silence. They were too deep for even a faint breeze to disturb the humid, stagnant air. At least this section of the tunnels didn't smell too bad—just musty and dirty, with only an occasional whiff of decay.

Dax wanted to check his watch to see how long they'd been waiting but resisted the urge. Boudreaux yawned and leaned up against the concrete wall, crossing his arms. Tomi, his hands slipping into his pocket, moved to put his back near a wall without touching it.

Off in the distance, Dax thought he heard faint squeaking. Then another squeak, but this one from the other direction. A moment later, something latched onto the leg of his jeans.

"Just stay still and calm," Boudreaux said, his voice smooth and relaxed.

The weight skittered up his pant leg and onto his shirt, shimmying under his arm and up his back. Finally the creature settled on his shoulder and snuffled his ear and hair. Dax gave a little twitch; its whiskers tickled. Flicking his eyes over, he saw a rat sitting on Tomi's shoulder, though Tomi had his eyes clamped shut, his lips moving in some sort of silent prayer or curse.

The scratching of thousands of rodent claws on concrete rose and shattered the earlier silence. An occasional squeak punctuated the scurrying of the animals as some bumped him or ran over his feet. Another decided to seek the advantage of height and joined his pal, but on Dax's other shoulder.

A high-pitched chuckle echoed from Dax's right. "My little friends are curious. They wonder who has come down into their domain. Will they be food?" The voice steadily grew louder at the approach of the man they were here to see.

A shape formed out of the shadows, becoming a short man in dark clothes. Dax had met The Rat once before, but in a different neighborhood's entrance into the city's underground tunnels. It had been outside and less spooky, though the horde of rats had been similar—except bigger now. Dax hoped The Rat would be as helpful this time.

"Ah, you've made friends," The Rat continued, scooping a large brown rat off his own shoulder and cupping it gently in his hands.

He gave it a little kiss between its little rounded ears and a scratch under its chin.

Dax gave the slightest of nods to acknowledge he'd been spoken to. The rats had settled down, stretching out across his shoulder like two furry epaulettes, their heads nestled against his neck.

The Rat sauntered by, his minions moving about him in chaotic orbits, and stopped in front of Boudreaux, who pushed off the wall and extended a hand for a shake. "It's good to see you, as always."

"You know, Boudreaux, you're one of the few people I believe when they say that." His words tumbled out of his mouth quickly in a high-pitched voice. He chuckled squeakily. "What brings your friends down into my realm with you?"

Boudreaux gestured toward Tomi and Dax. "You remember Tomi and Dax?"

"The gentlemen who own a dive bar up in north Red City. I do. I do. How did your little adventure into the richer environs of Red City fare? I didn't stick around too long. Too clean. Too bright."

"Well enough," Dax said, turning carefully so as not to dislodge his furry riders. He didn't want to hurt The Rat's minions nor incur their wrath and earn a bite. "We managed to free those who'd been wrongfully detained while you and your little friends raided the kitchen."

"I hear rumor that the city is light one rich prick."

"I've heard the same," Dax replied. The Rat had helped them find their target before and had sent his rats to disable the mansion's security systems, but he'd missed most of the action and then disappeared after he checked to see if the rats were finished for the night. Dax didn't trust the odd man well enough to speak of matters he hadn't witnessed himself in more than vague terms.

The Rat chuckled. "Excellent. I like to see the scales balanced. And I'm glad that my information proved valuable." He made eye contact with Dax. "Though I'm assuming you're not here to bring a gift basket."

Dax narrowed his eyes. They probably should have sent some sort of gift in appreciation for The Rat's help, but Boudreaux had never mentioned there'd be a price. Dax wasn't naïve. He knew it would be added to the tally Boudreaux was no doubt running, but he'd assumed his connected friend would take care of balancing the scales with The Rat, then add it to the running balance Dax had. He'd guessed their first meeting had been done as a favor to Manman Delphine. Then they'd hooked up Boudreaux and his boys with a lot of loot. But Dax had never considered a separate piece he owed to The Rat. Tomi usually handled things like this. He'd have to check in with his best friend to ensure he kept himself favor debt free.

Dammit. He just wanted to keep his head down and run his bar. Why couldn't everyone just leave him alone?

Tomi mumbled something.

The Rat's head swiveled toward Tomi. "What now? A nice cheese basket wouldn't go amiss. I like blue cheeses. A nice Stilton." He made Hannibal Lecter like yummy noises. "Or a Cambozola Black? Yes, please."

Boudreaux snickered.

"My apologies for my friend," Dax said. "I'll ensure you receive a nice gift for your efforts."

The Rat bowed his head regally. "It is appreciated. Now. What can I do for you this time?"

Tomi cleared his throat. "I'm sorry for making the joke."

The Rat nodded graciously, acknowledging the apology.

Tomi continued, "I don't know if you heard, but Dax was shot twice a few months ago and one of his employees was killed, likely because of a passing resemblance."

The Rat shrugged, his eyelids drifting to a bored half-mast. "Gunshots in Red City are more common than stars in the sky. Why should I care about a small cluster revolving around you two? I don't know either of you from a hole in the wall."

"They say there's little in the underbelly of this city that doesn't escape your attention," Boudreaux said.

"This wasn't a series of random shootings," Tomi added. "This was several people trying to assassinate Dax, including a gang of Nazi werewolf bikers and a Red City cop."

"Or someone doing it at the behest of a Red City cop," Dax added.

The Rat whistled, his eyebrows raising. "Whose breakfast cereal did you piss in?"

Dax shrugged. "I don't know, at least not exactly. I know why the bikers might have a beef with me, but this doesn't feel related, or at least not entirely."

"Did this have anything to do with that biker bar that burned down a few months ago?"

Tomi snorted. "Dax burned it down."

"But that was after they tried to kill me." He left Jamie's name out of it. The kid had gotten mixed up in the whole affair because of her deadbeat dad, and she deserved a chance to escape what had happened. She hadn't been the attempted killer, just the weapon. "And technically, I didn't burn it down. Not intentionally. Some sparks set off some broken liquor bottles in the fight."

The Rat turned to Boudreaux. "And you helped him? That doesn't seem your style."

"Nah. He did all the work. We just did a little containment on the outside. Maybe picked up some abandoned stuff after all was said and done."

The Rat laughed. "Now that sounds more like your style." Then his eyes narrowed and slowly panned toward Dax. "You and your pal here took on a whole biker gang and won?"

Dax shifted his weight to his other foot and crossed his arms. "Tomi waited outside with Boudreaux."

"No shit?" The Rat smirked. "What kind of badass are you?"

"You're going to have to show him, or this is going to take forever, boss." Tomi rolled his eyes. The Rat didn't see it since he faced Dax, but he had trouble keeping a smirk from his lips at his friend's impatience.

"Can he be trusted?" Dax directed the question to Boudreaux.

"Can you be trusted?" Boudreaux asked The Rat.

"A rat is a loyal creature to those in their pack, but a rat is also a survivor." The Rat winked at Boudreaux.

"He's no friend to those in power. He's more trustworthy than most people in Red City, though that's not saying much." Boudreaux wrapped the bitter undertone in a coat of joking.

Dax flicked his eyes to Tomi, making eye contact. His friend nodded imperceptibly.

"Alright, I'll tell you who I am. Or perhaps show is a better word." Reaching up to his shoulders, Dax carefully scooped the rats up and gently set them on the ground.

Drawing in a deep breath, he reached into the nether realm—the place in between—and found his other form, the form he'd been forced to take in exile. He could make the switch in an instant but chose to draw it out to make a point. Dax the human slowly faded as the stereotypical Grim Reaper image humans had assigned him took its place. Tall and skeletal, a black robe made from a rough and holey fabric wrapped him from the top of his bleached white skull down to his bony feet. The only parts of him visible were his skeletal hands and the front of his skull.

Reaching out next to him with his right hand, he snapped his fingers, though the sound was made of bones scraping and clacking against each other. A full body shiver ran down Tomi, causing him to twitch.

"Damn, I've seen that before, but it still makes my blood run cold," Boudreaux said in low tones.

"Right?" Tomi nodded vigorously.

The Rat blanched and took a faltering step backward, then another. Before he could turn and run, he ran into Tomi, who placed his strong hands on The Rat's shoulders, supporting and stopping him.

Tomi leaned forward so his lips were close to The Rat's ears. "You wanted to know who he is. Behold."

"Well, Mr. The Rat, can you aid us?" Dax's voice wheezed from the aether, hollow, airy, and as cold as the grave.

The Rat's eyes went wide, then rolled up into the back of his head. He promptly fainted.

SIX

JAMIE

Jamie brought up the rear of the small parade moving through the city morgue. The coroner, a white woman whose name she didn't catch, the pair of cops, a detective, and her mother all walked in front of her. Jamie barely heard a word anyone said. They all sounded like adults from one of the old Peanuts cartoons—wah wah wahwah wah.

Instead, her eyes flicked around, looking at all the concrete, stone, and shiny stainless steel. All cold surfaces. Hugging her arms around herself, she marveled at the bright, shiny, sterile surfaces and dark, uninviting corners and nooks. The contrast was almost off-putting.

Every time she looked for too long into one of the dark recesses, a shiver ran up her spine and her whole body shuddered. She couldn't tear her eyes away, but if she stared too long, her reptilian mind forced her to look away so she couldn't make eye contact with whatever lurked just outside of her conscious vision.

The whole place gave her the squick. But what would you expect from a place where the city stored its murdered citizens? This was where tragic stories started their final phases. The clean and polished stone and shiny stainless steel felt like lies. The dark, sketchy corners and recesses held the truth.

Misery and fear and despair—that was what this place dealt in. What it represented.

The bright voice of the coroner, Winnie, that was her name, bounced off the hard surfaces. Between the echo and the affected joviality, Jamie wanted to plug her ears or do something to shut the woman up.

"Sorry, there's only room for four of us in the elevator. Weight restrictions," Winnie said, sweeping a few stray black hairs that had escaped her bob out of the way. "You'll have to leave your officers up here, Detective."

The white man in the cheap suit mumbled something to the cops, and they posted up on either side of the elevator doors. The detective waved her mother and the coroner in, waiting for Jamie. With a sigh and avoiding eye contact with the cops, she forced herself to take the last three steps and cross the threshold of the elevator, worming her way to the back so she could resume her place as the procession's caboose.

"I'm glad you have your jackets," Winnie said. "We don't bother heating things down there. City says it saves on the power bill." She shrugged, reaching forward to push the button to the lower levels of the morgue.

Jamie gasped when the elevator bumped to a start. As the four of them stood silently, the motor and cables ground and groaned as they descended into the bowels of the building. She rubbed her arms as the air became noticeably cooler. Their breath hung in the air as it grew thicker with each exhalation. Finally, the elevator stopped with a small jerk.

Winnie gestured toward the opening door. "You know the way, Detective Ryan."

He grunted and swaggered out of the elevator. Jamie's mother followed him. Seeing that the coroner wasn't going to step out first as she reached to block the door, Jamie gritted her teeth and exited the elevator, tucking herself against the wall just to the side.

Steel drawers and doors lined all three walls except for the one she stood in front of. Despite all the light reflected off the shiny surfaces, the room felt dark and ominous. A feather's wisp dragged over the back of her neck, and she shuddered, rubbing it with her hand until the chill went away.

"Let's see... Which one is he... Tobias Rodriguez." She dropped the clipboard back into place against the door and pulled the drawer out.

The metal sliding against rollers echoed around the room filled with hard surfaces, an occasional squeak and screech making everyone cringe.

"Sorry. I'll have to leave a note for maintenance." Winnie shrugged apologetically.

The drawer finally thunked to a stop.

"Mrs. Rodriguez?" Winnie grabbed a white sheet and stepped away, making room for Sharon to step in.

The cop slid up behind her, peeking over her shoulder. "Is that your husband, Mrs. Rodriguez?"

She answered with a wobbly nod, trying to stifle a sob. "Yes." She turned around and took a couple lurching steps away from the drawer containing her dead husband.

"Miss Rodriguez, we'll need you to confirm the identity as well," Detective Ryan said, staring at her.

She could have sworn his eyes did a quick sweep up and down her body. She pulled her jacket closed and took a few hesitant steps forward, doing her best to avoid eye contact with the cop.

"Does she really need to do this?" Sharon asked. "She's only a child."

Det. Ryan shrugged. "Legally, she's an adult. In the case of homicides, more confirmations help."

Sharon gulped, brushing a tear off her cheek, and nodded weakly, backing away.

"It's OK, honey. It'll just take a moment." The coroner tried to affix a reassuring smile on her face, but it seemed a bit cold and overly practiced. It was only for a moment, but Jamie thought she caught a quick predatory flash from the odd woman.

Keeping her eyes pointed at the tile floor, Jamie stepped up to the spot where her mother had stood moments ago. Slowly, she raised her eyes to the bottom of the drawer. Then her eyes darted to the sheet the coroner held up which blocked the rest of his body while revealing the face. Steeling herself, she looked up.

Her father always tended to be pale. There weren't many underground gambling halls in the sunlight, but he looked even worse. He hadn't shaved in a while—the stubble at the not quite a beard stage. Though at best it was patchy, anyway. Across his neck ran a jagged line from side to side. Someone had cut his throat, and he'd probably either drowned in blood or bled out.

She couldn't look away from the wound. She hadn't wanted to see him ever again when he left, but she hadn't wanted him to die. Not like this.

"Is this your father?" Detective Ryan asked, his voice too close to her ear.

She twitched away from him, her eyes still locked on the gash across her father's neck. "Yes," she mumbled.

"It's OK, honey. You don't have to look anymore." The coroner reached out and touched her hand.

A zap of static electricity surged into Jamie's hand, and she pulled away from the weird coroner, but bumped into the detective. He set his hands on her shoulders and squeezed. That jolted her away from her father's visage.

She twisted away from the cop and stepped around her mother, using her body as a shield. The unwanted touches made her want to crawl out of her skin. The detective radiated creepiness, but the coroner seemed…wrong somehow. The brightly chipper expression felt almost sinister. Jamie sighed as her eyes flicked back and forth between them.

She'd met the grim reaper, and though he scared the shit out of her, he'd never felt creepy. She'd thought that the master of death would have felt like the grave—bugs, worms, and decay. He just seemed like an awkward human. But when he slipped off his human costume, he felt like finality. Terrifying, but honest.

The coroner felt…dirty. Jamie didn't like her. She wanted to reach down and rub the spot where the coroner had touched her.

Maybe it was just the situation. This room. The cold. The dead body of her father three feet away.

Her mother cleared her throat. "Is…is there anything else I need to do?"

"I just need you to sign some paperwork upstairs," the coroner replied.

Sharon nodded, swallowing hard.

Everyone stood frozen in the moment, no one daring to make the first move. A shiver ran down Jamie's back as the cop's eyes ran slowly up and down her body. Bile rose in the back of her throat. She forced her eyes away from the cop, his greasy stare making her skin crawl.

The coroner's gaze wasn't much better. Though it was more clinical than lascivious, there was still an appraising ownership Jamie didn't like. Placing her hand on the flat of her mother's back, she gently nudged her toward the elevator.

Sharon took the hint, moving her foot in the first hesitant step. A second followed the first until she was walking briskly toward the shiny stainless-steel doors of the elevator. Jamie swung around her mom, keeping her mother's body between her and the creepy cop and the weird coroner. Behind her, the drawer slid shut. Crisp, clipped footsteps followed them. The coroner reached out and pushed the button and the door opened.

Not waiting, Jamie stepped in and tucked herself into the corner, pushing her back into the wall as hard as she could. Her mother followed her in, moving to the side of the elevator. Her body blocked Jamie's. The cop and coroner walked in, the coroner pushing the button to take them up.

The ascent took forever, at least in her head. Being confined inside a morgue elevator with people she wasn't fond of, including her mother, wasn't a delightful experience. Normally, she wasn't a claustrophobic person, but this elevator… The walls were closing in on her. The smell of death contrasting with high-powered cleaners didn't help as they assaulted her sensitive nose.

When the elevator binged and the door opened, she pushed past her mother and walked halfway toward the exit.

"Honey, where are you going?" her mother asked.

"To the car."

"We'll need her to sign the paperwork, too. Since she's not a minor." Detective Ryan leered at her.

Jamie's shoulders slumped, and she trudged back toward the small group, keeping her eyes glued to the floor. When she neared them, the coroner turned and led the way toward an office. The space was entirely too small to be confined in. She walked in last, pulling the door only partially closed so she could flee if she had to.

Her mother sat in a chair with a clipboard on her lap as she filled out paperwork. The office was entirely too small for four people, a fact the cop used to stand too close to Jamie. She tried to block out his unwashed scent but couldn't. The dash of day-old cologne did nothing but highlight his rank odor.

When it was her turn, she snatched the clipboard from the weird coroner, filling out the lines as quickly as she could. She didn't care if her answers were legible. After she finished the last line, she dropped the clipboard on the desk, tossed the pen after it, and shoved her way past the creepy cop who'd placed himself to partially block the door. As she passed, he pressed into her, sniffing loudly at her.

Gagging, she set a brisk pace but did her best to avoid breaking into a run as she headed toward where her mother had parked the car. As fresh air—as fresh as the dirty air in Red City ever was— washed over her, she inhaled deeply but couldn't complete the breath before exhaling in a shallow gasp.

The stench of the cop stuck to her, slithering its way up her nose. Hurtling forward, she barely made it around the back of the car before her stomach asserted control, and she vomited over the cracked pavement.

SEVEN

DAX

Boudreaux bent over The Rat, checking his pulse. "Huh. I would have never figured him for the fainting type."

"Is he OK?" Dax asked, shifting back to his human form. He looked into the aether and found The Rat's life thread. It was strong and showed no signs of ending in the immediate future, so he let it disappear from sight.

"Yeah. He sagged on himself so he didn't crack his head too hard. He might have a sore spot, but I doubt he'll even get a bump." Boudreaux carefully straightened out The Rat's limbs so the crumpled form of his body looked more natural.

The rats circled around their master in waves like a furry whirlpool. They'd allowed Boudreaux to attend to their master but had lunged at Tomi and Dax if they tried to get closer. So, they stepped back and let the man trained as an EMT take care of their master.

Boudreaux looked up at Dax. "Want me to get out the salts?"

"Not unless it's necessary." He stepped back.

A few moments later, The Rat stirred, weak mumbles falling from his lips. Tomi reached into his messenger bag and pulled out a bottle of water and handed it to Boudreaux.

The Rat's eyes fluttered open but looked unfocused as he looked around. When his eyes settled on Dax, he whimpered and flopped up, pushing himself backward in a crab walk. The rats surged between Dax and The Rat, forming a protective wall, Tomi temporarily forgotten now that their master was back at the reins.

"H-h-have you come for me?" The Rat whimpered, terror filling his unsteady eyes.

Dax shook his head. "No. I'm retired." He wasn't sure why that wording formed in his mind and fell from his lips, but it felt appropriate, all things considered.

"R-r-retired?" The Rat stopped scuttling backward but didn't visibly relax.

"I'm only here for the reasons stated. We're trying to track down who wants me dead."

A shrill laugh erupted from The Rat. "Everyone?" The blood drained from his face and his eyes went wide in shock at what he'd said. "I'm sorry, please don't…"

Tomi chuckled. "Relax, dude. We ain't gonna hurt you. We're just looking for information."

Dax nodded. "That's it. I was merely demonstrating why I was different from other gunshot victims in this city."

"You want me to track down someone powerful or insane enough to put a mark on the fucking Grim Reaper's head? Nuh uh. Rats don't stick their necks out. That's how they get snapped in traps." He shook his head vigorously. "Rats are survivors. You don't survive by being that foolhardy."

Air hissed between Dax's teeth. "There's nothing I can do to persuade you to at least ask around?"

"No. I ask the wrong question to the wrong person, then my name makes it onto a hit list. I don't want to end up a chalk outline. I don't have much, but I'm not interested in acquiring one of those." He looked around frantically at his rats, mumbling, "Tiny little chalk outlines…"

It wasn't the first time he'd heard something like this. He'd consulted with a man named Gunnar about the runes carved on the bullet they'd pulled from Dax's body. Though Gunnar had given him a bit of information, he'd bowed out beyond that, citing a favor owed to Manman Delphine as the only reason he was there in the first place.

Dax sighed. No one in this festering shit hole of a city wanted to stick their neck out to help someone else. Each time he encountered this, he felt more grateful to Adele and Tomi for actually helping him when he first appeared in Red City.

"Thanks for your time, Mr. The Rat." Dax extended a hand to help the man up.

The Rat stared at the hand. "You're not going to smite me, are you?"

"No, I'm retired. I'm just offering a hand up, that's it."

The Rat nodded, and the sea of rats parted, making room for Dax to approach. The Rat accepted the help. Patting the dirt off of his pants and shoulders, he shifted his jacket into place and stood tall —as tall as a man of his short stature could—and looked quizzically at Dax.

The Rat tipped his head to the side and narrowed his eyes. "No threats? No attempts to force me to help?"

"Nope," Dax said, looking at Tomi. "It's not my style."

The Rat chuckled, the sound high and clipped. It extended into a full-on laugh. Dax quirked an eyebrow up. When the laughter ended, The Rat bent over and slapped his knees, picking up a rat to pet. "Not your style. That's funny."

"If we're done here, we should get back to the office, boss." Tomi tipped his head back the way they came.

"Right," Dax replied. "Boudreaux, I think we're ready to go." He turned to The Rat. "Again, thank you for your time. If you happen to pick up any information in your normal"—he looked at the rats moving about the tunnel floor—"foraging, please let me know. I'll buy you a drink or two. And, I'd appreciate it."

"What kind of favors can a retired man offer?"

Dax chuckled. "I guess we'll never know if you don't attempt to collect on the offer."

"I guess that's true." The Rat nodded as a bow of farewell. "Until we meet again."

Without a word, he turned toward the direction from which he'd emerged and stalked away, his rats scurrying around him in random orbits. Dax and his companions waited until he was no longer visible before starting their own trek out of the tunnels.

Another dead end. He wanted to sigh and complain to Tomi but kept it to himself in the presence of Boudreaux. At least the walk back would give him time to think about his next move.

EIGHT

DAX

Once they parted ways with The Rat, they kept quiet for a while until Boudreaux started whistling quietly. At first it was atonal, but as the volume grew, he added in a slight melody. Dax wasn't familiar with the man or his moods, they'd only met a handful of times and they'd kept pretty busy, but the whistling sounded nervous. Though it wasn't annoying to him, it did add to his growing tension about his lack of progress.

"You OK there, bro?" Tomi asked, picking up on his new friend's nervousness as well.

Boudreaux chuckled. "Sorry. I'm not that fond of tunnels. They make me a little anxious."

Dax had never had any issues with confined spaces before becoming a human, but after the incident in the basement of the morgue where the ghosts had pressed in on him like collapsing walls, he found himself focusing on the low ceilings of the tunnel and seemingly endless darkness a bit more than he was comfortable with.

Tomi shrugged. "They're not that bad. But I guess I've grown up in some small places. Well, at least this place. I didn't like the tunnels that stank of sewage."

"After being in Afghanistan, anything cave-like makes me a bit…apprehensive." Boudreaux shivered, though it wasn't that cold.

"Ah," Tomi said. "At least it's safe down here."

Boudreaux snorted. "I wouldn't place any bets on that. We're here at The Rat's invitation. What do you think would happen if he decided he didn't want us here? He could turn every rat in this place against us. And that means *every* rat, not just the few he had with him. And I'd bet there are others lurking down here that are at least as dangerous as he is."

Tomi looked around nervously, drawing closer to Boudreaux. Dax wanted to laugh but found his own anxiety elevating at the thought of what else might be hiding in this labyrinthine jumble of tunnels.

"What is he?" Tomi asked, now walking beside Boudreaux.

"The Rat? No idea. I've never asked him, and Delphine has never elaborated. Though I'm not sure she even knows. All I know is that he's a man with absolute control over rats. At least those around these tunnels." He stopped and looked up and to the side, rubbing his hand over his shaved head. "I have no idea if it's like a pack thing or a clan thing or what. Maybe his pack of rats has other rats that are their enemies. I've only met him around this part of town. Though never in the same place twice."

"I guess the more important question is, who is Delphine? She seems to have connections all over the magical community of Red City." Dax snorted. "I didn't even realize there was much of a magical community here, let alone multiple ones all seeming to connect through Manman Delphine."

He'd known there were supernaturals in Red City—they were spread out over the world—but hadn't realized how diverse and sizable it was. He guessed in a place like this where chaos and corruption were the order of the day, it was a good place to hide in plain sight since everyone seemed to want to keep their heads down and not get involved.

Boudreaux laughed and started forward again. "I wish you luck exposing those depths. Those waters run *deep*. But you could do far worse than staying on her good side. She's well connected, and I suspect she has a deep reserve of her own power."

Dax nodded but realized Boudreaux wouldn't be able to see the gesture since he was in front. "That is something we can agree on."

He'd only had the most basic of interactions with the manbo, but what he'd felt without probing deeper had indicated she was indeed quite powerful. He didn't wish to investigate further; he felt that would be considered rude, though he didn't know much about the etiquette between supernaturals. He imagined that similar rules he'd learned about consent and privacy from Tomi and his family would translate to those in the paranormal community.

Keeping to himself had seemed like a good idea when he first landed in Red City, but he was at a severe handicap now that some members of the magical community were after him, or taking orders from someone who wished him grave harm. What was it the mortals said? Hindsight is twenty-twenty?

He had to be thankful that Delphine had connected him with several members of the magical community who could help him now that he needed it. If it weren't for Tomi's mother and her friendship with the voodoo practitioner, he'd truly be up shit creek. Though, Boudreaux had turned out to be the only one willing to regularly assist him, besides the manbo that is. He tried not to be frustrated about the lack of aid, but right now, it was becoming a serious obstacle.

He wasn't entirely sure what her reason was for being so helpful. Sure, he'd facilitated the peaceful end-of-life transition of one of her parishioners, who couldn't afford hospice care, as repayment for healing him and arranging for medical treatment after the two times he'd been shot. But he couldn't help but wonder what her end game was.

He snorted quietly. He'd been shot. Several times now, including the bullets that struck him during the melee with the bikers. That was something that'd never happened in his entire existence, and he couldn't say that he ever wished to experience it again. Getting shot wasn't even a possibility when one was a primal force of the universe.

He just wanted to be left alone to run his bar, hang out with his friend, and watch his kitten grow. But with each passing incident, those goals were looking more and more distant. He could either hunker down and be cranky about the whole situation or keep doing what he was doing now—trying to put himself out there to find some way of ending the attacks.

Tomi and his mother, he could trust. They had a mutual bond forged out of saving each other's lives and years of friendship. Dax had naturally extended this bond of trust to Delphine because she was Adele's friend. And Adele had introduced them to each other when he needed help with a wound that wouldn't quite heal and when he needed the bullet that had done it examined by an expert who could read the runes carved into it.

Going forward, he'd have to be more cautious about who he trusted and why, including Delphine and Boudreaux. He didn't know if it was the general mistrust he'd encountered in the last few months when he needed help that had caused his growing wariness or if it merely had reinforced that which had been lying under the surface, tucked away from when he'd been betrayed and cast out to live as a human in this dark, fetid city.

Tomi's sigh of relief drew him up from his dark thoughts as a soft glow of natural light greeted them in the distance. When they stepped out of the tunnel and back into the light, his own shoulders relaxed. Boudreaux escorted them to Tomi's car before departing.

Dax held out his hand. "Thanks for helping out, Boudreaux. Next time you're at the bar, your tab is on me."

Boudreaux shook Dax's hand firmly. "Hell yeah. Thanks, Dax."

"Just yours, not your crew's," Tomi added quickly.

The bald, muscular Black man laughed. "Don't worry, bro. I'm not going to fuck up a good offer like that. That's how you ensure it's only a one-time deal."

"Thanks," Tomi said. They exchanged the same elaborate handshake they'd shared earlier.

"Anytime. You two stay out of trouble. And let me know if you need anyone to run the streets with you. It's always good for a laugh." He turned around and walked off, stuffing his hands in his pockets as he walked away.

Neither Tomi nor Dax felt like chatting after they climbed into Tomi's car, at least not until they were back in the north part of town.

"Want me to drop you off at your apartment?" Tomi asked.

Dax ran his hand through his hair and squeezed the back of his neck, the muscles tight with tension. "Yeah. I need the rest of the day off to figure out what the hell our next move is."

"You sure? Suzie's acquaintance Becky was supposed to stop by, along with a few other applicants. I thought you wanted to be there."

"You can handle it, Tomi. You know what kind of person we need behind the bar. If one of them has the skills and will fit in with the clients, hire them. Suzie can help you out."

"I can handle that." Tomi nodded, pursing his lips. "I'll take care of the orders today, also."

"Thanks." A beer, some music, and Morty's antics would go a long way to relieve the day's frustrations. He just hoped he'd be able to figure out his next move before someone else made theirs.

NINE

DAX

"Ugh." Dax waved his hand in front of his nose as he cracked the door to his apartment.

The cat box needed cleaning again. It didn't help that Morty liked to leave particularly stinky turds unburied. Dax almost thought it was a warped game the kitten played with him.

He was fond of his kitten, surprisingly. Having the little furry friend to come home to had filled a hole he wasn't aware of. After more than five years in Red City living as a human, he'd barely scratched the surface of what it meant to live inside his human meat suit beyond the basics of food, drink, and regular visits to the bathroom. He was quite fond of the drinks. Tea was one of the few mortal luxuries he really reveled in.

Whiskey had been a nice addition.

Grabbing a baggie and the scoop, he bent over to the litter box, grumbling about the stinky kitten. As if planning the timing, Morty bounced along chasing a toy mouse, looking for all the world like a silly monster with his ears down and his back arched.

Dax chuckled at his antics and stood up to watch. "Wait… You don't have a toy mouse. Fuck!"

A terrified squeak drifted in from the kitchen. Dax jogged in after it. Morty, hissing and growling at it, had the mouse cornered under the counter. Listening for a moment, Dax shook his head. His ears must be playing tricks on him, or it was a coincidence that some of the kitten's hisses and growls sounded vaguely like words.

A mouse must have made it into the apartment. The tenants on the lower floors had been complaining about the incursion of rodents forced out of their field from the nearby construction project. They'd finally made it to the fourth floor.

Squatting down, he looked closer at the mouse. "How is the poor creature still alive?"

There were several large wounds and what looked like guts poking out of a wound on its side. Dax reached out to the mouse in the aether and found its terribly frayed life thread. With a quick mental twitch of his reaping scythe, he put the poor critter out of its misery.

Sneaking forward, Morty patted at the mouse a couple times then turned on Dax, swatting at him with a growl.

"Hey!"

The kitten sniffed then walked away, his head held high and disdainfully.

He didn't know what normal behavior was for a kitten, but Morty certainly had a load of personality. Once he saw his kitten's spiky tail disappear around the corner, he plucked the mouse's corpse from the floor by its tail and dropped it into the garbage. He'd take it down to the dumpsters after he finished the litter box.

With that task finished and his hands washed, he fired up the water kettle for a cup of tea. He pulled down a tin of Ambra Thieves, wanting something black and robust and easy. A hit of caffeine would go a long way after the long morning of crawling through Red City's underground. He chuckled to himself. Morty wouldn't have been as aggressive with the rodents there, several of which were bigger than he was.

After he set his tea on a coaster on the coffee table, he turned on the stereo system and put on some Buckethead, wanting some instrumental metal to think over his predicament to.

At some point, Morty must have forgiven him his trespasses with the mouse, curling up next to him on the couch for a nap. He absent-mindedly stroked the kitten's back, the feel of his soft, silky fur soothing him, despite the dark thoughts ruminating in his head.

Some still wanted him dead. Several someones actually. The bikers could still be counted on to collect on the debt he'd created by killing most of the local chapter and burning down their clubhouse. No doubt they'd been paid to put him in their crosshairs. Unless the cold trail on their lost enforcer had finally led back to him...

Then there was the perfidious Detective Randall Ryan. The cop had been harassing Dax since he purchased the bar not long after washing up in Red City. Ryan had only been a beat cop, running the normal bullshit protection racket the low-level badges ran on every street in the city.

He'd advanced up the ranks to become a homicide detective, although he kept his fingers in the pies he'd baked earlier in his career. A detective had more time on their hands in a city where the police didn't give an actual shit about solving murders, especially since they had their hand in a fair few of them directly or through their surrogates like the bikers, as many rumors had it.

Then there was a potential mystery third shooter. He suspected that Ryan might have been the one to pull the trigger on Jason, Dax's bartender, mistaking him for Dax in the dark, but he had no actual confirmation of it.

If he'd had more time and awareness at either the scene of the crime or later in the morgue before he became overwhelmed by the angry spirits pressing in on him, he could have more thoroughly investigated Jason's life thread to see if it intersected with his killer's near the moment of death. Perhaps he could have traced that line to its owner. But for now, suspicion and a desire to avoid adding more complications to the equation kept ol' Rand Ryan in pole position.

Perhaps the manbo might know a way to get in touch with the more distantly deceased. He doubted the TV psychics were the real deal, but if anyone was, Delphine would likely know them.

But neither the bikers, at least with their first attempt—it seemed unlikely that they'd cracked his identity after all this time—nor Ryan would take him out on their own initiative. Ryan wouldn't do anything without extracting profit from it. Someone put them up to it, likely for a handsome fee. Out of a sense of morbid curiosity, he wondered what the price was for the head of the Grim Reaper. If the boss actually knew who they were targeting.

The bikers might have had a reason to come after him on their own. He'd killed and taken the body of one of their numbers when he was first dropped off in Red City by the death gods who'd teamed up to force him to accept banishment as a human. But after this long with no attempts, he had assumed they'd given up looking for their gang's enforcer and debt collector.

If they'd been serious about collecting that debt, they wouldn't have sent in a green kid to do it in a morbid bid to pay back the kid's degenerate gambler of a father.

So, that left him with a sinking feeling, especially when coupled with the warning from Baron Samedi, that one or more psychopomps were trying to get around their deal to let him be by employing mortal agents in Red City.

"Fuck me sideways," he grumbled. "Why can't they just leave me alone? It's not bad enough they stripped me of my power and forced me to live in this bag of meaty water, but they're trying to take even that away from me?"

He felt the fire ignite in his eyes. The hand stroking the kitten shifted from flesh to the bleached bones of the reaper form he'd been forced to take as an alternative to the human body. He'd been too powerful to contain in just a human vessel, so as a joke, they'd allowed him the second form. The tattered robe-covered skeleton had never been his favorite depiction humans had given death, so that's the one his exilers had selected. It allowed him room to maneuver a little but with little power unless he violated his word.

He might be death, but he had no desire to meet his own oblivion.

Without The Rat's help, he didn't have many avenues left open to him.

TEN

JAMIE

"Jamie?"

"Jamie," Cory hissed. "You're being asked a question. Jamie."

"Cory, that's enough," Mr. Baker, her history teacher, snapped. "Ms. Rodriguez. If I could have your attention, please."

She sighed loudly, shaking her head slightly. She'd gotten lost in her thoughts again. Anytime her focus slipped, her mind drifted back to the morgue and the sight of her dead father's body. He'd always tended toward an unhealthy shade of pale, but with his throat cut, he looked practically sepulcher.

She snorted. Sepulcher. That word had to be worth a few points on the SAT. And despite the lack of blood, the cut glowed dark red in her mind's eye.

"Is something amusing you, Ms. Rodriguez?" Mr. Baker's words sounded clipped and irritable, though that wasn't a far trip for him at the best of times.

"Sorry," she mumbled.

"Can you tell us what year the last Roman emperor was deposed in Rome?"

She used to like history class, but Mr. Baker only seemed to want to talk about dates and names, never the why's and how's. "476 CE."

Mr. Baker narrowed his eyes at her, then turned to stalk back to his desk. Opening his mouth, he didn't even get a syllable out before the bell rang. Anything else he might have wanted to say disappeared in the din of students shifting their chairs and preparing to vacate the room for their next class.

Shoving her book into her backpack, she joined the scrum trying to vacate the classroom. Cory's familiar presence tucked in behind her. It had been ages since she'd seen him outside of school. Not since she and her mother had moved out anyway, and they hadn't been allowed to go out on their own in case the bikers might have been looking for them. At first, she'd almost been relieved to move out of Cory's house with the increasing tension as Linda grew cold. The added tension of her mother's unwillingness to rely on the almost stranger hadn't helped. But things had only gotten worse when Cory had been banned from seeing her after school.

As soon as they squeezed through the door, they took the turn toward their lockers to dump their books before their break. They maintained their silence as they made their way to the library and their favorite table buried deep in the back corner.

She did her best to ignore the strange glances and the behind-the-hand whispers that had followed her since returning to school after leaving with a police escort. At times, she wished she could disappear. She'd spent so many years trying not to be noticed. Being perceived was just one more insult to the steady stream of injuries. Before following Cory in, she cast one last look around her to make sure she didn't see the unwelcome and unwanted visage of Travis.

They hadn't seen him since that fateful night. She didn't recall seeing him at the bar when she'd been dragged in with her parents, but it's not like they let her get a good look around. It was possible he could have been one of the bodies Dax had left to the fires.

She wasn't sure how she felt about that possibility. She didn't like Travis. He'd been a piece of shit well on his way to a criminal life in a Nazi motorcycle gang, but she'd known him for a lot of years—since elementary school. He'd never gotten a chance to find a new path.

She shrugged. She couldn't devote any emotional bandwidth to him. With her own life swirling steadily downward, she barely had the energy to shower and show up for school. But at least it was a relief from the shitty motels and her mom. Her mother barely talked to her. They'd moved a few times already, looking for weekly rental motels in random parts of the city. She lived out of a bag, her clothes smelling like a laundromat washing machine. Groaning inwardly, she wondered what her father's death would do to her mother's justifiable paranoia.

The drive home had been uncomfortable, her mother swerving between coldly numb and falsely cheerful like a metronome—

"Ouch!" Cory said.

She'd slammed into his back after he stopped.

"Almost crushed my giggle berries into the table…" He gestured toward his crotch.

"Sorry," she mumbled. Normally, the silly euphemism would have gotten a groan or a halfhearted chuckle out of her.

"What's going on with you?" Cory sank into the seat he usually took.

Not saying anything, she dropped her bag and slipped into her chair. Staring at the table, she leaned forward, resting her forehead against the knuckles of both fists. "My dad is dead."

"W-what?" Cory slumped, leaning closer.

"Someone killed him. Slit his throat." It all came out of her mouth flat and robotically. "I had to identify his body last Thursday."

The blood drained from Cory's face, and his jaw dropped. "Holy shit… Was that why you weren't at school Friday?"

She gave a half shrug. "I guess we don't have to worry about him gambling away everything now…"

Cory slowly brought a hand up to cover his mouth. "I'm so sorry, I…"

"I feel like I'm supposed to be sad. But I'm just swinging from numb to angry. Just one last indignity my father forced on me. Like that's how his life ends. Dead on a slab, an unredeemed gambling addict." She should probably worry about being overheard, but it was almost the end of the year and few people chose to gather in the library when the sun was shining.

"Do you think… I don't know. Did you want to give him a chance?"

"No. Yes? I don't know. We'll never know now." She raised her eyes from the scratched wood of the library table and met Cory's gaze. "I guess Mom was right to keep moving us." She barked half a hysterical laugh. "I better start watching behind me."

She sank in on herself and let her head fall to the table with a sold thunk of bone against wood.

"Shit. I-I don't know what to say."

Raising her head an inch, she let her head bonk back onto the table a few times. "Fuck my life. What's left of it."

She jolted slightly as Cory's hand rested on her shoulder. Once she relaxed, he gave it an affectionate squeeze. Taking in a deep breath, she held it for a while, then let it out explosively as she sat back up.

Cory swallowed and licked his lips. "Should you go…you know…go see Dax?"

She scoffed. "What's he going to do? I'm not sure he'll be exactly excited to see me darkening his door."

"I mean, he showed up to help you once. You're kind of bonded now. And"—Cory looked around to check if anyone had moved into their area—"if he's as scary as you say he is, he's the only one that can look after you. Lord knows I can't." The last bit sounded a bit bitter.

"It's never been your job to protect me, you jackass." She shook her head, her cheeks flushing with a touch of anger. "Just be my friend. That's all I've ever asked of you. Damn, I could use a run and a burger."

Cory eye's flicked back and forth nervously.

"Please tell me your mom has ungrounded you. It's been a while now. You've never been in trouble this long before. I need a run with my best friend." Pleading filled her eyes.

"I'm real sorry." He swallowed and looked down at his hands as he clasped them tightly in front of himself. "I'm so sorry…"

"Why? Still grounded. It's not your fault. It sucks"—she shrugged—"but it'll be over eventually, then we can hang out again."

Cory shook his head, still refusing to raise his eyes. "I can't hang out with you anymore. Not outside school. She-she won't let me see you anymore." He reached out to her, but she jerked back. "I'm sorry," he mumbled.

She'd pulled back like he'd just hit her, her mouth hanging open in shock. Her heart squeezed in her chest. Linda had been like a second mother to her. Sometimes a better mother than her own who seemed too distracted by solving the problems her husband's gambling had caused.

Now, Linda had escalated the prohibition against Jamie and told her son to not see her anymore. Not only that, but did it in such a manner as to enforce it.

"Can't..." She didn't know what she wanted to ask. For him to sneak out? To defy his mother? Some part of her wanted him to risk it for her. They'd been friends for most of their lives. Now...this?

"I can't. She got rid of my car. A tow truck showed up and took it away last night. She cancelled all my cards."

"But you're eighteen..."

He snorted bitterly. "Fat lot of good that did. They're all under her name. I have no wheels and no funds. I can't even access my bank account."

"I-I've got bus money..."

"Jamie... I can't." He hung his head low so he could avoid her eyes.

"You can't?" She lurched up from her chair, knocking it backward. "We've always been there for each other? Now this?"

"Jamie, I'm sorry."

"Sorry?" She snatched up her bag. "No. I'm sorry."

Spinning around, she stalked out of the library and through the halls. Behind her, the door to the library slammed open.

"Jamie! Wait," Cory called.

She held up her fist and extended her middle finger, not trusting herself to say anything. Tears burned at the corner of her eyes, and she worried that if she tried to speak, it would only open the floodgates. She hadn't cried when she saw her father or later when she'd returned home. But Cory? Abandoning her? Her one rock?

That was too much. He was the one thing she could always count on through all the bad times she'd been forced to endure. Focusing her senses forward, she didn't want to see if he was following her. She wasn't sure what she'd do, and she didn't want to say anything she'd regret. At least more than anything else in her life.

Her feet carried her toward the nearest exit. She was done.

"Ms. Rodriquez, where are you going?" a woman with authority in her voice asked as she passed.

"To deal with my dead dad." She slammed her palms into the door's crossbar and shoved it open, ignoring anything or anyone behind her.

ELEVEN

At some point, Jamie had slung her backpack over her shoulders. She wasn't sure when. All she knew was her feet hurt. She probably needed new shoes, but where would she get the money for that? She'd been walking for a long time, just wandering over the dirty streets of Red City.

She stopped. While the neighborhood the school was in wasn't great, it wasn't as dirty and rundown as this one. She didn't know when the transition had happened, as caught up in her own internal world as she'd been. Sighing, she dragged her arm across her forehead, smearing sweat and grime across herself.

Something felt vaguely familiar. Looking around, she saw the city morgue she'd been to last Thursday. Why her feet had carried her there, she couldn't be sure. Nearby, a bench offered a tantalizing place to get off her feet. It even had enough slats to make it somewhat comfortable.

Sinking onto it, she grunted as her backpack blocked her from the backrest. She shrugged it off and set it next to her, making sure to sling an arm through the strap in case someone tried to make a snatch and dash.

Even in the warm spring sunshine, the morgue made her shiver. She'd grown up in Red City. Violent death was a normal part of life here. But it had just been part of the background—the sinister ambience—of the place, not a direct reality for her. She'd been too young to remember or really be affected by the death of her mother's parents. She'd never met her father's.

She'd seen dead bodies in the bar just a few months ago. Bodies Dax had killed. But her adrenaline had been pumping, and she'd been more focused on surviving and getting out of the bar than really looking at the results of death, even though it was her nominal ally.

But her father's body. Looking at the jagged cut across his neck. Looking into his vacant eyes. That was the first time she'd directly confronted mortality. Even during their near disastrous car chase with Dax, she'd been too terrified of everything happening, including the oncoming train, to really grapple with death.

In her pocket, her phone buzzed a couple times, but like all the previous times, she ignored it. She had no desire to hear Cory's voice or her mother's.

She looked up. It was later than she'd thought. The sun was drawing near the horizon. Soon, darkness would descend over the neon polluted sky of Red City. Even the morgue had a tacky neon sign announcing itself.

Looking down at the ground, she wondered how deep the elevator to the room full of bodies went. How far under the ground was her father? Did it run under the street? She might be sitting directly above her father's body at that moment.

She snorted and shook her head. At least for now, she'd never have to guess where her father was when he didn't come home in the evening. She had his exact address.

Sparing some focus, she turned her body toward the west, letting the colorful sunset paint her in its vivid colors. All the pollution at least made for beautiful sunsets.

Her whole body cringed in a sudden shiver. "Ugh."

She didn't think the temperature had dropped that much, but temperatures were more variable in the spring. She waited until most of the color had been leached out of the sunset until only the deepest purples faded into the somewhat darker night sky.

Another shiver wracked her body. It felt too directional to be the air. Her back almost felt clammy. A good walk would warm her blood. It was probably time to head toward the motel her mom had procured the other night.

Sighing, she spun around for one last look at the morgue. "Wha!"

A figure sat next to her. She shook herself back into awareness. She hadn't heard him walk up. Nor had she felt his weight on the bench when he sat. Pushing back, she tried to open more space but bumped into the armrest. Her eyes darted around, looking for an escape.

So far, he hadn't addressed her, but she didn't want to make any moves that would inspire him to pursue her. As she waited, a car came down the dark road and turned so its headlights pointed in her direction. The man on the bench washed out as the lights poured through him.

In shallow gasps, her breath whistled in and out of her mouth. Now that she focused on the man, she realized she could see the planks of the bench through him. She swallowed but found her mouth as dry as a desert.

So far, whatever it was—it couldn't be a person; people weren't see through—hadn't noticed her. Gathering her feet under her, she placed her hand on the armrest, bracing herself to stand and dash away.

"Ja...mie..."

It had to be the wind. But the air felt dead and stagnant, with no breeze touching on the sweat blossoming from her skin. A piece of nearby plastic trash sat perfectly still.

Slowly, the thing turned its head toward her. She squeaked and pushed herself further back into the armrest. It looked at her through her father's eyes and face.

"Ja...mie..."

She clamped her eyes shut, trying to think who she should cast a prayer to. Could she pray to Dax to protect her from a...a ghost?

"Ja…mie…"

It had to be a figment of her imagination. She'd been staring at the morgue for hours, thinking about death and her life and her father. She'd barely had lunch nor much water. She had to be hungry, thirsty, and hallucinating. Reaching down with her free hand, she rested it on her thigh. Forcing her eyes open, she brought her thumb together with her fore and middle fingers in a brutal pinch.

"Ouch! Fuck!" She let go and shook her head and her hand. The thing with her father's face stared at her still.

"Ja…mie…"

"What? What do you want from me? Haven't you taken enough from me already?" She groaned. "Now you're taking my sanity."

"Jamie…" The syllables were a bit closer, the sound more substantial.

She sagged back on the bench, putting her head in her hands.

"Ssssorry…Ja…mie…"

Raising her head, she pursed her lips. "Typical. Trying to apologize after it's way too late."

He shook his head, wisps floating away. "Be…ware…"

"Beware? I know. Murderous gang of motorcycle wolf shifter Nazi fucks are trying to kill me. I don't need M. Night Shyamalan for that twist, Dad."

"No." It was the most substantial word he'd said.

She thought a wave of anger had passed over his spectral face.

"Be…ware…fake." His spectral skin faded a bit, revealing veins and flesh under it.

"Fake what?"

"Im…poster…" His skull flashed, almost baring his teeth.

"Who? Damn you, can't you even be useful in death?" She reached out to grab him and shake him, but her hands passed through him. Shivering, she tried to right herself before she fell all the way through him.

She pushed back into the corner of the bench, trying to get her breath under control. Once she quit blinking rapidly, she thought her father looked less substantial than he had earlier. At best, he was an insubstantial man in life. In death, he seemed even more so.

"Ja…mie…be…ware…the…imp…" He failed to finish the last word before another car came along, and the glare of the headlights forced her to closer her eyes.

When she opened them, the…ghost…spirit…whatever…was gone. Reaching out, she waved her hand through the air where he'd been earlier. Finally, she pressed her hand onto the wood slats where he'd been sitting—if a ghost could be said to sit. The planks were ice cold. She yanked her hand back, shaking it. Now that he was gone, the night felt practically balmy.

Despite the sudden increase in temperature, she shivered, her body twitching exaggeratedly, and huffed out a noisy sigh.

It's not like she had enough on her plate without some new warning, if she even believed it. Who was the imposter? Why should she be aware of it? Snorting, she slumped. Cory was an imposter, pretending to be her friend.

That wasn't fair. He'd participated in her attempted murder of Dax. It wasn't his fault, except for agreeing to get involved in the first place, that his mother wasn't letting him hang out. Her first priority was to protect her son, not the stray he'd brought home all those years ago. It hurt like hell, though.

Staring at the morgue, she wondered if she'd actually seen a ghost. A few months ago, she wouldn't have believed a ghost could exist. Now… She'd been chased by the Grim Reaper and seen the terrifying flames in his eyes. She'd watched as he demolished a bar full of scary outlaw bikers and survived. If the angel of death could exist, it made the existence of ghosts far more possible.

Someone had killed her father, and now his ghost—if it was indeed his spirit—had visited her and provided a warning. But without more definite information, she'd just have to continue her hyper vigilance and look forward to an ulcer by the time she was nineteen.

Off in the distance, another car approached. Squinting, she looked away to avoid having the headlights blind her completely. As the car passed, she returned her attention to the building across the street. How many ghosts were stuck in the limbo of the morgue besides her father?

Blinking, she realized the red glare breaking into her peripheral vision was the brake lights of the car as it slowed. Then its reverse lights added a touch of white light to the mix.

A new shot of adrenaline dumped into her veins. "Fuck."

TWELVE

DAX

Dax sat at the end of the bar against the wall, the usual spot he liked to occupy while he wasn't behind the bar or in the office. It was his turn to train Little Suzie's friend Becky. Even though the budget was tight, they just didn't have enough bodies to cover all the shifts, especially if he or Tomi weren't available for whatever reason, such as recovering from lead injections…

Now that she'd had a couple days with Tomi and Suzie and knew most of the bar's basic procedures, she could run the front of the house well enough. She knew her business, and the crowd seemed to like her—both the daytime blue-collar crowd and the evening hipsters, punks, and metal heads.

She looked like a preppy cheerleader from down the block, but her bobbing head and mouthed along lyrics to the punk and metal songs blaring out of the jukebox spoke to different depths. Most importantly, Tomi and Suzie liked her and thought she'd work out. He'd come to trust Tomi's assessment of people, especially since his own ability to judge people was somewhat limited due to his background.

"Another can of Rainier, Dax?" Becky asked, leaning against the bar.

"Sure. Why not."

She reached into the undercounter cooler and pulled one out for him. He pushed his empty can toward her and took the can, downing a drink before placing it on the now damp coaster.

"Hey, Dax. Haven't seen you in much lately." Geoffrey pulled out a stool in the middle of the bar and sat down.

"Been a bit busy on a personal project." He turned to Becky. "Becky, this is Geoffrey. He's a newer regular. Likes the whiskey. Let him know if we've got anything new."

Geoffrey, in his typical business suit, nodded and smiled at Dax.

"And to that effect, we have a new Irish whiskey that's quite nice." He pointed to the bottle on the shelf.

"Oh! I'll take a dram of that, please, Becky. Neat." He winked at Dax. "Thanks for the tip."

Becky pulled down one of the nice whiskey glasses they kept for the connoisseurs who came in. Whiskey had gotten popular, even with the young alternative set. He and Tomi had built the collection more for their own enjoyment, but they'd gotten a rep in the neighborhood as a place for the whiskey lover who wasn't looking for a pretentious overpriced atmosphere. The shabby decor definitely solved that atmospheric problem.

After Geoffrey settled into his glass of whiskey and casual chitchat with Becky, Dax returned to brooding over his can of cheap lager. He was considering ordering a whiskey and leaving the motorcycle in the alley when someone cleared their throat behind him.

"Hey, Dax," a familiar deep voice rumbled behind him.

He swung around on his barstool. "Boudreaux! Come into take me up on the offer?"

"I mean I will, but that's not really why I'm here." He sounded nervous, something Dax had never heard in the limited time he'd known the confident, self-assured man.

Just behind Boudreaux and to the side, a pretty white woman with a black bob stood. She gripped her hands tightly, wringing them. Something felt vaguely familiar about her, but he couldn't place it.

"This is Winnie," Boudreaux said.

Ah. The coroner at the city morgue Boudreaux had snuck them in to. Dax hadn't seen her. He'd been zipped up in a body bag in his skeletal form, but he'd gotten a whiff of her essence since she spent so much time there that the building had absorbed a bit of her over the years.

Dax stuck out his hand. "Nice to meet you, Winnie." He couldn't acknowledge that he at least had kind of met her, not under the circumstances.

She shook his hand briefly, then looked down, mumbling, "Nice to meet you, too."

He raised an eyebrow, directing it to Boudreaux. "In for a date night?" Though he doubted it. He wasn't the best at reading human signals, but he was smart enough to pick up on the nervous vibe.

"Not exactly," Boudreaux replied. "Do you have a place we can talk privately? I think I might have a problem you can help with." He nodded slightly toward Winnie.

"Sure." He turned to Becky. "Can you handle the bar for a while? I'll just be back in the tearoom."

"Sure thing." She smiled brightly at him.

"Good. Boudreaux, Winnie, do you want a drink before we head back? All I have in the back of the house is tea."

Boudreaux looked at Winnie. "Whiskey?"

"Make it a double," she mumbled.

"Whatever they want, Becky. On my tab." He slid off his barstool to make room and grabbed his mostly full can of beer. "I'm going to go open the tearoom. Once Becky gets you your drinks, head down the hall over there."

Boudreaux nodded as Dax slipped by. After opening the door, he turned the lights on and found some light acoustic music to fill the silence and cover their conversation from eavesdropping, though he doubted he would need it. Being hunted had made him more paranoid. Tomi had even made several passes around the bar after closing looking for things like bugs or hidden cameras to satisfy Dax's fears.

"Serve a lot of tea in a dive bar?" Boudreaux said by way of letting Dax know they'd arrived.

Dax shrugged. "Not really, but maybe someday. If either of you would like a cup, let me know."

Boudreaux held up his glass of whiskey. "I'm good for now."

"Do you have some chamomile?" Winnie asked.

Dax nodded and stood up, heading behind the bar to start the water and prepare a pot of chamomile. "So I'm not sure how I can help you. But if you wouldn't mind shutting the door and flipping the lock, you can tell me what's going on."

"Well, I'm not really here to see you as the owner of the bar. But more in your…uh…your other capacity." Boudreaux looked around the room.

He'd seen Dax in his skeletal form for the first time when they'd broken into The Collector's compound to free some supernatural creatures and people he'd abducted. Then again, a few days ago when they'd visited The Rat.

"Please have a seat." Dax gestured toward long rectangular table and benches that ran down the center of the tearoom. "I'll bring the pot of tea over when it's ready, then you can tell me how I can help you."

Once the water kettle dinged, he filled the pot and brought it over, fetching three cups to go with it. He pulled the strainer from the pot once his timer sounded, pouring a cup for Winnie. She nodded her thanks, then poured half the remaining whiskey down her throat, coughing at the burn. Dax grabbed her a glass of water. The tea would be too hot.

He kept his gaze on Boudreaux since Winnie seemed to be extremely uncomfortable for whatever reason. "So tell me why you're here."

THIRTEEN

DAX

Winnie wrapped her hands around the teacup, staring down into its pale depths. "I feel so stupid even being here. I'm a doctor. A scientist." She sighed. "But Boudreaux thinks you can help me. I don't know how. You're just the owner of a dive bar."

Boudreaux cleared his throat lightly.

She looked up quickly, her eyes wide. "Oh… I'm sorry. I didn't mean 'just' in that sense. Only that you're…" She huffed. "I don't know. I'm discombobulated."

"There are more things in the world than explained by science," Boudreaux said calmly.

She reached over and patted his forearm. "I know you're superstitious, but I have a medical degree. I'm an agnostic. That world just isn't for me."

Boudreaux laughed. "You may not think you're for that world, but it seems to be coming for you whether you like it or not."

Winnie scowled at him before turning back to Dax.

He suspected he knew what her issues were, at least partially. Ghosts. The morgue she was in charge of was infested with murder victims whose souls were pinned to their corpses, or at least, to the morgue. He didn't know the situation of every spirit there. Some were no doubt victims of the same bullets he'd nearly been a victim of, but many might be stuck there for a whole host of reasons. Winnie's morgue collected the city's violent deaths.

What concerned Dax more was the fact that the psychopomps who wanted the power of collecting souls for their own purposes seemed to be neglecting their duties. Those unhoused but imprisoned spirits deserved peace and transition, or at least transition. Some might have a reservation in the punishment side of their believed afterlife.

He thought about broaching the subject and making it easier for Winnie, but that would mean revealing Boudreaux's role in sneaking him into the facility to inspect Jason's body. Giving his head a quick shake, Dax focused in on his two guests who were staring at each other, apparently in some sort of wordless conversation or battle of wills.

"Do you want me to tell him? Dax and I have worked together on a couple things and I trust his opinion—"

Winnie opened her mouth to interrupt.

Boudreaux held up his hand. "You're going to have to trust me, Winnie. You've never had reason to doubt my integrity."

Her mouth hung open for a moment, then she closed it and nodded. "You've always been honest with me."

Boudreaux smiled fondly at her. "Thank you."

Dax refilled his cup. Chamomile wasn't his normal preference, but the anxiety of the tense interchange and the undercurrent of several someones wanting him dead made the tea a nice balm. The sudden motion outside their circle ended their brief exchange.

Shifting his attention to Dax, Boudreaux rested his elbows on the table and leaned forward. "I'm guessing, and this is from my own experience after our little adventure up on the bluff and knowing Manman Delphine, but I think you're uniquely qualified to help Winnie out."

He nodded, offering more tea to Winnie, who'd polished off most of her cup now that it had cooled enough. She set her cup down so he could fill it.

"To be blunt, Winnie is seeing ghosts at the morgue."

Winnie scoffed and looked away.

Boudreaux raised an eyebrow. "That's what they are. How long have you been seeing them?"

She sighed. "I don't know. It's hard to say. It's a spooky old building at the best of times. Lots of dark nooks and weird sounds. Not a lot of people around... Living people, anyway. But all that is to say, I'm not sure when."

She checked Dax out from the corner of her eye, probably to see if he his expression betrayed amusement or skepticism at her situation. Even if he disbelieved her, his inscrutable face wouldn't have betrayed anything. Tomi had often said he'd be "great at poker with a mug like that."

Taking in a deep breath, she straightened up, opened her mouth, then her shoulders slumped again. "Um, I started noticing weird temperature variations in the actual morgue and then on other floors. I take that seriously, because...well, dead bodies. I have to keep them preserved and safe. So I called in maintenance. They didn't find anything wrong with the morgue's systems, though they couldn't explain the variations."

"The drawers were fine, so that was all good to them," Boudreaux added with a shrug.

Winnie nodded. "I started carrying a quick read thermometer gun and recording the spots and temps. I had maintenance down a couple more times, but still nothing wrong with the refrigeration. They told me to stop wasting their time."

"She's not kidding, I mean, about the temperatures. She showed me. There are all kinds of weird super cold spots." He raised an eyebrow and exchanged glances with Winnie. "Want me to say this next part?"

She nodded shakily and looked down at the table.

"Let me preface it by saying I've felt it a few times myself. Maybe not as intensely as she's described it to me, but enough so that I have no doubts. I'm just"—a dark expression briefly washed over his normally jovial face—"inured to such things after seeing some of the things I've seen. Um, but she started feeling intense emotions that didn't feel quite like they originated with her. Like they were pressing in from the outside and forcing her to feel them."

"Anger, hate, terror, agony." She hugged her arms around herself. "So intense. I had to flee to my office more times than I care to say and just sob." She tossed a quick glance at Boudreaux. "Dreaux found me like that last week, and I broke down. He said I should talk to you. I still don't know why, but here we are."

Boudreaux reached out an arm and gave her an affectionate squeeze and a side-hug. "You'd better tell him about the other part."

She scoffed again. "How is that related?"

"I don't know. It might not be, but it's definitely worth mentioning because of everything else going on."

With an exasperated sigh, she unwound her arms and sat up straighter. "I lost a day."

"What?" Dax had no idea if a human spirit could take over a living body. He reaped souls and dealt death to those whose time had come. He rarely looked into what spirits did. When he found one unhoused, he just cut its life threads and sent them to the next part of their journey.

"I lost a whole day. Or most of one." She stopped to take a few sips of tea.

Boudreaux reached behind her and rubbed her back gently. "We had a date, so I showed up at her place. When she didn't answer the door, I let myself in. She was laid out in her bed in her bra and undies. She was groggy and starting to come to. It was like she was coming out of general anesthesia."

Winnie nodded. "I have no idea what happened to my day. I had gotten dressed. I know I was dressed. I'd put on normal work clothes, and I was about to leave. Then the next thing I knew or remembered was Boudreaux's face. Just the whole day"—she swiped her hand through the air—"gone."

Dax rubbed his chin, the texture of his scruff on his palm centering him. "Let's just say, I one hundred percent believe you about the first part of your story. Boudreaux is right. Your morgue is infested with angry and distraught spirits." He shook his head, pursing his lips. "They shouldn't be there. Someone should have been along to collect them and move them to their next steps, but…"

Boudreaux raised an eyebrow, the corner of one side of his lip quirking up sardonically. "Isn't that your job?"

"I'm *retired.*" The word held a bit more disdain and annoyance than he usually infused into it. He found the situation at the morgue deeply offensive, both professionally and personally. The psychopomps had betrayed him for the right to take more souls—banning him from doing it in the process—but here they were, letting the unhoused spirits marinate in their own misery.

"'Retired'? How the fuck does that work, Dax?" Boudreaux asked.

"It's a complex situation, and that's as much as I can say about it." Dax sighed. "Fuck."

"Can you do anything about it?"

Dax chewed on the inside of his cheek, mulling over the question and the situation. "I might have to. And if not, maybe Manman Delphine can cook something up as a stopgap to protect you." He caught Winnie's eye. "I don't know if the unhoused spirits 'possessed' you. It's not something I've ever investigated. But it certainly can't hurt to eliminate the one thing we know could be a potential cause." He'd have to ask if she'd let him look at her life thread to see if he could find anything of note.

"What are you? Some kind of medium or exorcist or some other bullshit?" Winnie asked, a bit of color returning to her face.

"I'm a bit more than that," Dax replied.

Winnie shook her head sarcastically and stared at him with expectant eyes.

Boudreaux rested his elbows on the table and leaned in closer to Dax. "Just show her. She's a skeptic and a thoroughly *modern* woman when it comes to the sort of things I believe in and you are."

Dax held the Black man's gaze until he finally looked down. "I trust Tomi out there. And his family trusts the manbo. I'm coming to trust her as well. But to how many people do I extend my circle of trust before it's broken? So far, you've done right by me and Tomi, and Delphine trusts you."

He didn't know if this would come back to bite him in the ass, but who would believe her if she started telling people she'd seen a skeleton man? They'd laugh at her and call her kooky after working with the dead for too long. And it would get him closer to being able to investigate the morgue with her approval to find out what the hell was going on with all the trapped dead.

Boudreaux raised his eyes to Dax. He'd never seen him look more earnest or seen the depths of the open windows into Boudreaux's soul.

"I've seen some shit in my life. Too much. Too fucking much. But I have an educated guess about who or what you might be. I saw that little piece of you… I'm still having nightmares about it. I could never betray you. You don't mess with the lwas." He made a sign against evil.

Dax wasn't sure if the gesture was to ward off any ill will from him or the lwas, of which he was not one, but he'd let it slide. Boudreaux, despite his normal cool and smooth facade, was clearly nervous and trying to cover his fear of Dax. He felt bad that he'd scared the man so badly when he'd gotten angry at The Collector's brutality. But he did feel a bit better about having Boudreaux as a provisional part of his circle.

"Show me what, Dreaux?" She sounded skeptical, but there was also a nervous quiver running through her voice, no doubt triggered by the shift in the man she knew.

Dax straightened up and rolled his back up, eliminating the slight stoop he usually had. "Show you who I am and why I might be the best and maybe only option for helping you deal with your spirit problem."

"If there are even such things," she mumbled, a bit of her earlier starch coming back.

Drawing a deep breath, Dax exhaled, slowly letting go of his human facade with the exhalation. His human suit gradually melted away, leaving only bones. As the breath shifted to a raspy wisp, the robe fell into place. With a quick thought into the aether, he settled his scythe into this plane where it could be seen.

The color slowly drained from Winnie's eyes as her eyes widened and her jaw dropped. Then she wilted, slumping backward.

FOURTEEN

JAMIE

Looking around, Jamie stood up and walked away from the car backing up. She couldn't quite see what kind of car it was because of the brightness of the reverse lights. It just looked like a basic sedan, as far as she could tell. She headed toward the nearest side street, walking briskly. With a quick look over her shoulder, she saw the car stop next to the curb. Once the door opened, she gave up the pretense of calmly walking away and broke into a run.

As soon as she hit the corner, she sprinted down the side street. This wasn't a neighborhood she knew, but her enhanced wolf shifter vision helped reveal what would be hidden to a normal human. Her eyes could penetrate the dark shadows cast by the night-shrouded buildings, and her ears would let her hear all but the most silent pursuers.

The flap of running feet followed her down the side street. Looking for her next move, she planted and darted into an alley on her right. She hoped it came out somewhere. The dumpsters on both sides did an effective job of blocking her vision.

Turning on a burst of speed, she dodged around empty boxes and garbage, slaloming between the dumpsters. When she figured she'd gone far enough, she slid to a stop and ducked behind a dumpster.

Despite being in good shape from all the running through the woods, the adrenaline and the mad dash had robbed her of her breath. Concentrating, she worked to control her breathing in case whoever was chasing her had supernatural hearing like she did.

She longed to peek around the edge of the dumpster to see if her pursuer had followed down the alley, but that would give her away quickly. Instead, she slowed her breathing and listened as hard as she could.

"Hey."

Jamie choked off a scream, covering her mouth, and kept it to a quiet squeak.

"What are you doing?" someone entirely too close whispered.

Swallowing the saliva that had pooled in her mouth, she turned her gaze into the shadows behind the dumpster. The pale face of a person poked out from under a blanket or a sleeping bag.

As they opened their mouth, Jamie quickly brought up a hand and laid a finger across her lips. The person closed their mouth.

"Did she go down here?" a male voice called out.

"I don't know, but it seems like the best option," another male voice replied.

Jamie made eye contact with the person and pleaded silently for help. The person narrowed their eyes for a moment, then nodded, crawling out from the pile she'd likely been sleeping under.

"Come here," she — it was a white woman who looked to be in her forties — mouthed, waving her over.

Jamie, keeping slow, moved silently toward the woman as she shuffled around sheets of cardboard and blankets. When she seemed satisfied, she waved Jamie over and signaled she should lie down.

"Fuck, it stinks down here," one of the voices called out.

"Shh, she'll hear us," hissed the other.

Jamie slid onto the cardboard and pushed herself up against the brick wall, lying still. The woman quickly covered her in cardboard and plugged the end with a blanket.

Despite her terror, she tried to keep her heart from beating out of her chest and alerting the creeps chasing her to her hiding spot. Next to her, the woman wiggled back into her bedding and settled down, affecting a steady, even breath that would hopefully be taken as a sleeping person.

The scrape of feet on asphalt caused Jamie to cast a silent prayer to whatever divine power might be listening.

The woman next to her jerked as if nudged. "What the fuck?"

"Hey, bum, wake up," an arrogant male voice said.

"Fuck you, leave me alone," she replied.

"Did you see someone come down this way?" the other man asked.

"I said"—a gun was cocked—"leave me the fuck alone, douche bags."

"Whoa, whoa, whoa. There's no need for trouble."

"Bro, let's go."

"Listen to your friend," the woman said.

"Come on, it's not worth it."

A second later, two sets of feet jogged away. Next to Jamie, the woman held still, but the silence of a gun not being uncocked spoke volumes to her readiness. Jamie risked a light, panting breath, hoping to calm down now that her pursuers appeared to have gone away.

She didn't know how long they waited, but the strain of listening was starting to wear on her.

"Hey," the woman hissed quietly.

Jamie nearly jumped out of her skin. She'd been so focused on listening for the sounds of the men that the nearness of the whisper had caught her completely by surprise.

"Are they gone?" Jamie whispered.

"Yeah. I think so," the woman replied. "It's been about fifteen minutes. You can come out now." She pulled the blanket away and moved the cardboard.

Jamie rose to her knees, blinking her eyes to let them adjust to the low light of the alley, which felt startlingly bright after the darkness of the improvised cave. "Thank you."

The woman shrugged. "No problem." She uncocked her gun,

which in the dim light looked similar to the one Jamie had used to shoot Dax.

No doubt those old police revolvers were readily available to anyone who wanted a small, easily concealable piece.

"Is there another way to get out of this alley?" Jamie asked.

"Yeah. Keep going that way." The woman pointed deeper into the alley. "About two buildings down, there will be a walkway on the left that leads out to Oxford Avenue."

Good, that would take her away from the morgue and where the car had parked.

She stood up and stretched the tension out of her muscles from lying on the ground and looked around. She wanted to give the woman something for helping, but she didn't have any money. The woman was a bit shorter than her and a little skinnier.

Shucking off her backpack, Jamie quickly pulled off her black hoodie and set it down next to the woman. "Again, thank you." Then, she took off before the woman could refuse or say anything else.

Once she found the walkway, she checked down it cautiously. When it seemed clear, she jogged on, stopping before it opened on Oxford Avenue to see if she could spot any danger. It was going to be a long, anxious jog home, stopping often to make sure she wasn't being pursued. Sighing, she waited for a break in traffic and darted across the street and into the night.

FIFTEEN

DAX

With a speed born of experience and trauma, Boudreaux leaned backward quickly and caught Winnie before she could fall to the floor. Once he stopped her descent, he shifted and more firmly braced her until he could move her to the floor and set her down gently. Laying her out flat, he shifted into professional EMT mode and checked her vitals.

After he seemed satisfied, he shifted back so he squatted next to her, his elbows resting on his knees. Chuckling, he shook his head. "Should have thought of that. Seems like I've been doing this a lot lately."

"Is she OK?" Dax rasped in the hollow voice his skeletal form possessed.

Boudreaux nodded. "You just gave her a real shock there. It was a bit of a surprise when you turned to bones when we were chaining you into the van, but I nearly shit my pants when you called down judgement upon The Collector." He shivered. "She wasn't ready for that heavy of a shift in her belief system."

Winnie rolled her head to the side, whimpering and mumbling.

"Should I turn back?" Dax asked.

Sighing, Boudreaux ran a hand over his smoothly shaved head.

"As much as I'd like to spare her from that fright again, she needs to have your identity reaffirmed." He shifted around so his body blocked her line of sight to Dax. "That'll at least let me get her back into the light before she faints again."

"W-what? Why…" She groaned.

He reached down and gently helped her sit up with a large hand. "Slowly, Winn. You had a little shock."

"Why am I on the floor?" She reached back to feel her head.

"You'll be fine in a moment. I caught you before you hit the floor."

She tried to look around Boudreaux, but he shifted to block her.

"I'm sorry to have frightened you," Dax said, trying to control the hollow, spooky harmonics that filled this voice.

Winnie whimpered, contracting her body to let Boudreaux's body block her more effectively.

"It's OK. He's our friend. He can help you." He squeezed her shoulders and leaned down to kiss her forehead.

"Are we d-dead?" Her teeth chattered a bit.

Dax clamped his teeth tightly, suppressing the chuckle he wanted to release. People didn't like it when he laughed. It universally sent shivers down the spine, at the minimum. He didn't want to scare the woman any more than was necessary, not that scaring her had been necessary at all. It had just been a natural byproduct of revealing the truth to her.

"No. We're all alive. Well, you and me, anyway." Boudreaux's eyes slipped toward Dax briefly, a twinkle of mischief in them.

Dax snorted. "You had to come give me medical attention after I nearly died. I'm as alive as you two are." He tilted his head to the side and back up. "In my own way."

Winnie shivered at the sound of his voice.

"Are you ready to move back to the bench?" Boudreaux slipped a meaty hand under her neck.

"C-can he put it away?"

"Will I have to convince you of my identity if I do?" Dax asked.

"I-I think I can suspend my disbelief for a bit." She chuckled weakly. "I may need to go home and crawl into a bottle of whiskey after."

Dax made eye contact with Boudreaux who gave him a slight nod. Inhaling, Dax brought his human flesh out of the place in the aether where he stored it, wrapping it around his bones. Once everything slipped back into place, he exhaled and shuddered. The sudden return of his meat suit and its accompanying functions always felt odd. Though he didn't care for the robe-wrapped skeleton, it was a bit closer in nature to the form he'd inhabited before being exiled.

Boudreaux helped Winnie up, guiding her back onto the bench. As soon as she got herself settled, she grabbed her glass with its double whiskey and took a gulping drink. Coughing, she shook her head and went back for another gulp. This time, she exhaled heavily afterward without the cough.

"Let me know if you need another." Dax lifted his drink and saluted her.

Winnie swallowed. "So…you're the Grim Reaper?"

"If you wish to call me that. It's the appearance I'm bound to. The functions were similar, I guess."

"For the angel of death, you don't seem too sure about what your job is." A bit of her spunk seemed to be returning.

Dax gave a noncommittal shrug. "Like I said, I'm retired. Others are supposed to be minding the shop."

" 'Supposed'? Again with the wishy-washy language."

Boudreaux cleared his throat.

"No, it's OK. It's a fair question." He leaned forward resting his elbows on the table as he fixed his gaze on the coroner. "If you'd like it in human business terms, there was a hostile takeover by certain parties, and I was forced into retirement. I was allowed a human body and forced into the semblance of the robed skeleton."

"Why not just the human body?" Winnie was a sharp woman, and a bit bold now that she'd recovered some.

Dax shrugged. There were probably many reasons. Containing the amount of power he had in a mortal shell with no other outlet would likely burn out the limited capacity of the flesh suit. Maybe they wanted to keep him around in case they needed him. Maybe they just wanted to be dicks and let him see pieces of his former self.

"I'm not privy to that information."

Her eyebrow cocked up. "Are you even able to help me?"

"I think so. And to tell you the truth, I've been concerned about the morgue for a while now." His eyes drifted toward Boudreaux, who gave a quick shake of his head.

"What do you mean?" Her brow furrowed as skepticism washed over her face.

"I've driven by the morgue. Those feelings you've been having. The unexplained sightings. For those of us in the business, we can sense them outside the building. There's something profoundly wrong in your morgue."

Color flushed her pale skin. "I run a clean ship."

Dax held up a hand to mollify her. "I'm not saying you don't. This has nothing to do with you, at least as a cause. Though your lost day might speak to something even more sinister than I'd thought initially."

The color raised by her momentary flash of anger quickly washed away. "You're saying there are ghosts in my morgue? And they what? Possessed me?"

Dax nodded his head slowly. "Yes. There are definitely ghosts in your morgue. As far as the possession? Possibly. If so, that's even worse than I thought."

The morgue had been an itch at the back of his mind, constantly there since he discovered it but not front and center. But if ghosts were possessing humans… That would be a whole new level of trouble—an itch he couldn't ignore. If he continued to ignore it, Winnie could be possessed again. Or it's possible someone else coming into the morgue might be. And as angry as the trapped spirits were, they might do more to their unwilling hosts than take a day's worth of memories.

He didn't really want to wade into the mess at the morgue. At least not until he had a better grasp on what was causing it and how to solve it without bringing about his own destruction if the psychopomps took offense and decided to carry out their threats.

"So… Ghosts are real? Like Caspar? The Ghostbusters?"

Boudreaux chuckled, but stopped abruptly when Winnie turned a baleful glare on him.

"I don't know Caspar. And I can't speak to the veracity of *The Ghostbusters*"—Dax inhaled slowly through his nostrils, pursing his lips—"but yes. There are unhoused spirits in your morgue. Violently unhoused."

Winnie grasped her hands, trying to control a slight tremble that had appeared. "Will they turn into poltergeists?"

Dax furrowed his brow in confusion. "I'm not sure what you mean."

"Violent ghosts that can hurt you," Boudreaux supplied.

"I've got to be honest with you; I don't know much about the varieties of unhoused souls—"

"Souls? Like for real souls?" Winnie interrupted.

"What did you think we were talking about? The body dies, but the spirit, the soul goes on, moving to its next steps." He held up a hand to forestall any further questions. "Don't ask what those steps are. My duty was to bring them through the veil, where their believed afterlives claim them. It was not my place to interfere in the beliefs of humans and the gods they created."

"OK, OK, OK." Winnie covered her eyes with a hand. "I'm going to need to you stop with the revelations for a bit. Please. I'm struggling enough with ghosts. Don't bring anything else into the equation."

"Fair enough. Ghosts." He sighed and rubbed his temples. "I was shot with a bullet a few weeks ago. It was—and I'll need you to continue with your suspension of disbelief for a bit more—a magic bullet."

Winnie rolled her eyes but didn't say anything.

"Once it was removed"—he shuddered—"painfully, I had it analyzed by an expert. It was designed to pin my soul to my body and to keep me from shifting. I've also seen its effects on an acquaintance. His spirit couldn't move on. It was tethered to his body. I had to step in and use my abilities to set him free. Once I did, he was able to move on." Sighing, Dax tapped his finger on the table, then took a drink of his whiskey.

"I've had a suspicion that those bullets have been in play for a little while. I don't think I was the first victim of them, nor were me or my friend the last. Your morgue, at least the long-term residents, are victims of violence, correct?"

She nodded once curtly. "Mostly, yes. Once the murders are solved or the police move the cases out of active investigation, the bodies go to their families or to processing for those whose bodies aren't claimed."

Boudreaux snorted. "How many cases are solved in this city?"

She sighed. "Too few."

"Hardly any at all would be more like it. Seems like the only ones that get 'solved' are if the victim is important or rich enough for the Police to care. And even then, solved is a pretty euphemism for pinned on someone to satisfy the news cycle." Boudreaux shook his head, a look of disgust contorting his features.

They all nodded and looked at each other briefly before looking away.

Finally, Dax found Winnie's gaze again, his jaw flexing. "I think you have a surfeit of bodies murdered with those bullets."

Winnie sat back, looking over Dax's shoulder as she mulled over what he'd just said.

"Have you extracted any odd bullets lately?" Boudreaux asked, breaking the silence.

She shrugged. "I don't know. I pull them, bag them up, and the cops collect them with the rest of the evidence after I've catalogued caliber and such. I never look at the bullet that closely. That's the investigator's job." She turned back to Dax. "What am I looking for?"

"Markings. Norse runes to be specific. Though I guess others could be using their own magical systems. But the two that were pulled out of me had Norse runes on them. Though, it might be hard to see them when they're mixed in with the normal damage a fired bullet takes. And the signature of the one that killed my friend matched those." He took another drink. "They were used by a violent outlaw motorcycle gang with ties to white supremacy."

Boudreaux barked out a harsh laugh. "Ties? They're fucking Nazi bikers who claim to be Norse pagans."

Dax tipped his head toward Boudreaux, acknowledging the point. "They're very bad people."

He decided to keep the wolf shifter aspect in his pocket for now. Winnie had been asked to suspend her agnostic disbelief a lot this evening. That might be one bridge too far. Besides, he wasn't sure if Boudreaux knew that fact either. He'd just been there at the end of the fight at the biker's bar, coming in to ransack any valuables. Dax didn't remember telling his new acquaintance if the bikers were wolf shifters. He'd only found out himself when Jamie's friend had let them in on that information right before the fight.

Winnie shook her head, a look of skepticism returning to her face. "And they're killing people with magical bullets? Why? What does it matter if they're killing them with magic bullets versus regular old bullets? Dead is dead."

"Cruelty?" Dax pursed his lips. "I don't know. There's a deep, dark world out there that you're unaware of. And there are powerful beings who have all kinds of motives. A soul is power. Collecting it. Possessing it. Harvesting it. There are those who want to interrupt the normal cycles of life and death for their own means."

It had been something he'd been thinking about for a while. He'd been exiled so he couldn't interfere with those who wanted to benefit from the power of a soul. He'd never interfered in the normal cycle. Hadn't used the power collecting a soul could have accrued to him. His duty was to start the transition and escort the soul to the next step. He'd had enough power. He didn't need to steal that which didn't belong to him.

But there had been those who wanted the power he left alone. They'd been willing to form a cross-pantheon alliance to bring him to his knees and exile him from the world of the gods to get access to it.

"For someone who can't access the power of the soul... If someone wants to build a safe reserve for later use, circulating magic bullets in a city where crime is high and goes unsolved would provide for a rich feeding ground. Well, let's just say your morgue is currently a large deposit of power. Like a reserve bank."

"Damn…" Boudreaux muttered under his breath.

"At least that's my hypothesis," Dax said, completing his thought.

"But why would they possess me?" Winnie asked.

"I don't know. I'm not even sure if they can possess a human." He held up a hand to stop her from interrupting. "But let's say they can, because right now it's the best idea we have." He shifted his focus to Boudreaux. "Though, I'd like to check with a more knowledgeable source before I go too far down an incorrect path.

"As to the why? I don't know. To be an unhoused soul pinned to its body, unable to move to the next step, is agony. Your morgue is practically bursting at the seams with pain, frustration, fear, and hopelessness. That's what you described feeling. That building is awash in those feelings. The spirits are angry about their circumstances. It's like a bad bottle of home brew. The morgue is fermenting with the torment of the dead, and I'm afraid it's going to explode, metaphysically speaking that is."

SIXTEEN

DAX

A pregnant silence hung in the air between Dax, Boudreaux, and Winnie. Bits and pieces of ideas had been percolating around in his head since he first stepped foot in the morgue. Being able to air his thoughts to the coroner had allowed some of those pieces to fall into place.

"What happens when it explodes?" Boudreaux asked quietly.

Dax shrugged. "I don't know. I don't know if it will explode. And if it does, I'm not sure what that means exactly. It might be like the end of *The Ghostbusters* when they shut down the containment unit and it blows the top off the building, or it might be something along the line of a spiritual explosion. I just don't know enough at the moment. It's only a collection of thoughts stitched together with a thin thread. But I'd rather act as if that were a real possibility and not have it happen than the reverse."

"Can..." Winnie ran a hand over her eyes and sighed. "Can you do anything about it?"

"Again, I don't know. I really need to consult with Manman Delphine. I'm just not sure what will happen if I shake that beehive."

Boudreaux raised an eyebrow and smirked. "The bees will come out and sting you?"

"I'm more concerned about the beekeeper."

Winnie rubbed her temples. "My morgue is a ghost hive?"

"I guess it's as good of an analogy as any."

"Well, what can you do?" Her words were quick and clipped.

"I'm not sure, not until I get a chance to poke around a bit. Get a lay for the hive, if you will." He leveled his gaze at Winnie. "I'm going to need some time in your morgue."

She pursed her lips, blinking rapidly, before she shook her head and sighed. "Why not? If I've got to believe in ghosts, I guess I have to let a man who claims to be the Grim Reaper investigate them." She looked ruefully at Boudreaux. "I wish I'd never said yes to that first date once upon a time…"

Boudreaux laughed. "No, you don't. Especially now that you need my unique connections."

A faint smile spread across her lips. "I guess so. I don't under-stand everything I've heard tonight, but it makes sense in a certain weird way." She snorted. "Ghosts. Fuck me."

"Putting aside the suggestion"—Boudreaux winked at her—"when can we get Dax into the morgue so he has the time and space to work?"

"I don't know off the top of my head. I'll have to check the schedule tomorrow." She slumped a little. "Assuming I even make it into work this time."

"I could see if the manbo would make a gris-gris bag for you." Boudreaux turned to catch Dax's gage and flicked his eyes toward Winnie. "Can you…uh…check to see…" He left it hanging. "Do you have a way to see what's going on with her?"

He thought about it for a minute. He didn't know. He'd only looked into a few threads, mostly of those who were dead or shortly about to be. Investigating back into a person's past via their life thread would be a new experiment for him.

"I might be able to." He made to stand up. "I'm going to need to touch your head, if that's OK."

Winnie nodded, slumping a bit more.

He doubted he actually needed to, but it couldn't hurt. The few times he'd looked at life threads over the last couple months, he'd done it without contact. He'd never actually tried this with direct human contact before. Perhaps the process would be easier or provide clearer results. Also, based on what he'd seen of humans so far, it seemed like they needed something more in the process to believe in. If he just sat there in his seat, it wouldn't look like he was doing anything. A touch could provide the little bit extra to help her skepticism.

It also meant he could investigate whether contact would allow him access to greater depths of knowledge.

He walked around the table and stopped behind Winnie. "I'm going to touch your temples. Just relax and try to clear your mind."

"Will I feel anything?"

"Only my fingers on your temples." He hoped that would be the case. He wasn't actually going to be manipulating anything, but being vague might shake her confidence in the process.

"OK." She sat up straighter and looked toward the wall of tea.

Reaching forward, he gently pressed the index and middle fingers of each hand to her temples and closed his eyes. It was easy to find her life thread. It pulsed strongly.

Taking a moment, he oriented himself to figure out which direction things were going. Once he slipped along the thread leading toward her death, he stopped. That information he didn't need, nor did he want to possess it. It would be the kind of thing that would taint whatever relationship he'd have with her going forward. And more importantly, it might affect his relationship with Boudreaux, who'd become a reliable person to call when there was potentially profitable trouble on the horizon.

Now that he knew the direction he needed to go, he moved backward down her timeline slowly, not wanting to blast past the events he needed to look for since they were so close in the timeline. There it was—a weird disruption from what should have happened.

That in itself was odd. People's life threads almost never shifted from their courses like this. Most people were unimportant in the scheme of the universe. Their timelines didn't move, nor were they able to move someone else's beyond the normal things one could get at a local municipal vital records office—births, marriages, and deaths. Those life threads only touched a few other threads to form a basic weave in the tapestry of existence.

Something or someone had temporarily moved her thread out of alignment.

Pressing slightly harder, he homed in on the disturbance and followed along with its forward process. It still hadn't quite reunited with the main core of her life thread. He wasn't quite sure, but whoever had caused the deviation might still be tangled with Winnie, though he couldn't be sure if it was intentional or not.

"Hmm," Dax said.

He pinched the spot where he was and zoomed out. Just past where his aethereal fingers had marked his place, he saw tonight's intersection where his line crossed hers. While hers was strong for a human, his dwarfed hers and pulled it further out of alignment with the trunkline of her central being. While his life created a bowing in her lifeline—like a greater gravitational force pulling on it—the one created by whoever or whatever had possessed her, assuming it even was a possession, was only a very tiny shift. But the fact that deviation had been created in the first place was the interesting thing.

"What, dude?" Boudreaux asked quietly.

Dax gave a light shake of his head to wave him off.

The angle would eventually rejoin her original line, but if he pulled any harder against the small change, he risked shifting her line in possibly a new direction. He didn't want to do that. So, he let go of the thread and returned to the place where the deviation intersected with the main thread.

There should be an actor. A mover. Something to have generated the small shift and spur off in a new direction.

He added the touch of his ring fingers to her temples, hoping the additional skin to skin contact would let him find what he was looking for. Something eluded him. He could almost feel a foreign influence at the intersection of Winnie's thread deviation, but he couldn't quite get it to resolve into visibility, as if it was capable of twisting and avoiding him even at this level.

Pressing harder, he tried to find a point where he could get some information from the new thread. He thought there might be something familiar about it. Like a faint whiff of perfume on the wind. Frustratingly elusive.

Winnie whimpered lightly, and he sighed, letting off on the pressure slightly. He decided to track further back in her timeline. Perhaps if he got to know her better, he'd be able to find what separated the foreign thread from hers. They were incredibly similar in a lot of aspects.

The further back he went, the more odd and interesting her life became. So much death. So many broken threads touching hers. Her career tending to the bodies of the violent dead of Red City had left an indelible mark on her life, certainly in ways she couldn't grasp or comprehend.

Stopping to savor the uniqueness of her being, he could see where some deaths had pressed more firmly across her thread. It was a hodgepodge. Some faint with only the most minimal influence. Some that touched in more firmly. Some even weaving back and forth over several points in time. Those, he suspected, were the ones generating what she didn't want to believe were hauntings.

Though he suspected those hauntings weren't directed specifically at her but had only glommed on because of the sheer amount of time she spent in the building in the presence of dead bodies and the spirits unwillingly tethered to the cadavers.

The thicker lines and the multiple intersections, those he focused on, carefully sipping their flavor. Most felt completely unfamiliar, but one felt... He wasn't sure. Maybe like the one who'd caused the deviation. But one, one felt all too familiar, though he couldn't put a name on it or find where it met with his life thread.

At first, he worried it could be Jason, still trapped even though Dax thought he'd finally freed his murdered bartender when Boudreaux had snuck him and Tomi into the morgue. But the flavors weren't right. It wasn't Jason. He'd interacted with Jason enough that he'd recognize his old employee. He couldn't find a hint of him in the most recent intersections. If he went far enough back, he was sure he'd find it, but that wasn't today's task.

Beneath his fingers, Winnie twitched and exhaled shakily. He was running out of time if he didn't want to force her to sit still with her increasing discomfort. Since he had the feel of what was happening in the more recent month of her life, he slipped back up to the thread. He could get a bit more from the mysterious line, though it still remained more slippery than an eel. Intertwined within the deviation—he focused in as tightly as he could—was just the slightest hint of the strong familiarity he'd just discovered further back in her life.

But they both—the deviation and the strong, familiar influence—remained tantalizingly close and yet so far away.

Sighing, he removed his fingers and stepped back.

With a raspy exhale, Winnie slumped down on herself. Slipping over on the bench, Boudreaux braced her back so she didn't tip over backward again. Dax moved back around the table to give them space but didn't resume his seat.

Winnie, her hand shaky, reached for her whiskey, slamming the rest down. The empty glass thudded onto the table.

"Would you like another?" Dax asked, keeping his voice low and calm.

She nodded vigorously, then groaned and reached up to massage her temples. Boudreaux threw back the rest of his glass and slid it toward Dax. With the glasses in hand, he slipped out the door and came back with three more glasses. After he set those down, he went behind the bar of the tearoom and poured three glasses of water. He wasn't sure what she'd need after he'd gone exploring in her life. But booze and hydration would cover her most likely immediate needs.

"Let me know when you're ready for me to tell you about what I found." He said it quietly and calmly, hoping she wouldn't feel pressured or startled.

Winnie nodded, reaching for the water and taking deep, noisy gulps. Boudreaux took his whiskey, though he left his other hand on Winnie's back, rubbing it soothingly.

"What did you do to me?" she asked finally.

Raising an eyebrow, he leaned over the table. "How much do you want to know?"

She thought about it for a moment, then shook her head. "Not that much." She sighed. "What did you find out?"

"A lot and not enough. Something definitely caused you to miss your day. I couldn't figure out who or what it was though. I also found something familiar a bit further down the thread."

"What all does that mean?" Boudreaux asked.

"It means I'm going to want to investigate more. Let me know as soon as possible when I can meet you at the morgue."

She rubbed her temples again, then nodded. Weariness suffused her movements and her expression. "Can we go now, Boudreaux?"

"Sure, baby." He stood up, extending a hand for Dax to shake. "She'll give me a time, and I'll relay it to you. Good?"

This was all new to him. As a human, Dax'd had never played around like that in someone's life thread before. He wanted to ask her what the experience had been like, but it was clear she'd had enough of tonight. "That works for me."

Winnie stood up with an assist from Boudreaux. Not wanting to waste good whiskey, they both took their glasses and threw them back, both sighing after. Though, his was one of satisfaction and hers one of weariness.

Dax moved toward the door, sliding it open. "I'll walk you both out front."

Boudreaux nodded, his face in his phone. "We'll have a taxi here in a couple minutes."

"Good." Dax opened the door for them and followed them out to the front but stopped by Tomi on the way. "There's a full glass of whiskey back there if you want it. Untouched. I'm going to head home and check on Morty."

Tomi grinned and waved Dax on.

"Thanks for letting us interrupt your evening, Dax. I do appreciate you looking into the issue at Winnie's morgue," Boudreaux said once the bar's door had closed behind them.

Winnie nodded in agreement.

"No problem. It's the least I could do after all the help you've provide. And you've given me an opportunity to look into something that's been bothering me, so it's a win-win." Though he wasn't really sure if it was a win-win. He knew the morgue needed to be dealt with, but he wasn't sure it would be the best idea if he did it. He still feared drawing the attention of whichever psychopomps were secretly hounding his trail.

In the past—before his exile—he'd been singular in his path and his decisions. Now? It seemed like everything about being a mortal human involved decisions that left him feeling conflicted and pulled in multiple directions.

Boudreaux winked at him, giving him a friendly smile. "Best kind of deals."

Dax chuckled. "Now, I think I'm going to head home, too. You two OK waiting here?"

"Later, Dax."

Dax had a lot to think about. A glass of whiskey, some music, and his kitten would go a long way to helping him sort out what he'd experienced tonight. Maybe then he could come up with a better plan than just "poke around the morgue until he found something useful." But if all else failed, it was at least a plan, even if it wasn't that good of one. He nodded at Boudreaux and Winnie, then headed for the alley and his motorcycle.

SEVENTEEN

JAMIE

Jamie finally slowed down as she entered the neighborhood where the extended-stay motel she and her mother were staying was located. The cool breeze puckered her sweaty skin into goosebumps. As the wind shifted into her face, a faint scent of something familiar teased at her senses.

Her stomach dropped as her reptilian brain sent a signal to run. Her goosebumps forgotten, she dropped behind a bush, pulling its shadows around herself like a shroud.

This was the fourth time that evening her adrenaline had spiked into fight-or-flight levels. Taking a moment to regain control of herself, she concentrated on her breathing. Once she felt like she was in charge of her own body, she crawled out until the breeze once again drifted toward her.

Raising her nose, she inhaled lightly, feeling for the dangerous but familiar scent. There it was. The scent wasn't quite strong enough. She couldn't place it. If she shifted into her wolf form, she could bring her powerful nose into the situation.

Glancing around, she noticed the open windows, light spilling out. A shadow moved across one of them, pausing to look out.

Across the street, a door opened and someone wheeled out a garbage bin. A dog barked.

She sighed. She'd never be able to get away with it. Plus, she couldn't wear her backpack, and it had her school stuff in it. It was way past the point where she should have been home. A yawn escaping from her mouth announced her fatigue.

Slipping into the shadows, she backtracked and turned toward the road that led to the backside of the building. When they'd moved to this place, she hadn't even waited an hour before leaving her mom so she could explore the neighborhood.

Before she turned onto the small lane, she waited until the breeze came from the same direction and took a long sniff. Then another. She didn't smell that familiar scent.

Her shoulders dropped, and she sighed in relief. Picking up her pace, she jogged toward the back entrance of the motel but still kept to the shadows, just to be cautious.

Once she neared the parking lot, she found a tree to hide behind and scanned the cars for any movement or lurking shadows. Just as she was about to step out from behind the tree, that familiar scent returned but much stronger.

Panic surged through her veins. A bit of movement out of the corner of her eye drew her attention.

Ivar.

Patting down her pockets, she pulled out her keys. Careful not to make any noise, she reached around and pulled off her backpack. A fresh gust of wind hit her back, and a shiver ran through her body. Her back was covered in sweat where the backpack had been. She zipped the keys into one of the pockets of her backpack and poked her head out quickly. He seemed to be focused on the backdoor, the glow of his wolf shifter eyes collecting enough light to reflect.

She looked around. There. Her mom's car was parked one car back from the edge of the parking lot. Dropping down, she crouch-walked around the first car and hid behind her mother's car. As slowly as she could, she slid her backpack under the trunk of the car. If she had to run, at least she wouldn't be encumbered or lose the bag.

Patting her pockets, she pulled out her phone and opened it, shielding its light as best she could.

She sent a text to her mom. *"Mom. We need to move. The biker found us. He's hiding in the back of the building. I might have to run. Backpack under the back of the car."*

After she sent the message, she stared at the phone. If she had to run, she'd lose it if she had to shift into her wolf form. But if she didn't have a phone, she wouldn't be able to call anyone for help. But who did she have to call? Her mom was in the building and in danger herself. Cory? She couldn't bring him back into this. His mom would put a restraining order on her.

She reached under the car and slipped the phone into the bag's pocket. She inhaled sharply at a skittering piece of gravel and the grind of a foot fall on the pavement.

"Well, hello. If it isn't the little rat."

She whipped her head around. Ivar stood ten feet from her. It only took her a split second; turning, she coiled her body and took off.

"Fuck!"

Out of the corner of her eye, she saw that Ivar had slipped on the loose gravel of the shittily paved parking lot. She aimed for the nearby grass. As soon as her foot hit the spongy surface, she increased her speed. He'd worn his typical biker boots while she had on her sneakers. She had no idea what kind of shape he was in.

"Come back here, you little bitch!"

She had a bit of a lead on him thanks to his poor footwear choices and the decaying parking lot of the cheap hotel. Risking a look over her shoulder, she gasped. He'd gotten back on his feet surprisingly quickly and was gaining on her slightly. She had to make a decision and fast.

Reaching down, she unbuttoned her pants. She lunged to the right and jumped over a fence, dropping onto the ground. With a speed born of desperation, she kicked off her shoes and yanked her pants and socks off and sprang up, shifting to her wolf. Her bra stretched tight against the barrel of her chest. At least she'd been wearing a cheap, stretchy sports bra.

As she moved out from behind the fence and bush, she flicked her eyes to the side before she left the questionable protection of the fence. He'd stopped and was tearing off his shirt. It would take him a few moments to yank off the boots. She dug deep and stretched out. All those times with Cory, running through the woods. Sprinting and chasing each other. They'd prepared her for a moment like this.

Digging in, she sprinted away from her quick hiding space, leaving her clothes in her dust. She aimed for the edge of the sidewalk where she could stay on the turf but avoid the kinds of things people put in their yards, like bushes or broken washing machines.

She chuckled in her mind. If someone looked out their window, they'd see a wolf wearing a T-shirt sprinting down the street. She'd enjoy that thought later, after she'd escaped the vengeful Nazi biker wolf shifter.

No cars were coming, so she darted out into the street and angled around the corner. She could do some fancy navigating later. Right now, she had to preserve her speed and open up some distance.

She took the next turn away from the hotel. Then another. After several more erratic turns, she found an alley and slipped down it. It had been a while since any shifts in the wind had carried his scent to her or the sound of his pants or feet padding on the ground as he chased after her.

It had been a long day, and her muscles burned. All the running earlier had sapped her, and she needed to find a place to hide. She took one more turn then stopped behind a building. Poking the tip of her nose around the corner, she sniffed, trying to find the breeze. When it shifted a bit and came from the direction she'd just come from, she let her wolf nose take charge. There were a lot of scents, and most of them were bad—garbage, sewage, pollution—but none of them sparked the terror Ivar's scent had.

Now that she had a moment, she surveyed her surroundings. She'd run into the industrial part of Red City. Turning, she jogged down the alley. But when she rounded the next corner, an angry growl rumbled toward her. A big wolf stepped out of the shadows, his teeth bared and drool dripping from them. He must have guessed her direction and come at her from around the other side of the building.

Spinning around, she sprinted away. Ivar, at least that was her assumption, let off a pissed-off yip and tore off after her.

He probably had fifty pounds on her, maybe more. He'd be able to dominate her if it came to a fight. She didn't want to have to rely on luck. He'd crush her neck and shake her like a rag doll. Her only defense was swiftness of paw. And in her wolf form, she was faster than the bigger wolf.

Her lungs burned and her muscles strained to find every bit of speed and maneuverability she could, but she was nearing the end of her body's ability to run. Another turn, and she saw a dark maw in a wall of concrete. Digging deep, she made for the dark rectangle.

Normally, she'd never go near a giant dark chasm, but right now, it looked like salvation.

As soon as its dark confines slipped around her, she felt a momentary sense of relief. But she kept running, slowing only to allow her eyes to adjust to the poor light. An intersection in the tunnel rapidly approached. Without thinking, she slowed and skidded through a left turn and barely kept her feet, nearly slamming into the wall. She didn't care that she could barely see anything in front of her.

Clinging close to the concrete walls, she stretched out, hoping she'd have enough warning to turn or stop. Most of all, she prayed she wouldn't run into a dead end.

A brief increase of the shadows to her right was the only warning that she'd found another split. Slamming on her metaphorical brakes, she slid around the corner and actually hit the wall this time. Fortunately, it wasn't too hard. Air puffed from her lungs, but she righted herself and tore down the new tunnel as it grew darker.

As the light faded to almost total blackness, she was forced to slow to a walk. Her chest heaved like bellows as she tried to pull in enough oxygen to replenish her depleted muscles. But at no point did she think to stop. Stopping or backtracking meant death in the jaws of Ivar.

Snugging up to the wall so she could feel her way along it as her fur brushed against it, she walked forward. And when the last of the light behind her finally failed to follow, she kept walking.

Without light, she felt like she was moving through some infinite abyss. But forward meant a chance at survival.

For the second time that night, she lost track of time due to being trapped in a dark, silent space. She took a turn to the left when the wall disappeared from her fur's touch. Then a right when she hit a wall with her nose, knocking dust into the air.

After a couple sneezes, she froze, listening. Nothing. She let out her held breath and turned into the change in direction. It could have been minutes or an hour, but she kept moving forward.

Her paws hurt and her muscles burned with fatigue. After a day of walking, running, and more shocks than anyone should have to endure, she didn't have anything left. She had to stop soon. When the wall along her left side disappeared again, she took the turn. Then another one when the wall on the left dropped away. This time, she stopped, turned around, and poked her head out, perking her ears up to listen. When she was able to ignore her breathing and her pounding heart, she found no sounds to concern her. Or even sounds at all.

Backing up, she jumped when her butt bumped into a wall after less than a dozen steps. Feeling along the side, she found herself in a little alcove. Once she'd marked the space of the alcove, she returned to the back corner and curled up in a ball. With a yawn, she lowered her head and tucked her nose into her tail.

EIGHTEEN

DAX

The night was cool, but Red City seemed to be done with most of its Spring rain for now. Summer was in sight. It would be a pleasant ride home on his motorcycle.

Despite the quiet on the "kill Dax" front, he still felt nervous about the alley. Getting shot two different times by two different people would do that to a man.

Narrowing his eyes, he peered into the depths of the alley, but the shadows remained inanimate. He sighed and strolled into the alley, fishing his keys from his pocket. He was nearly to his bike when he heard his name called.

Spinning around, he headed for the mouth of the alley.

"Dax?" Boudreaux called.

He wondered what his friend had forgotten. Maybe it was news about his Lincoln Continental. It had to be—

An explosion shredded the quiet of the night. Heat slapped into his back and flung him forward. He flew out of the alley and landed in a heap just past the sidewalk.

His eyes and ears weren't functioning—stars blocking the one and a deep whine dominating the other. The stench of burning hair and fabric, along with the burning metal and hot chemicals, told him his nose was working fine.

A moment later, pain slammed into him. Burning heat spread over his back, and his front felt like ground hamburger from scraping across the pavement.

Something slapped his back several times. He tried to push his way up, but something shoved him back down, adding the back of his head to their smother fest. Dully, throbbing pain wound its way up from his palms.

"Dax?" The word sounded like it was coming through thick water while someone else took a sheet of tin and wobbled it. "Dax. Stay still."

He tried to grunt an affirmation but only whimpered. A moment later, water flopped down on his head, sending excruciating pain over his burned back. The shock of cold water forced an inhale, bringing droplets with it. He sputtered, his cheek grinding into the harsh pavement. Someone threw more water on him, then another. After the initial agony of the impact and the temperature shock of the water, his back throbbed dully with only occasional spikes of agony.

"Dax? Don't move, buddy." The voice sounded familiar.

"Tomi?" he rasped out.

"Everybody get back," Winnie called. "Let Boudreaux through. He's an EMT."

"You heard the man! Back your shit right up!" Tomi said, taking charge.

"Cuz, call 911?" A note of panic filled Suzie's words.

"No. Let me call my partner Alejandro. He's on duty tonight," Boudreaux replied.

"Tomi?"

"Listen to him, Suzie. Boudreaux knows what to do."

"Right, Cuz. Alright you looky-loos, unless one of you is a doctor, get your asses back in the bar and let the trained people do their job. First round is on me."

Dax groaned, trying to move.

"Dude, keep your ass down," Tomi said. "There are not enough people left to cost us much money, anyway. I need to go hook up the hose and see if I can put that fire out before it moves to the building." Sneaker-clad feet slapped on concrete as Tomi ran to dig out the garden hose they used for spraying down the beer cooler and the alley when it needed it.

"How is he, Boudreaux?" Winnie asked.

"Alive. He'll have some burns and probably some road rash from hitting the ground. He'll need a haircut. But he's damned lucky."

Off in the distance, the first hints of a siren alerted them to what he hoped was Alejandro and his ambulance. He grunted and tried to push off the ground, only to be held down. With the agony of his shredded hands, he gave in.

"You stay still, Dax. That's my bus. Alejandro is on the way. I'm going to call the manbo and see if she can roust that doctor she sent you to last time." Boudreaux removed his hand from Dax's shoulder.

"He needs a proper emergency department," Winnie said, her voice forceful.

"Baby, do you think he should be in an ED? We know a doctor —a proper doctor—who's helped him in the past with far more serious injuries. Trust me."

Winnie sighed. "You're probably right. This whole fucking thing is so weird."

Blinking, a bit of his vision returned. Boudreaux's blurry form squatting over him blocked most of his view, not that he could probably see much of anything beyond a very limited range. The approaching siren displaced the whining in his ear as the dominant sound. A moment later, it screeched to a halt nearby.

"Dreaux, buddy, what's up?" The EMT replaced Boudreaux by his side.

"Alejandro. My buddy needs some help. I'll have an address to take him to in a minute."

"Not the nearest ED?"

"No. Not this one. We got a doctor who'll take care of him."

"Gotcha." He laid his fingers across Dax's neck. "Can you hear me? Understand me?"

He rubbed the side of his head along the pavement in what he hoped was a nod. "Yes."

"Are you OK going to the doctor Boudreaux wants to send you to?"

"Yes."

"Good. I'm going to check you over and make sure we can move you."

Dax did his best to wait patiently as they checked him over, poking and prodding where they needed to. The only thing keeping him steady, such as it was, was his brain's lack of proper function and his growing trust in Boudreaux. He just had to keep his focus long enough to get to the doctor who'd helped him before.

"How's he looking?" Boudreaux asked.

"Looks like a concussion, some bad burns—we won't know how bad until we can get him to the medical facility—and some scrapes and bruises."

"Yeah. That was my assessment, too." A phone beeped. "Good. I'll text you the address now."

Alejandro squatted next to Dax's head. "We're going to move you onto our gurney. We'll leave you face down so you're not laying on your burns."

He grunted in pain as Alejandro and a second set of hands lifted him gingerly onto a gurney. Once he was secure, they raised the gurney and moved him into the back of the ambulance.

Alejandro leaned down so he was in front of Dax's face. "Dax, we're going to give you a little something to take the edge off the pain. That OK?"

"Please," he rasped out.

"It might make you a little drowsy. Try to stay with us until we can get you to Boudreaux's doctor."

He grunted. " 'K"

Scissors ran up his arm, cutting away his leather jacket to reveal his arm from the elbow down. Compared to the heat of his burned back and legs, the alcohol swab felt like paradise. A moment later, a needle slipped into his arm. It didn't take long after for the first cool waves to spread through his body, bringing the pain down from a blazing roar to a dull general throb.

The rest of the ambulance ride passed in a semi-awake haze, enjoying the pain relief while trying to keep awake until he arrived at a destination he felt was safe, at least more safe than an ambulance with Boudreaux's friend and whoever else was working with him.

NINETEEN

JAMIE

Something drew her from the depths of her dreams. Even there, she'd not been able to escape being chased. Without moving, she let her brain try to find a bit of wakefulness. There it was. A slight, delicate scratching of something natural against hard concrete.

Lifting the ear that she'd pointed toward the entrance to the alcove, she waited. A couple more delicate scratches drew her attention. Holding perfectly still, she tried to maintain the even, easy breathing of the deeply asleep.

Something…small…sniffed at the air. She thought it was about four or five feet away. Quickly, she tried to block it out while not losing it entirely to see if anything else accompanied it. Nothing.

The creature sniffed again, but this time it was closer. She kept herself perfectly calm and still. But when it brushed against her whiskers, she couldn't help but let out a low, rumbling growl. The creature squeaked in terror and scrabbled away.

Leaping to her feet, she loped after the rat. She knew a mundane wolf would snap up a rat for a meal in a heartbeat, but she had no interest, even though her stomach rumbled, in breaking her fast on a Red City sewer rat.

With the faint click of her own nails on the concrete, she had trouble following the scratching sounds of the rat running away from her. Lowering her head, she found its scent trail easily enough.

She wished she'd had time for a good stretch before dashing off to follow the rodent, but it represented a chance at…something. Maybe it would lead her back to its nest or toward a tunnel with some light. As she tracked the rat, she tried to remember what the combination of turns she'd made was but couldn't quite put it together.

If she turned around, maybe she could feel her way back. There weren't that many turns, at least that she could remember in her panic tainted brain. But that way also meant a chance of running into Ivar. What if he'd gotten lost in here, too? Forward with the rat and away from Ivar seemed like the better plan at the moment. At least that's what she tried to convince herself of before panic set in. Besides, the rats probably lived close to a water source. She could do without food for a while, but skipping water wasn't an option.

The rat led her through a series of turns down the tunnels, keeping up its pace as it ran away from her. Each turn sent another dagger of uncertainty and fear through her heart. If too many more landed, she'd slip into a full panic.

It wasn't until she saw a faint crack in the concrete she kept her nose to while trailing the rat that she realized they'd returned to the light. Lifting her head for a moment, she saw a faint change in the darkness further down the tunnel. Before she became too bemused by the light, she returned her nose to the trail. Since the rat seemed to be heading toward a section of the tunnel with light, she'd keep following. A bit of the panic receded.

After a couple more turns, the light increased enough that she could see a bit further down the tunnel, including what looked a potential source for the light. The glow seemed to be coming from above, near where the ceiling was. Just ahead, she could see the rat's backside as it continued leading her down the tunnel.

She had to keep slowing herself down, otherwise she'd overtake the rat or maybe cause it to panic and become erratic. And then the rat disappeared.

Confused, she took a few more steps until she realized the floor ahead of her was moving, writhing. A moment later, a pair of eyes near the floor appeared, reflecting the dim light. Then another pair joined it. And another. And another. And another, until dozens of pairs of tiny eyes stared back at her.

The earlier fear and dread returned and then some. Her body shuddered. Backing up a few steps, she spun around but was greeted with even more eyes staring back at her. She was trapped.

A growl rose in her throat, and she bared her teeth. A wave of squeaks and little rat claws scratching on concrete answered her.

Turning, she backed into the nearest wall to protect her flanks, though that many rats would eventually overwhelm her.

Slowly, they advanced on her. When one ran out and got close, she snapped at it, flecks of spit flying from her mouth. Squealing, the rat darted away, hiding in the pack, and the rest of the rats stopped.

The little rat had been the scout to see where her line was and now that they'd found it, they stayed behind it. Though they didn't stay still. The whole mass vibrated and squeaked and shifted as rats moved around their companions.

Her eyes moved over the horde, trying to make sure none of them sneaked up on her, but she saved the growling for when she might need it and just panted. She had no idea what the rats wanted. Would they actually attack a large predator like a wolf? She could snap them in half with her powerful jaws, but eventually she'd be overwhelmed. Especially if they bit through any sensitive areas like her tendons. Then she'd drown in a sea of rats.

Her neck was becoming tired from swinging it back and forth quickly to watch all the rats. She wasn't sure, but she thought the volume of squeaking was rising, as if more rats were showing up to reinforce their friends. She didn't know if this was normal behavior for rats. Her high school biology classes had been absent of curriculum around rats and rat behavior, even in the advanced class she was taking this year.

The little rodents didn't seem to want to advance on her, so she risked sliding back until she could sit. It would protect her hind quarters a bit and would give her a slightly better vantage point to watch from.

Now that her eyes had adjusted to the low light, she tried to find the backside of the rat swarm, but all she saw was more rats. There must be hundreds, maybe thousands, of the little creatures surging around her. If she could leap over the mass and start running, she knew she had more speed than they did. And she felt much better after a full night's sleep, though she couldn't be sure how long she'd actually slept in this lightless, timeless tunnel she'd escaped into.

But she couldn't find the back. She just saw more rats. If she launched herself from a running start, could she leap far enough and hope they'd scramble out of the way of her landing? But she didn't know how many more rats were coming. Maybe every rat in Red City had been called in to deal with the predator in the T-shirt. It seemed like she'd gone from last night's frying pan into the fire, then several more fires along the way.

Her panting increased, drawing drool from her mouth as it dripped to the concrete. As thirsty as she was—her water had run out the previous night when she'd been sitting on the bench across from the morgue and she'd left her empty water bottle with her backpack—it might be dehydration that got her before the rats did. She snapped her jaws closed, but the need to pant took precedence, and she was forced to open her mouth again.

This was not how she wanted to end her life—dying in a tunnel to become rat food. Maybe if she didn't fight them, it would go quicker, and she wouldn't have to suffer as long.

She laid down, resting her head between her outstretched paws. Yet the rats didn't move. She couldn't help but flick her eyes around at all the movement with an occasional hopeful glance toward what she thought might be a slightly less dark part of the tunnel. They stayed behind their imaginary line and continued doing whatever it was they'd been doing.

Huffing, she sat up. She didn't want to die as a wolf. She shifted back to her human form and pushed back so her back was against the concrete wall. The rats still didn't react, at least that she could see.

The concrete floor felt rough and cold on her bare butt. Reaching down, she tugged the back of her T-shirt down enough that she could sit on it. Next, she drew up her knees to her chest and pulled the front of her T-shirt over them. It would likely stretch the old cotton beyond recovery, but at least it was one more layer between herself and the cool, still air of the tunnels.

Folding her arms on top of her knees, she rested her head on her arms. She didn't want to die, but at least accepting the very distinct possibility that it could happen at any moment if the rats decided they were ready to attack her had brought a bit of calmness. And with it, her heartbeat and respiratory rate slowed. At least it wouldn't be at the hands of Ivar.

Rats weren't compassionate, but at least they'd kill her quickly to prevent her from lashing out in her pain. The Nazi biker would take his time and make the pain and torture last.

Jamie guessed Linda, Cory's mom, was right to keep him away. Likely, no one would ever recover her bones, and her mother wouldn't know what had happened to her. Cory deserved better than to be gnawed upon bones lost to time. She sighed. She deserved better. After all the work she'd put into surviving and her plans to escape as soon as high school was done, and she'd end up spending eternity as rat turds in a shitty tunnel in an even worse city.

"Fuck my life," she mumbled.

Off in the distance to her left, the direction she'd been heading toward, the faint light increased its glow. She closed her eyes, not wanting to know what new hell was coming her way. The rats squeaked louder, and the speed of their claws scratching concrete picked up. Something had caused them to become more excited.

She rocked gently, humming atonally to try to block out the noise, but it was futile. There were just too many rats.

A high, squeaky, but rough voice broke into the din created by the rats. "Well, well, well. What have we here?"

TWENTY

JAMIE

"Hmm, what have you led me to, my pretties?"

Jamie didn't bother looking up, trying to delay learning what new trouble she'd found herself in. Nothing seemed to be going her way. Ever. Whatever was about to happen would no doubt make her life worse than it was five minutes ago. She was so tired of everything. What new hell was the squeaky voiced man going to bring into her life?

The voice wasn't in and of itself scary, but the incongruity of the high-pitched squeaky voice that nearly mirrored the squeaks of the rats made her skin crawl. Had she wandered into the lair of the king of the rats? She had no idea if rat shifters existed.

She knew next to nothing about the supernatural community. Wolf shifters were what she knew about since she was one, as was her best friend. She could recognize most other wolf shifters. There were rumors of witch covens in Red City, but she didn't know if their magic was real or not.

She'd also met the Grim Reaper, which was an experience she had no desire to repeat. He'd starred in a few of her post-rescue nightmares. Those flaming eyes…

If she never saw him again, it would be too soon.

"Is she scared? Of little ol' us? Hmm."

Inhaling slowly and deeply, she risked opening her eyes. A pair of scuffed boots and baggy, threadbare jeans interrupted the line of the rats as they moved around him, some climbing up or down his legs. It was the king of the rats. But at least it might be a human or have a human form.

Sighing, she raised her head.

He looked homeless with his dirty, baggy clothes and unkempt hair and beard, but he didn't smell bad. Not enough to overwhelm the scent of rats dominating the tunnel.

"Yes, yes. Scary wolf, sharp teeth. Snapping. Growling. Scared girl. Cringing. Waiting."

She wasn't sure if was talking to her or his rats. "What are you going to do to me?" Jamie asked timidly.

"Nothing. Too skinny for a good meal." He cackled. Though, she cringed and shivered. "Jokes. Jokes. Hmm. Lost, are we?"

Annoyed at the joke, she narrowed her eyes. "I don't know. Are you lost, too?"

She put a bit too much sarcasm in her voice. Her mom was right. Her mouth was going to get her killed one of these days.

"Never lost in my tunnels, but are we speaking philosophically? We're all lost in Red City." He cackled squeakily. "Want to be unlost?"

"I'm not sure unlost is a word." Damn it. She shook her head at herself.

"Sure, it is. I spoke it. In the aether it now exists." He tilted his head to the side. "But my question was left unanswered. Shall I help you to become unlost?"

She looked him over. He wasn't very tall. She probably had a few inches on him. He also didn't look very powerful physically. Though, if he were some kind of shifter, looks could be dangerously deceiving. And that was even assuming he didn't have magic to augment himself.

"Please. And thank you."

"Hmm. Politeness. Courtesy." He bowed deeply, a smirk breaking the line of his mouth and peeking out from his beard.

She eyed the rats. "Um, will they let me pass?"

"They'll let you pass. Unless you are a Balrog. Are you Balrog?" He titled his head again, raising an eyebrow.

She snorted. "No. Just a…" He knew she was a wolf shifter. He'd said it. Somehow, he knew about it. Maybe the rats had told him. "A lost wolf shifter."

"Yes. Yes. Lost." A rat climbed from his back onto his shoulder and squeaked into his ear. "Mhm. Mhm." Then he returned his focus to Jamie. "Chased. By a bad man. A very bad man."

She nodded, unsure how to respond.

"According to my little friend, you led him a merry chase, but it is safe now." Another rat climbed onto his other shoulder, squeaking at him.

Her curiosity outweighed her fear. This little man could talk to rats, or at least pretended to. But he also knew she'd been chased into the tunnels by "a very bad man," indeed.

"Do you know the man who was chasing me?" she asked.

The man shook his head vigorously, nearly dislodging his rat friends. "Wolf man, like you, but worse. Very bad. You don't hurt my rat friends, even though they scare you. He hurts for fun. For pleasure. For profit." He shuddered. "You've made a very bad enemy."

"Don't I know it." She drew in a deep voice and launched into her next question. "You don't work for him, do you?"

He sniffed as if he smelled something deeply unpleasant. "The Rat works for no one, except"—he raised his arms and gestured to the rats swirling around him—"for my friends." He bent over, so he was closer to her. "Are you my friend?"

She swallowed. "I'm not your enemy."

He cackled. "Wise. Very wise. Good answer. Beware fast friends in need." He narrowed his eyes at her, then sighed. "Come. Come. It's time my not enemy becomes unlost."

Nodding, she carefully stood up and tried to do her best to keep herself covered. At least the stretched-out T now hung low enough to cover her business.

He looked her up and down. "Hmm. Outfit too cold. Come.

Come. Will help you become uncold too." He turned and waved her after him.

The rats parted like the Red Sea and turned to follow him. Closing up behind them, they made a barrier of fur between her and their master, though not a massive one. Willing herself forward, she took the first hesitant step. Then the next.

Warring with the need not to get lost again and being too close to the rat army, she tucked in at the back, but left a good five feet between her and the back of the group. Though the swarm quickly rendered it moot as they shifted yet again to wrap around her, leaving her what she guessed they thought was a respectable bit of space.

The squeaking never stopped. It was like all the rats had to tell each other the latest gossip. Some of them would climb up the back of the man, replacing the one that had been there moments ago on his shoulder, and speak into his ear. He always acknowledged what his little friends said. Sometimes with a noncommittal grunt. Sometimes with an interested hum. Others warranted a bit of conversation. A few even elicited that cackling laugh.

Did rats have a sense of humor? She wondered if a rat joke would translate to a human's sensibilities. The man seemed to find whatever it was they'd said amusing. But she didn't know if he was indeed a human. Maybe he'd lived with the rats for so long he'd picked up their mannerisms.

She swallowed nervously at this thought. What if he couldn't understand them and he was just playing along? Or worse, he thought they spoke to him. She shook her head. She had to hope this was just going to end up one of the weirder experiences she'd had in Red City and not just another horror to be overcome. She didn't need to go borrowing trouble at the moment since she already had too much to deal with already. If things got weirder, she'd make new decisions then. Be wary. Be ready. Be fast.

The tunnels seemed to go on forever. Some intersected with other tunnels that smelled bad, like sewage. Those they didn't navigate. Her shepherd seemed to know which way he was going, never hesitating when there was a choice to be made. His confidence in this dimly lit maze was slowly leaking into her. Occasionally, a rat or a group would peel off and scurry down a side tunnel, no doubt on some important mission for their pack or their master.

She stifled a chuckle, not wanting to offend him or his friends. Right now, he was helping her. If he decided she wasn't worth helping, she'd be right back where she was, but with thousands of rats who might decide she wasn't too skinny for the dinner menu. She stopped herself before she could sigh in exasperation. Cast into the wind, she had to rely on this rat man if she hoped to see the light again, no matter how frustrating it felt to be almost entirely reliant on a weird, total stranger.

Her stomach rumbled. Reminding her it had been a long time since lunch at school the previous day. And with that reminder of bodily functions, her bladder jumped in as well. She hadn't had time for a quick break when the rat woke her. She'd been up and following instantly.

"Um, sir."

He stopped, turning around. "Yes? Yes?"

"Is there a place I can go to the restroom?"

"Soon, soon. Keep following."

She nodded and sighed as their little rat pack continued down the tunnel. Soon. Soon. Her bladder was beginning to hurt, and she didn't want the indignity of having to stop their procession to pee in front of a horde of rats.

TWENTY-ONE

JAMIE

Jamie's feet ached from walking barefoot on the concrete of the tunnel warren. She had no idea that all of this lay under Red City or what purpose it served. Some of the tunnels, when she had more light to see with, looked old, while some sections looked newer. Some had pipes and other signs of utility works.

"Where are we going?" she asked the man leading her along with his rat army. She hoped they arrived soon. The ache in her feet coupled with the poor night's sleep made her want to whine, but she held it back, not wanting to annoy the person who hopefully was helping her.

"Almost there. Safe place. Patience."

Grinding her teeth, she stopped the snarky words from leaving her mouth. He was helping her; there was no need to be antagonistic. She could be patient. A couple minutes later, they turned, then stopped at a dead end.

The man stopped and looked over his shoulder. "Turn around and close your eyes. Secrets. I must protect myself and my friends."

Sighing, she folded her arms across her chest and turned around. She didn't want to close her eyes, but she'd be willing to extend him a bit more trust. She'd gotten used to finding things to mistrust about people, but as odd as he seemed, he didn't feel like someone who meant her any ill-will. If he'd wanted her dead, he could have just left her where she was or swarmed her under immediately with his rat army. Instead, he'd been courteous and almost respectful, something unusual in this hellhole of a city.

A few moments later, a series of thunks were followed by a grinding noise like heavy stones rubbing against each other.

"Turn. Turn. Safe now," he said.

When she spun around, he waved her after him as he ducked under a short passage that hadn't been there a moment ago. Shaking her head, she dropped to her hands and knees and peered into the dark space but couldn't see anything.

"Come. Come. Safe for rats and for girls."

A light flicked on. All she could see was a sea of rats moving around and the man from the knees down. She had no idea where she was. If she decided to stay where she was, she'd be just as lost as she'd been earlier. If she entered the man's...lair, she might be trapped. But her only hope at the moment rested on the other side of the door with the odd little man. She'd come this far...

"Fine. Coming." She crawled in, ignoring the discomfort of the rough concrete on her knees and palms. When she cleared the small door, she scrambled to her feet, tugging at the T-shirt to keep herself covered.

"Please, close your eyes again. Must protect my safety and secrets." He smiled, though it felt a bit too wide and forced, as if he wasn't quite familiar with how a natural smile should work.

Sighing, she stepped out of the way and placed her back to the wall next to the door and closed her eyes. "OK."

The clunks and grinding repeated themselves.

"Safe again."

Now that she was stuck there for the moment, she looked around. The room appeared to be a long rectangle, the far walls shrouded in shadows. As she squinted into the distance, more lights flared on, and she closed her eyes against the sudden glare.

"More light. Surface dwellers like it bright." He wandered away from her, spreading his arms wide as he spun around slowly. "Welcome to my home!"

The light did make her feel more comfortable as the shadows in the back corners receded. There appeared to be little rooms cordoned off with blankets or curtains, most of which weren't open.

"Excuse me, sir. Um, do you have a restroom?"

"Yes. Follow." He took off toward one of the curtained off sections.

"How do you keep all the rats from chewing up everything?"

He stopped and turned around, his eyes narrowed in what looked like a mix of annoyance and confusion. "Why would they chew my stuff? They are my friends. Plenty to chew elsewhere. Plenty. Good rats."

When he swept the curtain back, he gestured inside. "Privacy. I'll go find some clothes for you." He didn't wait for her answer but headed off toward a different cordoned-off area.

Shrugging, she darted inside the room and pulled the curtain shut. She was surprised to find a toilet sitting on a short platform next to a bathtub with a shower curtain surrounding it. With a quick check under the toilet's lid, she found water and in the tank, too. A pipe ran up the wall, connecting into a large pipe running near the ceiling. A larger pipe ran out the back of the platform and off to yet another pipe.

Her bladder screamed at her to get on with it. She'd been holding it for a long time and had been OK, but as soon as she neared a toilet, it refused to wait any longer. When her butt hit the seat, she shivered at the touch of the cold toilet seat. It wasn't heated, and his underground warren wasn't terribly warm.

After she finished, she washed up at the sink he'd rigged up to the pipe system and poked her head out through the curtain door. A small pile of clothes had been set by the entrance to the restroom.

She grabbed them and made sure the curtain was fully closed. Staring at the pile of neatly folded clothing in her hands, she brought it up to her face and gave it a sniff. It smelled clean, like some sort of mild laundry detergent. That surprised her. She'd expected stinky rags smelling of body odor and rats.

Pulling off her sweaty, stretched-out T-shirt, she unfortunately had to leave on the bra since there wasn't likely to be one in the pile. There wasn't any underwear either, but the jeans, socks, T-shirt, and sweatshirt felt amazing.

When she stepped out of the bathroom, the scent of cooking food drew her attention. Following her nose, she found a small kitchen area with an old electric oven and stovetop. The man was contentedly stirring a pan.

"Better? Warmer?" he asked without turning around.

"Yes. Thank you."

"Oatmeal?"

Her stomach rumbled in answer, and he laughed.

"Yes, your stomach says." He lifted up a bag of dried apricots. "Tasty cut up in oats. Agreed?"

"I've never tried it, but I like apricots."

Dumping out a dozen onto a nearby table, he quickly chopped them into small pieces and dumped them into his boiling pan of oatmeal. Off to the side of the stove stood an old bookshelf covered in kitchenware. From it, he grabbed a couple of bowls and spoons.

"Sit. Sit." He sat the bowls on the table, nudging the single chair toward her.

"I can't take your chair. I'll stand."

"No. Our guest. Sit, sit." He removed the pan from the stove and divided the oatmeal into the bowls. Before he grabbed his bowl, he scooped a healthy dollop of peanut butter from a nearby jar and mixed it into the steaming oatmeal. Seeing where her eyes went, he slid the jar to her.

It was the best meal she'd ever had thanks to the sauce of her hunger. The hearty, warm peanut butter laden oatmeal filled her up and took away a bit of her anxiety. A full belly was a good place to restart the day.

"Thank you, sir."

"No sir. Just The Rat." He picked up the bowl and licked it clean.

"What?"

"The Rat. It's what I'm called."

"Oh. Um. I'm Jamie."

"Nice to meet you, Jamie." He smiled, setting his bowl down in what looked like a freestanding utility sink.

"I don't mean to be rude, but can you please lead me out of the tunnels?"

"Yes. Yes. But not now." He gave his head a twitchy shake. "Send out my rat friends to scout to make sure the bad man isn't waiting."

"Is that the only entrance?"

"No. But I've seen him in other parts of the tunnels at other entrances. I don't know how well he knows this place." He shrugged. "Safe here for now."

"Oh. OK." She didn't want to stay down there anymore than she had to. Her mother must be worried sick about her or thinking the worst had happened—that Ivar had caught her and killed her. "Do you have a phone I could borrow? To call my mom?"

He shook his head, his shaggy hair flying around. "No. No phones. Don't work. Too deep, too much concrete."

"Oh."

"Don't worry, you can call when we get near the surface. The Rat has a phone." He grinned broadly. "The Rat is up on burners! We'll get you home soon."

Home? She didn't have one of those, not that what she'd had before was much of one. She wondered if her mom was still at the hotel or if she'd moved on. If she had moved on, she hoped her mom had picked up her bag, though she wouldn't be able to call her since her phone was safely zipped in the pocket. She didn't even have a quarter for a payphone, assuming they could even find one that worked.

"I don't think I can go home. That's where Ivar found me."

"Ivar. That's a dark name. Nasty name. Hmm. So, our bad man is the infamous Ivar. I've never had a face to put with the name." He paced back and forth in front of the table. "You've got a powerful enemy. How did one so young manage that?"

"I kind of, um, helped burn down his gang's bar…" She'd not set the fire, but she'd been the one who'd drawn Dax to the bar.

"Oh." He laughed, his voice rising to a higher octave. "So you're a friend of the scary one?" He shuddered.

The burning eyes of Dax sent a matching shudder down her spine. "He's not my friend. It's a bit complicated."

"Does he know Ivar is back in town?"

"I don't know. I haven't seen him since the night of the bar incident."

He stopped his pacing long enough to allow a rat to scamper up his leg and rest on his shoulder. The rat squeaked into his ear, and he nodded. This had to be one of the weirder interactions she'd ever had. If she wasn't still a bit numb from watching the Grim Reaper mess up a bunch of bikers, this might have been a bridge too far.

She sighed. A few weeks ago, she'd wanted out of her crappy life. This wasn't the direction she wanted to go. She was waiting to hear back from colleges. Hopefully some would offer scholarships. At least the poverty created by her dad's gambling and inability to maintain a good job would help her qualify for needs-based grants. She shook her head. If she didn't have to go into deep hiding…

A paper trail of scholarships and college paperwork would be easy enough for even the dimmest dirtbag biker to follow. And there was the double-edged sword of the hole her dad had dug. Even if she got the grants, she might not be able to take advantage of them. She wanted to break down and cry.

"Damn. Damn. Damn." The Rat reached up to scratch the rat's head. "We didn't want to become involved."

"Involved in what?" Jamie asked, rubbing her eyes and using the distraction to prevent the tears.

He took the rat off his shoulder and set it gently on the ground. "Trouble is brewing in Red City. Bad trouble. Your friend is at the center of it, even if he's unaware of it."

She slumped and sighed. She'd hoped to never have to see Dax again, but they were too linked when it came to Ivar. And if she hoped to survive to get a chance to get out of this festering shithole of a city and life, she needed him to survive to help keep her alive.

TWENTY-TWO

DAX

Dax woke on his stomach, his head hazy with drugs. He yawned and tried to get up but couldn't move. Sagging back onto his stomach, he groaned, a dull throbbing of pain making itself known.

"Good morning, sunshine," Manman Delphine said. "Glad to see you're back among the living."

"Mmm."

"My, aren't we loquacious this morning?"

He still hadn't opened his eyes to locate the manbo, and his ears were fuzzy and thick feeling. Taking his best guess, he slowly brought down his forefinger, ring finger, and pinky while tucking in his thumb. He didn't quite have the coordination to properly extend the middle finger, but under the present circumstances, it would have to do.

Delphine laughed. Apparently, Dax had guessed the correct hand. He forced his eyes open only to slam them shut again at the explosively bright light.

He chuckled, the sound raspy and thick. He wasn't the kind of being to go into the light. He was the kind who escorted others to it. But it wasn't that kind of light. It was just eyes not ready for a brightly lit room. This time, he opened his eyes more slowly, letting them adjust.

Once they adjusted, he found Manman Delphine sitting in a chair, a closed book in her hand. The tall, Black trans woman wore a long blue, red, and green dress and a red and black head wrap that coordinated with her dress.

"Where am I?" His tongue felt like sandpaper in his mouth.

"You're in a clinic. One you've been in before."

That made sense. He'd been… "Was I in an explosion?"

"Wi, cher. Someone tried to blow up your motorcycle. Well, someone tried to blow you up. They succeeded in blowing up your motorcycle."

"Everyone OK?"

"Yes. You were the only one hurt. Your bar is also fine, save for a few scarred bricks and some singe marks. Some trash was set on fire. You'll have to decide if you want to file an insurance claim on that." She smiled and gave him a wink.

"Thirsty."

"I bet you are. Just hold on." She stood up and grabbed a cup with a straw in it. Carefully, she directed the straw into his mouth. "Go slowly. Just a little until you're sure you can swallow properly."

He followed her directions. The water dancing across his tongue felt glorious. He wanted to suck it all down, but resisted until he was sure he'd be OK. When nothing happened, he took a bigger drink, sighing happily when the straw drew in air from the now empty small cup.

"That's all for now, cher. Let's wait for the doc to examine you. And if he says it's alright, I have a fresh batch of poultice for you. It'll fix up the scrapes and help heal the burns faster."

He nodded gratefully. Her poultice would fix him right up, though he wondered what he'd owe her for the newest round of aid. "How bad?"

"The burns?" Her voice turned serious. "Nothing worse than a second degree. You can thank Boudreaux for that. He leapt into action and smothered the flames."

"Mmm." And again, he owed Boudreaux. Though the score on

The Collector's cars probably would more than cover this. And the promised aid to Winnie.

He sighed. He'd tried to keep his attachments to the bare minimum—Tomi and his family. They were the only ones he owed everything and nothing to. It was a two-way street. They'd saved each other's lives when Dax had been first dropped into Red City in a world he didn't understand. Now they were family, their fortunes tied to each other.

But now he was becoming tied into Delphine and Boudreaux, both connections from Tomi's mother Mama Adele. He didn't know how much longer he could keep fighting to be a loner.

Red City had quickly become personally very dangerous. If this explosion was indeed another assassination attempt, this was the third direct attempt in as many months. Without the help he'd received, he likely would be dead with his essence trapped inside a decaying mortal prison.

He sighed. For now, he'd have to accept the connections and the aid. He didn't have a choice if he wanted to live and protect those he'd taken responsibility for. And now that circle of responsibility seemed to be increasing in diameter.

"How long have I been out?" Dax asked.

"Not long. Your injuries may cover more of your body, but in total, they're not as severe as the bullet you took to the chest." She looked at her watch. "It's been about thirty-six hours. The doctor kept you sedated so you wouldn't move. He had to remove some shrapnel from the back half of your body and some bits of pavement from the front half of your body. You look like you've been well tenderized on both sides, cher."

He yawned. "Why are you here?"

"Well—"

He grunted. "My apologies. That sounded a bit abrupt."

"No worries, zanmi m. You're not a man of many words, and you've always been straight to the point. I take no offense. I'm here because Tomi has to cover your shift at the bar and Boudreaux has to work. Tomi wished me to pass on that Boudreaux had his boys pick up the remains of your motorcycle."

Dax perked up a bit. He knew he grumbled about his motorcycle a lot in the winter, but he loved the stupid thing. It was a much a part of his identity as a mortal human as anything. "Does he think he can fix it?"

Sympathy filled Delphine's eyes. "No, cher. Unlike you, your bike is beyond recovery. One of Bordeaux's associates is a bomb expert. He's going to look at the remains of the bike and bomb to see if they can find out anything about it."

"Oh…" He deflated a little. "I guess that's a good idea, though. Might lead us to who did it."

"Indeed. Sorry I couldn't bring you good news about your motorcycle. As to the why of my company, besides others being busy, we didn't want you to be alone."

"I was unconscious. Not sure I had much need for company."

She chuckled. "Cher, it wasn't friendly company we were worried about, not entirely, anyway. You've been the subject of three assassination attempts that I know of. We wanted to make sure you had proper protection while you were unconscious."

Though he could still feel the effects of the sedatives and despite his normal surface level approach to human emotions, his friends' concern for his wellbeing warmed his heart. And that made him think some more.

When had Boudreaux and Delphine moved to his friend column? Previously, that list had been exclusively reserved for Tomi. Everyone else, his employees, his regulars at the bar, and the new people he'd met through Tomi's family had been acquaintances or friendly acquaintances at best. Now he could add Delphine and Boudreaux in as new friends.

"Thank you." He lifted the corners of his lips without opening them as a full smile. That was the best he could do considering the circumstances of his injuries and the awkwardness he felt as the realization that there were a couple more people who seemed to care about his wellbeing.

"Cher, Dax. Not all people in this lwas forsaken hellhole are bad. In fact, I'd venture to guess most of the people living and working and trying to get by in this city are good, honest folk." She leaned forward, a gentle smile on her face. "And you're one of them. We're all just trying to get by. But someone has taken umbrage to your existence in this city. You've got to reach out to the other good folks and let them be there for you. You're lucky you have Tomi on your side. And his mama. They're some of the best people I know. And they've led you to other good folk. You just have to step forward and stop being aloof in the background."

He thought back to the last time he'd trusted someone and how badly he'd gotten burned. He'd lost everything and been exiled to live as a human in this shit hole. "Trust is a dangerous thing, especially when you place it in the wrong individual." He couldn't help the bitterness spreading across his face.

She smiled warmly at him, an understanding note in her eyes. "I know, cher, I know. I mean, not your situation specifically, but we've all been hurt by someone we trusted. Most of us many times by several people. Some were worse than others. But we've all keenly felt that pain of betrayal."

"How do you get over it?"

Her rich laugh filled the room. "Often, you don't. At least not entirely. You can never get back to that person you were before the betrayal. That person is a figment of your past. It's someone you used to know, even if the face looking back in the mirror is the same—as long as you don't look too deeply in the eyes. But—"

"But?"

"But what matters is how you deal with it. You can let that hurt, that betrayal fester until it consumes you and turns you into a husk of your former self." She stopped, narrowing her eyes at him and leaning forward to rest her elbows on her knees. "May I make a candid observation?"

He snorted, making a sloppy gesture with his hand that wasn't tied down with IV lines. "Not like I can go anywhere."

"But consent matters, cher. Some people aren't ready to hear honest but kind observations about themselves."

He'd come to value Tomi's opinions. They'd always felt delivered with honesty and in the spirit of their friendship. If he was going to count Delphine as a friend, he'd have to open himself enough to see if it would become a true friendship like he and Tomi shared.

"Please."

She nodded, the motion regal in its seriousness. "I know we've danced around each other about who we are and what we can or could do. But I don't think you came to live in that husk because it was your first choice. You tell people you're retired, but it was a forced retirement. You were betrayed." She shivered. "I don't want to know by who or what because… Well, who would betray one of your stature and win?"

He snorted. "Yet here I am. Pain meds wearing off in a hospital bed, a perpetual murder target."

"Trust was betrayed, Dax. Someone you'd been vulnerable to abused that position, and because of it, you are now here. A perpetual murder target, as you say. And because of that, you've hidden. Not just from those who put you here but from yourself. You've created a small little life to survive in and done little to figure out where you wanted to go during this stage of your journey."

"You do not know the ones who watch, Delphine. They are not to be messed with. A small life was my best defense."

"I understand, but you can be so much more than that."

He opened his mouth, but she held up a hand to stop him.

"I'm not saying you must seek to return to your previous heights. You have a business that has managed to survive in this town, even if it's not lucrative. You have a wonderful friend in Tomi and a family in his. Mama Adele is not one to so easily welcome someone into the lives of her children, yet when she came to me seeking help for you, it was as if she were coming to ask aid for one of her blood." She smiled kindly. "Dax, you are rich in the best way. You just need to recognize it and let that be the place you grow from."

Mama Adele had always looked out for him, making sure he was fed and had a place if he needed it. They could have gone their separate ways after he'd saved her life and the lives of her children. But she'd sent out Tomi to collect him, and eventually she'd made him one of her brood. He squeezed his eyes, a bit of emotion dampening them.

"You've just been existing, my friend. Maintaining yourself at a step or two above your lowest point. You can keep that up. I bet you'll survive this current round of assassination attempts. But where will you go from there? You can return to your current status quo, or"—she sat up straight and raised her arms to the side—"you can build a new, rich life with the friends and family you've found here. It doesn't have to be an either or of your previous heights or nothing. You can find a new path."

He wiped the dampness from his cheeks with his free hand. And though he wanted to look away from the Delphine's gaze, he forced himself to hold it. It wasn't unkind or for the point of dominance, but to let him know that she was offering genuine advice. And he suspected that she knew she was on the cusp of being part of his new life, if he chose to seek it out.

"I-I'll think about your words." His voice simultaneously sounded weaker than he'd heard it in a while and warmer than he'd maybe ever heard it.

Before he could say anything else, the door opened and a Black man of average height and slight build stepped into the room. His black hair was cropped short on the sides to form a donut around the bald top. "Ah, Delphine. So good to see you. If you can step out and give me and my patient a moment or two of privacy so I can examine him, I would appreciate it." He sniffed the air briefly. "I see you've brought a batch of your wonderful poultice. I'll see if he's ready for it."

"Of course, Konan." Delphine stood and squeezed the doctor's shoulder on the way out of the room, shutting the door quietly.

Konan bent down so his face was level with Dax's. "I'm glad you're awake, Dax. But to be honest, I'm a little disappointed to see you again so soon."

"Sorry, Dr. Ofori, it wasn't really my idea. Well, either time."

The doctor chuckled. "Fair enough. Do you mind if I take a look at your burns and other wounds?"

"Of course."

Dax zoned out while the doctor lifted the sheets and looked under bandages. A few times he winced or grunted in pain. After the doctor finished, he took the seat Delphine had vacated and slid it forward so he was closer.

"Well, Dax. You're a pretty fast healer. You're looking a fair bit better than yesterday."

"That's good. No offense, but this bed isn't so comfortable that I want to spend a week in it."

The doctor chuckled. "No. It's not a deluxe memory foam mattress, is it? Well, most of the open wounds are doing pretty well. The small stuff is closed up, and the blisters from the burns have receded. I think we can smear some of the good manbo's goop all over you and go from there."

"Can I go home after?"

"Yes. I think so. Nothing looks like it's infected, and her poultice will take care of the rest. Though I recommend you spend as much time on your stomach as possible. You've got a few wounds and burns on the back of your legs, buttocks, and back. It'll be quite uncomfortable, and I don't want you to open any of them or irritate them."

He grunted and nodded. "I think I can manage that."

"Good. Good." He walked to the door and opened it. "Manman Delphine, you can rejoin us now."

"How's he doing, Doctor?"

"Well enough. He can go home if you can arrange a ride for him."

Dax groaned. "My motorcycle. Now I'll be stuck riding the bus."

Delphine bent over and picked up the cloth bag she'd brought, pulling out a couple sealed ceramic pots. "I'll call Boudreaux and have him bring his bus by. It'll save Dax some back and butt time until he's a little more healed."

"Sounds like a plan." The doctor stepped into Dax's view and extended a hand. "If you think you can manage it, I'd prefer not to see you again, at least professionally, Dax."

"Thanks, Doc. I'll see what I can do to stay out of here, though it wasn't really my idea to pay you a visit."

The doctor chuckled. "Good luck!" The door clicked shut, signaling his departure.

"So, Dax, we're about to get a bit more intimate. I'll let you handle any application on the front side, if you need it. But I'll take care of placing the poultices on your back and elsewhere."

He sighed. "I guess there's no other choice." He wasn't particularly modest, at least he didn't think so. Though he'd never really been naked in front of anyone as a human. "What's in the second jar?"

"A salve. The poultice is great but needs a bandage to cover it and keep it in place. I can cover your burns with the salve. It'll speed up the healing process, moisturize the skin, and keep you from scarring or peeling."

"You're a talented individual."

She laughed. "I'm just practical. When you often work with fire, it's a good idea to have a remedy if things get a bit out of hand. It's one of my bestselling items with many of my more serious practitioners. Ready?"

"I suppose so."

The sheet covering him had been tented so it covered him without touching his skin. It kept in a bit of warmth and kept any breezes off his skin.

"Damn, that's cold." A shiver ran up his spine from where she'd placed the first dollop of goop.

The manbo chuckled and ignored him, working the salve over his burned skin. After the initial cold shocks wore off, the places where her hands had been felt cooler and the dull general throb of pain receded to the point it was easy to ignore. Again, her skills shined, and he appreciated having access to them.

Delphine was quick and professional, humming a tune while she worked. Soon, she'd returned the sheet to its previous position and resumed her vigil in the chair after she'd washed her hands.

"Thanks, Delphine. I really appreciate this."

"Anything for a friend." Her phone chirped. "Ah, Boudreaux said he'll be here in an hour. Are you going to need more poultice and salve for tomorrow?"

His nose twitched, getting used to the pleasant but pungent aromas of the manbo's products. "Hmm. Anything magical about the wounds?"

"Not that we could detect."

"Probably not, but if you don't have anywhere else to be, you might want to follow me home so you know where it is."

"Warded?"

"I think so, though I might need to have it reinforced or replaced." He sighed, shaking his head as much as he could with it twisted sideways on the clinic bed. "But I guess that's a problem for another day."

"If you'd like, I can take a peek."

He twisted to make eye contact. Delphine's face was a study in composed neutrality. She'd done right by him so far. Nodding, he gave her a closed-mouth smile. "It can't hurt."

"If nothing else, I can make a few gris-gris bags to beef up your supernatural security." She wrapped her ceramic jars in the towels that had padded them in her bag. "Now that we've taken care of that, what should we dedicate our remaining time to while we wait for our handsome friend to bring your horizontal conveyance?"

His brow furrowed as he held her gaze. A corner of one side of her lips curled up. It didn't matter to him. It just felt good to not be alone while he waited. An hour with his new friend would be good enough. "I'll leave it to your discretion."

She opened up her book, flipping back to the beginning. "It's been a while since I've had an opportunity to read to anyone…"

TWENTY-THREE

JAMIE

Impatience gnawed at Jamie. But at least it was better than being gnawed on by rats. She slammed the beat-up paperback shut for the dozenth time, eyeing the patch of wall where the entrance was.

When The Rat said he wished to send out scouts, the beady-eyed furry kind, it had sounded like a good idea. They didn't want to run into Ivar on their way out of the tunnels. Plus, she'd picked up enough hints in her questioning of The Rat to figure out there might be other dangerous beings down here in the hidden underworld of Red City.

But rats were not speedy creatures.

She was sure The Rat had sent out his sneakiest and wiliest rats on this mission. He'd held a little meeting surrounded by his squeaking minions. When he finished speaking to them, three small groups broke off from the maelstrom of rodents and skittered off in different directions, disappearing into the shadows of The Rat's lair.

While they waited for the rats to return, he'd shown her to his collection of books. It took her a while to look through it and find one that might distract her while she stewed in her own frustrations. Then he'd offered her a couple more simple meals. Finally, he directed her to a sleeping mat and a neatly folded clean blanket when he noticed she kept yawning over her book.

She stopped herself from tossing the book aside in frustration. It wasn't hers, and she was a guest in his rat-filled domain. Setting it down gently, she casually strolled toward the back of the cement room, away from where The Rat hummed to himself as he busied himself in his kitchen area.

Once she felt she was far enough to be out of sight but not too far away, she paced. Though she didn't get along with her mother, and the tension between them had only increased since the incident with the bikers, she knew her mother must be worried sick about her. Frankly, she was worried sick about herself.

If Ivar scared a being like The Rat, a man with a literal rat army at his disposal, perhaps she'd underestimated just how scary the biker was. And she'd been plenty terrified of him since she first met him.

A low growl rumbled in her throat, but she bit it down before it could become something that might disturb her host and his little friends. Rats probably had very good hearing, though she didn't know if The Rat had any of their abilities. If he didn't, they'd certainly tell him about it.

She felt cooped up more than usual. She was locked inside a concrete prison, even though it was a pleasant enough one, all things considered. But she needed to get out. Though, more than anything, she needed to run. To feel the wind through her fur.

The pain of losing Cory and their time together surged to the fore, escaping the dam she'd tried to keep on that particular hurt. Her eyes burned. Staggering to the darkest corner, she sagged onto the ground and pulled her knees up to her chin as she sat against the concrete wall.

Dashing the tears away from her cheeks, she sniffed hard. "Stupid Cory."

Of all the betrayals and hardships, that hurt the worst. Dealing with her dad's bullshit and trying to kill Dax had only been bearable because she had Cory by her side. Now she had nothing. She didn't have a home. She'd lost her home away from home and the person she considered as close as a parent in Cory's mom. And she'd lost her best friend.

She was stuck in the underworld of Red City, surrounded by the rest of the city's vermin. She snorted, half choking on her tears and snotty nose. She was just one more low-life vermin scrabbling around for survival.

With a great huff of exasperation, she let her muscles go slack as the last of emotional energy evaporated, her arms sagged and fell to the ground as she slouched against the wall. Focusing into the middle distance, she tried to find the place of numbness she'd been living in the last few weeks. Right now wasn't the best time to have an emotional breakdown. If she were numb, at least she could continue to function at the most basic levels.

No matter how hard she tried to find it, she couldn't get there. Each tear running down her cheeks pulled her back into the moment and her situation, though she didn't have the energy to lift her hand and dash them away, so she let them fall. Eventually they'd stop, or she'd dehydrate and turn into a dried-up husk. Either would work for her.

When something cold bumped her hand, she twitched enough for it to slip its furry head under her hand. Without thinking about it, she reacted as if she were an experienced pet owner—she'd seen it enough—and scratched the furry head. The head directed her to where it wanted her fingers, wiggling and shifting its position under her touch.

Blinking, the room came back into a vague focus. There were no kittens or puppies here...

She closed her eyes tightly, not wanting to see what she was petting, but she knew what it was. Sighing, she shrugged and continued providing scratches for the rat. Soon, one of its friends bumped her other hand, wanting to get in on the action. She hoped more of their friends didn't try to join them. She only had so many hands, and there were a hell of a lot more rats.

Off in the distance, a tall shadow grew larger as it moved toward her, finally resolving into the short figure of The Rat. "Jamie? Back there? Back where? In the shadows?" He cackled. "Hiding like one of my furry friends."

She made to open her mouth and answer, but under her right hand, the rat wiggled forward and squeaked loudly.

"What? Sassy rats. Disturbing scritch time. Greedy rats, imposing on our guest." He tsked, shaking his head. "Come away, let her be."

Both rats squeaked back in what she thought sounded like an affronted tone. Could rat squeaks have tones? Huffing, they both wiggled out from under her hands and scurried away.

"You've offended my new friends," she mumbled.

He chuckled, squatting down in front of her. The rats climbed up his body, settling on his shoulders.

Shaking his head, he smirked. "Such language, and right in my ears. They insist it was selflessness. Helping sad girl be less sad. Noble rats. Therapeutic rats."

She had to admit that being able to pet something furry had helped a bit. Sighing heavily, she sat up, wrapping her arms around her knees to hold herself upright. "Were you looking for me?"

"Yes. The scouts return. News to give. Routes to plan. Come, come! Time for girls and rats to be moving." He held out a hand to her.

Inhaling deeply, she extended her arm and clasped his hand, accepting his help to stand. He led her back toward his little cluster of improvised rooms, where he picked up a backpack and slung it onto his back.

"Snacks and water. Spare socks. Good for girl feet without shoes." He paused and stood up straight, though it didn't significantly add to his diminutive height, looking into the distance.

The rats who'd been milling about perked up then headed toward them in a sea of brown fur and bald tails. Once they formed up around them, creating an honor guard of sorts, The Rat pulled out her ratty T-shirt, holding it up. "Do you mind? I have ideas."

She didn't want it anymore. It was thin and stretched out and quite grimy. "No, keep it."

"Good, good." He pulled scissors from his pocket and cut into the

T-shirt, reducing it to a pile of small scraps. When he finished, he returned the scissors to his pocket. "Come, my little sneaky team. Get your mischief."

A small batch of rats scurried forward and grabbed the scraps, one each, except for one rat who proceeded to chew its scrap and swallow it.

"No, no, no!" The Rat scooped up the rat who'd eaten the scrap and set him gently back into the larger scrum of rats. "No sneaky team, not for you." The rat, seeming to hang its head, shuffled off to get lost in the big crowd.

With the last scrap dangling from the mouth of one of the sneaky team members, he led her toward the door they'd entered from. After she closed her eyes, he opened it.

"Ready? Lots of walking."

She swallowed but nodded wearily. "Where are we going?"

"Out."

TWENTY-FOUR

JAMIE

Once all the rats who were coming with them were through the door, The Rat closed it. "Now away, my sneaky team." The rats who'd picked up scraps formed a little cluster and darted away from the bigger group, heading in the direction from where The Rat had found her.

"What are they doing?" Jamie asked.

The Rat winked at her. "Smelly shirt, smell of girl and wolf. Lead the bad man on a right merry chase. They'll spread your scent all over the tunnels."

"Huh. That's smart."

"Rats are cunning, and so is The Rat." He cackled, turning toward a tunnel leading in the other direction.

Now that she'd been with the weird fellow for maybe forty-eight hours, she wasn't sure since she had no way of telling time, she couldn't tell if she was getting used to the man and his furry army, or if she was just numb to the never-ending weirdness that her life had become. She tucked in behind him, staying closer than when he'd found her. As they had the last time, the rats orbited around them, scurrying about in whatever shifting order they adhered to.

It didn't take long before she wished she had more than socks on her feet. She wondered if she could change to her wolf form, but that would require getting naked in front of The Rat and his little, beady-eyed buddies. Plus she'd have to ask him to carry her clothes for her. She'd just live with sore feet for now. Her enhanced healing would make short order of any blisters once she got out of these tunnels and found some proper food. Though The Rat had been more than generous with his supplies.

As they walked, The Rat hummed a tune, though it was a melody she didn't recognize. Occasionally at an intersection, he'd stop and let one of his rodent buddies crawl up his clothes to squeak messages into his ear. Then, he'd do whatever it is he did to communicate with the little creatures, and a pack would split off and disappear into the new tunnel before they continued on the path he'd chosen.

Finally, her curiosity overwhelmed her need to be quiet and follow along. "Why didn't we go down that tunnel? Why'd you send some rats?"

"Scouts. Lots of tunnels. Some go where we want, but some are unreliable. The Rat isn't the only one who lives here. Some beings aren't as nice as me. Lucky for girl my little friends found you before scarier creatures did. Lucky indeed. So…" He paused at another tunnel, his nose poking into the air as he sniffed carefully before he sent another rat crew down it. "So, rat friends go take a look-see if the ways are clear. If we run into trouble later, options are always good to have."

"Trouble?" Her eyes shifted around, focusing in on the dark spots and deeper shadows. "Is that likely?"

He squeaked and gave a half-hearted shrug. "Most avoid trouble, but everyone has bad days. Rats like safety, rats like caution." He paused again, scratching his chin as he looked back and forth between two tunnels. "Rats like to go…this way." He headed into the left option.

She followed in silence. After about ten minutes, the tunnels started vibrating as a dull rattle turned into a steady roar. Panicking, she looked around for a place to duck and hide.

The Rat chuckled. "No worries, all safe. Just subway tunnels nearby."

"Can we get out that way?"

"Not near here, and not without revealing where we came from." He shook his head. "Safe and secret, must protect my little rat friends."

She nodded, giving up on the idea. It would probably be faster and easier to pop out near random people, but if she tried to find the entrance to the subway system, she'd probably get lost. It was either risk running into one of the denizens of the underworld or continue to put her trust in the weird little man who'd done right by her, so far. And though he proclaimed a desire to protect his rats, which was certainly a partial truth, it was more likely that he wanted to protect himself and his home.

Of all the places she'd be willing to live, this was low on the chart. But The Rat seemed content to live in his secret home, siphoning off water and electricity from the city's grid. A small part of her appreciated that someone was taking something back from Red City, even if it was as simple as power and water.

Once he made the next directional decision, she tucked behind him and followed him into the next nearly dark tunnel.

TWENTY-FIVE

DAX

The ride back to his apartment had been unpleasant, though not excruciating. Except for a couple rough turns where the straps keeping him secure dug into some tender spots. But other than those moments, Boudreaux got him home quickly.

Once they parked, Boudreaux helped him to his feet. The clinic had let him borrow a gown and a robe. A bit of a breeze fluttered through the loosely tied strings on the back of the gown.

"Hey, Delphine. Did you put any SPF in that rub you put on him? He might get a sun burn on that pasty ass of his."

"Just help with the fucking robe, Mr. Funnyguy," Dax grumbled.

Delphine's rich laugh floated down the sidewalk as she approached. "I'm sure he'll be fine for a few minutes."

Shaking his head, he slid his arms into the sleeves of the robe and pulled the ties around to close it. "If you two can quit admiring my ass, I'll show you in."

"Need help?" Boudreaux asked.

"I think I can manage, but don't wander off too far in case I tip over for some reason." Dax started toward the front door, patting the empty pockets of his robe. "Fuck. Keys."

Delphine held up a set in front of him and jingled it. "Tomi gave me your keys when I showed up for my shift."

He took them with a nod of thanks and toddled up the few steps to the apartment building's locked main entrance. Fortunately, no one witnessed his choice of outfits or the man in an EMT uniform escorting him to his apartment.

As they exited the elevator on his floor, Boudreaux's radio burst to life. "Shit. I have to go. I have a call. You all good?"

"I think between the wall and Delphine, I can make it to my door." He held out his hand for Boudreaux to shake. "Thanks. For everything. Give me a day or two, and I'll be ready to investigate Winnie's ghost problem."

"Fair enough. You got my digits. Let me know when." He turned and disappeared into the elevator.

Dax's muscles weren't sore, save for around the few penetrating wounds he'd taken from motorcycle shrapnel, but the rub of cloth on tender skin kept his pace deliberately slow. "I hope you're not allergic to cats."

"No, I'm fine. I quite like the beautiful idiots."

"What?" He paused, raising an eyebrow at her.

"Cats? They're both brilliant and profoundly dumb, and always good for a laugh."

He shrugged. "I've only had him for a couple months."

"Your first cat?"

"My first anything." He opened the door and opened it carefully in case Morty was feeling like being a little shit who wanted to dart out the door. Normally, he didn't mind chasing the kitten, who seemed to enjoy the chase, periodically turning on Dax to pounce on him playfully. But today was not a day when he could give a proper response, nor would he ask his guest to chase the little troublemaker down. "Good. He must be napping."

They slipped into the apartment quickly and shut the door. Sure enough, Morty stood in the middle of the couch, stretching and yawning at being awoken.

"That's Morty." He gestured toward the kitten as he jumped off the couch and approached Delphine.

After a quick sniff at her hand, he flopped over on his belly paws in the air.

"Is it a trap?" she asked.

"What?"

"Have you watched any cat videos on the internet?"

Dax shook his head, trying to decide where he could get off his feet without seeming like bad company. While he thought about it, he sank onto the recliner. That was a mistake. "Holy fuck, that was not a good idea."

After a second, the shock settled into a dull throb, though still not as bad as prior to Delphine's ointment.

"Do you need help up?" She stepped around to face him, scratching Morty's chest as he lay upside down on her arm.

"I'm here now. It's not too bad." He let go of his clenched muscles and tried to ignore the discomfort.

"So not a trap." She nodded toward the kitten. "Cats like to flop on their backs, but a lot of them don't want to have their bellies touched. It's a trap because people can't resist trying to rub the belly, then they attack."

"Oh, I understand. Sometimes. Most of the time he likes it. Sometimes he uses that knowledge to lure you in."

"Ah, so a typical cat. Do you mind if I look into your wards? When I'm done, I'll check your bandages and throw on another round of the salve."

"Be my guest."

She wandered around his apartment with Morty in her arms, occasionally reaching out to touch the walls or squatting down to lay a hand on the floor. She punctuated her movements with an occasional utterance of interest or confusion. Once she'd made her round, she settled onto the couch on the side nearest Dax.

"So, what's the verdict?" Dax asked.

"I...I don't know." She snorted and shook her head, a smirk spreading across her face. "And not to brag, but it's been a while since I've been able to say that about something in the magical world."

Raising an eyebrow, he shifted delicately, hoping to find a more comfortable position. The manbo's declaration concerned him. "How so?"

"I've never felt a signature quite like it. It feels both ancient and foreign. Almost like it's not of human origins." She leaned toward him slightly without disturbing the purring kitten in her lap. "Did you lay down these wards?"

He shook his head. "Wards are not where my talents lay. Certainly not in this diminished form."

"It's certainly not one of the lwas. I'd know them and their *feel*, even if it's not one I've dealt with in the past."

"No." He chuckled. "I'd not trust that task to any of the lwa I know and have had dealings with. They're not to be trusted in such matters, even if they could do it."

"You're not wrong." Her eyes narrowed. "Who did it? Certainly not one of the covens in Red City. None of them have the power to do something this robust and subtle."

"I'm not one-hundred percent sure. It was a condition of my circumstances. Once I procured this place, I passed word to an intermediary, and another intermediary showed up."

Her eyes grew wide. "And you trusted them?"

"What choice did I have?" He rubbed a hand over his face and winced as the pressure pulled on the road rash on the palms of his hands. "I was brand new to the city. Tomi and Adele were the only people I knew. They'd have let me stay with them longer, but their place was already cramped with them and Tomi's sister. I had some money and needed a place to brood about my circumstances." He snorted. "I was still figuring how to use this damned body and navigate the limitations it placed on my abilities as well as the other hobbles placed on me."

"You're a brave man."

"Naïve, maybe. Hopeful the agreement would be honored. I wasn't completely ignorant of the situation. I tested it as best as I could. Unless you were invited, you couldn't find me. Not even following me. So I trusted that it was at least a deterrent against mortals. I haven't had a chance to test the wards deeper with supernaturals. Until recently, I didn't know any. So, here we are."

"What makes you suspect there's a hole in your defenses?"

"After Tomi and I survived the little fracas with the bikers, I came home drunk from the celebration and found someone here who shouldn't have been able to get in." He paused, trying to build up his courage to let out a big piece of information. While he was all for bringing her deeper into his circle of trust, his natural reticence and the basis for the conversation in the first place kept him from diving immediately in.

"You don't have to tell me. I know we've only just met to what amounts to a handful of weeks ago, even if they've been eventful"— she shrugged—"but I can't give you a professional opinion without all the information. Best I can do is an educated guess at your needs."

He nodded, holding her gaze for a moment before letting his eyes drop to the kitten, who was busy making donuts in the air. He couldn't tell if the kitten was a good judge of character. Only Tomi and Boudreaux had been in his apartment since he'd decided to keep the kitten after saving him in the alley by his bar. He adored Tomi. He didn't know about Boudreaux since the only time he'd been inside was when he'd come to rescue Dax after he'd been shot in the lung and was bleeding out.

But Tomi and Adele trusted the manbo. And he trusted them explicitly.

"It was Baron Samedi."

She whistled at the revelation.

He chucked his chin toward the other side of the couch. "That burn on the couch is where the fucking trickster dropped his lit cigar as he faded out. The traitor in your arms made him feel welcome with that little white belly of his."

Delphine laughed. "Any reason you haven't flipped the cushion to hide the burn mark?"

His brow furrowed. "Huh. Never thought of that."

She laughed louder this time, disturbing the kitten in her arms who flipped over and hopped away, his back arched and tiny annoyed hisses spitting from his mouth. "I'm sorry for disturbing you, my little furry friend. And I'm sorry for laughing at the low-level vandalism of your property, Dax. But, as the kids say, the Baron is gonna Baron."

"Yeah. But at least he left me with a warning."

That wiped the smile off Delphine's face as she instantly became all business. "Was it a threat to not interfere with his machinations? Or was he giving advice, freely given?"

"The latter. He'd come to pay his respects and offer thanks for the kindness I paid to Esther." He tried to appear casual, despite keeping the manbo tightly under his eye.

She nodded gracefully. "That's good. Esther always paid her respects to the lwas and kept them in her heart and her actions. She was a true woman of devotion."

He'd felt the same about the woman during their brief interaction. Few he'd dealt with deserved the comfort he'd given her. If he could have done more for her, he would have. Though he was glad to be in complete agreement with the manbo about Esther, it was the nearly imperceptible drop in her shoulders and slight relaxation of her body that spoke to him louder than her words. In some deep part of her consciousness, she'd worried that allowing him to take on the visage of Baron Samedi to help one of the Baron's followers might have invited his displeasure down on her.

"She was. I was honored to help her."

Delphine exhaled heavily. "The Baron gave you an honest warning." She chuckled, shaking her head slowly. "Dax, zanmi m, you're fucked."

He sighed. "I'm starting to get the picture."

Reaching up, he ran a hand through his hair, but stopped halfway through with a grunt of pain from his tender palm. He was ill-equipped to deal with a conspiracy. Now it looked like he might be dealing with two or maybe more. He'd received new revelations about one of the shooters thanks to Minh, adding to the mortal conspiracy. He couldn't say human, since it also involved supernaturals like wolf shifters. But with gods poking their noses in, and perhaps directing the mortal portion, he was in over his head.

He cast a quick glance over at Delphine. She was on the way to becoming a friend. Friends could be a liability. They could be hurt.

Targeted. Killed. But she'd seen what was happening to him and knew enough pieces of the equation. She could make her own decisions.

With a sigh, he shifted uncomfortably in his recliner. "So about those wards?"

Delphine nodded firmly. "I'm not sure if I can truly do anything to keep out the lwas, especially the Baron now that he's slipped through, but I'll see what I can do. As far as other supernaturals? I'll do some research and see what I can do about beefing up your security. There are always holes in any ward. Maybe if we put down enough layers of protection, we'll be able to plug most of them or make them harder to penetrate. It's the best I can do."

"And that's all one can do." He smiled fondly at her. "Thank you."

TWENTY-SIX

JAMIE

"Hmm." The Rat squatted low in the shadows and peaked around the corner. "Not good," he mumbled almost inaudibly.

Jamie tried swallowing, but her mouth was too dry. Backing up, she pulled out the bottle of water The Rat had given her and took a small drink. She didn't want to down too much, afraid a sudden inrush would cause her nervous stomach to rebel. And a noisy vomiting session was not what they needed right now.

The Rat's scouts had reported someone new in the tunnels in a typically uninhabited section—a section close to the exit The Rat had wanted to use.

"Guns," he whispered, pulling his head back into their hiding spot. With a wave, he stood up and walked back the way they'd come until he ducked into another tunnel and stopped.

Jamie leaned close to him so her mouth was near his ear. "What's going on?"

"There's a woman ahead. Many guns. Polishing them. Friends say many guns." He narrowed his eyes, clenching his jaw. It was the first sign of any negative feelings she'd noticed in the odd man. "Great big furry little fucks."

She snorted, then quickly clenched her teeth together to stop a laugh from erupting. She didn't want to give away their location or insult The Rat, though his curse was objectively humorous.

Clearing her throat gently to cover, she leaned close again. "What can we do?"

"We can't go that way. But rats are curious. Very curious. Who is in my tunnels?" A rat scrabbled up his leg and jacket, but before it could reach his shoulder, he scooped it up gently and held it up to his lips. After a few moments, he set it down.

A small group of rats assembled around that rat, then shot through the pack with purpose, disappearing toward where the stranger was. The Rat gave them a few seconds head start, then slunk after them, crouching low and sticking close to the wall. He stopped before reaching the corner and inched toward it. She slipped out to join him.

The tunnel erupted into flames and sound. Her ears ringing, Jamie grabbed The Rat and dragged him back and to the ground. Around them, the rats flooded away in a great furry tidal wave. Smoke drifted into the tunnel where they lay.

She couldn't tell if it was her ears squealing or if it was the rats. Covering the ear that was the worst, she turned the other toward the tunnel where the rats had gone. As her hearing cleared a bit, the sound of squealing rats—rats in pain—assaulted her.

Whatever had set off the explosion, likely the rats sent in to take a peek, had punished them severely. The Rat raised his head, looking at her. Tears streamed down his cheeks. Shaking his head, he tried to push himself up. But she grabbed his shoulder and stopped him.

"Fucking rats," a woman's voice said. "Damn it all. Their guts are everywhere."

Jamie cringed as a gunshot popped once, twice, thrice, four times.

"Fucking waste of bullets," the woman mumbled. "Now I'm going to have to reset everything. Fucking rats. I should've charged Ivar triple for this shit." Her mumbling grew quieter as she seemed to be walking away.

Jamie exhaled a pent-up breath slowly and looked down at The

Rat. His face stood frozen, tears scrubbing tracks in the dust that had settled on his face. They needed to get moving before she came back to investigate further. No doubt more heavily armed than the small gun she'd killed the wounded rats with.

Reaching out, she tugged his jacket, trying to get him moving. For a diminutive man, he was hard to move. Growling low in her throat, she raised her hand and popped him lightly across the cheek a couple time—not hard enough to be a slap, but enough to probably jar him out of his stupor.

"Come on," she mouthed.

Slumping in on himself, he exhaled and pushed himself up. Before he made it all the way to standing, he slumped but caught himself on the wall. He shook his head, wincing at the motion. Turning around, he gave one last look toward the room where the woman was. But as he made to turn around, he froze then darted down, picking something up.

A weak squeaking emerged from his hand. Answering it, more squeaks sounded nearby. If they didn't stop, the woman would come back and put them out of their misery too.

Jamie was ready to bolt. Exhaustion and stress had stretched her thinner than the threadbare T-shirt The Rat hat cut up earlier. When she looked toward escape and back to him, the pleading in his eyes stopped her. She gave him a single nod.

He thrust out his hand, and without thinking about it—because if she did, she'd scream and break for it—took the rat from him. Soon he bent down and scooped up more rats, handing them over to her. She didn't know how many more rats she could handle, but seeing she might be full-up on rats, he shoved his jacket into his pants and started placing rats in his pockets or inside his jacket. After a couple more bends and stuffs, he looked around frantically.

Now that her eyes had begun to adjust from the burst of flames, she looked around but didn't see anything. With a final sad sigh, The Rat slunk toward the tunnel that had brought them here.

"Shit," she mouthed, holding up her hand to stop him. She heard the mumbling again. "Go!"

Unable to sprint away like she wanted to because of the delicate need to not drop the rats in her arms, she walked briskly, sticking next to the wall so she wasn't as out in the open. The Rat, more capable of juggling his load, jogged ahead of her and disappeared around the corner. With a look over her shoulder, she made sure it was safe to dart across the tunnel to the next corner. It was now or never...

Walking as fast as she could, she hustled after The Rat, only stopping after she was sure she was out of sight. The Rat waited for her as did a large portion of the rats who'd fled at the initial explosion. Turning around, she slowly slipped to the corner, cast a quick prayer to whatever god might be listening, and moved the side of her head around the edge.

She gave her head a little shake to get the hair to fall across the side of her face, hoping it would obscure her skin and help her blend into the shadows a bit more. Holding her breath, she peeked out. She could see most of the tunnel leading to the chamber where the woman had been but didn't catch any movement. About ready to pull her head back, she paused when she saw a shift in the shadows.

Looking around cautiously, a figured emerged from the entrance into the woman's chamber and resolved into a feminine shape. Jamie froze, holding her breath. She hoped the woman wasn't a shifter or some other kind of supernatural being who had enhanced senses.

The woman advanced with a gun held in both hands and pointed toward the ground. Slowly sweeping her eyes around, she focused on the nearest tunnel—the one they'd been in when The Rat sent the scouts. Finally, she lifted her head and a stray beam of light landed on her face.

Jamie stifled a gasp before it could give her away and forced her eyes from wide open in surprise to slits. Once the woman's head swept away, Jamie yanked her head back behind cover. Turning around, she stalked quietly toward where The Rat waited.

"We have to go. Fast!" she mouthed, adding a whisper of volume, hoping he'd be able to hear it with whatever rat special powers he might have.

He nodded and turned briskly, jogging ahead. Doing her best to keep the rats stable, she followed as quickly as she could, taking far more turns and twists than they had to get here. He must be trying to take a more circuitous route. Sweat poured down her face and back, and her arms ached from the awkward weight of carrying several rats. She did her best to keep her panting as quiet as possible to avoid alerting the woman if she was following them.

Focusing on what might be coming up behind her, she nearly slammed into the back of The Rat, not noticing he'd stopped. He held up a finger to his lips. Around them, the rats stopped orbiting and looked up at him.

Goosebumps rose on her arms, and the hairs on the back of her neck vibrated. Every set of beady little rat eyes was firmly fixed on him. It was the creepiest thing she'd ever seen. Nodding, he pointed aggressively back the way they'd just came. About a dozen rats scurried off.

Leaning in closer, he drew near her ear. "I told them to make sure we're not being followed."

She nodded, trying to bring some saliva into her dry mouth. If her arms weren't full, she'd reach for her water bottle. Unfortunately, she'd have to make do as is.

The waiting felt interminable as she stood still, her muscles twitching with fatigue. Every sound, no matter how faint or from whatever direction, sent more adrenaline into her system. Her chest ached from the tension of short, shallow breaths.

When the first rats skittered around the corner, she swung her gaze to The Rat, waiting for one of the rodents to climb up. After it squeaked into his ear, he nodded, his face relaxing.

"He says the bad woman has returned to her den." He sighed. "And unfortunately, so must we for the moment. Let's be quiet, though, just in case. There are more than bad women lurking about."

She nodded and fell in behind him. Though they kept up a brisk pace, it lacked the frantic nature of their earlier flight. Finally, when they reached the safety of his hidden den, she exhaled noisily, her shoulders sagging.

"Follow me. We must see if we can help my brave little friends." He led her toward another one of his curtained off areas.

Carefully, he relieved her of the rats. When she looked down, the dark blood staining her borrowed clothes shined in the bright light. She did her best to hold back the urge to throw up. The Rat was similarly covered in stains from the wounds of his friends, at least that's what she hoped. He had been closer and might have taken a wound from flying debris and shrapnel.

Seeing where her eyes had landed, he smiled sadly at her. "Another shower. We both need one, but my friends need help. Go. Clean yourself. Find clean clothes in my room. Please." He bowed his head gracefully. "And thank you. On my behalf, and that of my little friends. Jamie is a true friend to the rats."

She smiled softly at him. "I'm sorry about your friends. If you need help, yell at me."

"Will do."

She turned and headed toward the bathing area of his den, but stopped when he cleared his throat. "Do you need my help?"

"No. But did you see the face of the bad woman?" His jovial face grew hard and angry, almost scarily so.

"I did."

"Did you know? Did you recognize?"

She nodded. "It was the coroner. The one from the city morgue."

TWENTY-SEVEN

DAX

Reaching down, Dax pried the kitten off his pants leg. Every time he got a paw or two unhitched, Morty seemed to sink in more claws. It didn't help that he was trying to gnaw on his knuckle, but at least he wasn't biting as hard as he could. Morty just thought it was fun.

"Look, you little shit, I need to get to work. Or you won't have any kibbles. If you want to catch your own meals like a common stray, be my guest…"

Finally, Morty relaxed and let himself be removed from the denim. Once Dax set him on the floor, he huffed, turned his back on Dax, and stalked off with his head held high, disappearing around the corner. A moment later, he came bolting out, chasing his favorite toy ball.

Groaning, Dax straightened up. Though he was mostly healed, he still had plenty of sore spots and stiffness to deal with. But moving around would certainly help that, along with the boredom of sitting around his apartment. At least the silly kitten brought a rare smile to his lips. Watching for a few moments as the kitten careened around, he checked his phone to make sure there weren't any messages, then headed for the door.

He paused before gripping the doorknob. He needed to go to work. Wanted to even. He'd asked his staff to cover for him while he recovered, and that meant pulling some long shifts. They were already staffed at their barest minimum. But it had been a rough couple months of assassination attempts at his business. It was getting so he was developing a complex.

He patted his pocket, making sure he had his wallet and bus pass. Without a bike—and his car still wasn't ready—he'd been relegated to Red City's public transit system. He wasn't looking forward to the hard plastic seats and the pothole riddled roads. It was sure to be a bad recipe for his sore ass. Sighing, he opened the door and locked it behind him.

He'd been right. The ride to work had pounded his sore body. The walk from the bus stop was short, but he still walked gingerly like a man twice his age. Well, the age of the body he'd taken.

A large yawn paused his hand as he unlocked the bar's door. It had been a while since he'd worked an opening shift. He'd like to hire someone to handle it, but the tips weren't great and he couldn't afford to pay someone extra to compensate for it. For now, he rotated it with the other bartenders so no one got screwed over.

He prepared the coffee and flipped the chairs down from the table tops where the closer had left them so they could mop the floor. Once he opened the door, he'd barely made it back to the bar before someone walked in.

"Hey, Dax. It's been a while."

Filling up a cup of coffee, he leaned up against the bar. "It has been, Bill. Usual?"

"Yup." The middle-aged bald man slid up onto a barstool and rested his elbows on the bar.

Setting his coffee aside for a moment, Dax poured the pint of Pabst before returning to his cup. Normally, he liked his coffee black, but it wasn't cooling down quickly enough, so he grabbed the cream and poured some in to take the edge off the heat. He hadn't slept well with the various wounds on his back, even though most were pretty much healed.

"What happened in the alley?" Bill asked after chugging down half his beer in a single go.

"What?"

"Saw the scorch marks on the wall and the door."

"Ah, yeah. Bit of a trash fire. No harm done." He winced internally.

Tomi had put the fire out and stashed the remains of the bike in the dumpster. Fortunately, like all services in the corrupt city, the fire department was slow to show up for whoever'd called them. By then, Tomi had arranged some cardboard and set it on fire with the aid of some high proof booze. When they arrived, jogging up with their fire gear in hand, they'd found a pile of soggy, charred cardboard and broken glass.

The RCFD wrote up the incident as someone messing around in the alley and drove off after checking to make sure the fire was indeed out and it hadn't sent sparks off elsewhere.

"How was work?" Dax asked, hoping to change the subject.

"Same shit, another day. Boss makes a dollar, I make a dime."

Dax chuckled, looking toward the door when it opened. "Hey, Ginger."

"Yo, Dax. Good to see you."

"Usual?"

"You know it."

Dax grabbed a bottle of Jim Beam, poured a shot, and filled a half pint of Pabst for the beer back. With Ginger and Bill at the bar, they'd entertain each other so he could continue brooding about everything else.

The rest of the morning went well enough with the usual overnight crew stopping in to wash away their workdays. It kept him busy enough that he didn't get carried away with being grumpy about yet another assassination attempt. To be fair, he had every right to be angry about it. But thunder in his eyes wasn't the best way to make a place welcoming, and he couldn't afford to drive off his morning regulars, especially when the evening regulars had gotten a bit sparse with all the chaos.

"Hey, Dax," Tomi said, coming through the front door.

"Tomi!" the regulars called out.

He waved at them dismissively. "I'm feeling like some pho. You want some?"

"Sure, that sounds good." Dax grabbed a bottle of vodka from the well to make someone another vodka soda.

Normally, they ate whatever Tomi's mamma had ready for them at her restaurant for free. But Dax suspected Tomi was more interested in buying pho from the convenience store across the street for reasons other than variety in his diet. Oddly enough, Tomi never had an urge to get pho when Thuc was working.

After Tomi stashed his stuff in the office, he headed back to the front door.

"Say hi to Minh for me." Dax smirked after his friend.

Tomi grabbed the door with one hand and flipped the bird with the other. Dax chuckled after the door swung closed. His stomach grumbled. Tomi's timing on lunch was impeccable. It was good to see his friend; the simple back and forth had done a lot to burn off a bit of his bad mood.

Since there weren't any drinks that needed to be poured, he slipped into the tearoom to get the kettle boiling for the ready-to-make pho the store made. As he emerged from the back, Tomi returned with a brown paper bag in his hand.

Tomi handed him the bag. "You can go first. You've been here for a while."

"Thanks." Dax left Tomi to manage the couple new people who'd come in after him.

The kettle beeped done just as he closed the sliding door into the tearoom. He quickly pulled out the ready-to-make pho and poured water in, mixing in the rest of the goodies. A few minutes later, he dove into his bowl of pho, scalding his tongue in the process. Growling, he wondered if the manbo's goop would work on his tongue. The silly mental exercise gave him something to distract himself with while he waited for his food to cool down.

Yawning, he winced over the scalded spot on his tongue. Maybe he'd make some tea to perk himself up after lunch. If he didn't scald himself again, he should be healed enough to enjoy a stiff black tea.

He reached into the bag to grab out Tomi's pho, but his finger bumped something that shouldn't have been in there.

Setting the pho aside, he stood up and peered down into the brown paper bag, holding it open at the top. Inside, he found a shiny round disk like the one Minh had slipped him a few weeks ago. A disc that showed evidence that Detective Randall Ryan might be responsible for the first time he'd been shot in the bar's alley.

Like the previous disc, there was a date written on the label side. Three days ago. The night his motorcycle blew up. Had the convenience store's cameras caught someone entering or exiting his alley to blow up his motorcycle?

When the sliding door rumbled in its track, he quickly stuffed the disk into the inner pocket of the faded black denim jacket he was wearing. "Tomi—"

"Why don't you bring that hand out where I can see it?" Detective Ryan, as if summoned by Dax's thoughts, sauntered into the room, a smirk plastered on his face.

Dax scratched his chest then slowly pulled his hand out. "Just had an itch, Detective Ryan." He held up his hand to show it was empty. If he hadn't been inhaling the fragrant steam from the pho, he might have caught the acrid smell of the unbathed detective. Dax wondered if Ryan only came in on days he hadn't showered. But judging by his unshaved face and greasy hair, week might be a more accurate time frame.

Ryan narrowed his eyes for a moment before stepping up to the table. "So, I hear you had a little issue the other night. Fire department reported that someone set a fire with some of your cardboard and a bottle of"—he pulled out a small notebook from the breast pocket of his mussed suit jacket—"high alcohol liquor?"

"Yeah. Tomi put it out by the time the fire department could get here. No damage other than some scorch marks on the wall."

The cop tapped a finger on his notepad. "What a coincidence? I heard from a witness that it was an explosion."

Dax shrugged. "Those one-ninety proof liquors can be dangerous."

"I guess you got lucky that no one was hurt. Even though an ambulance showed up."

Dax stopped, his eyes from narrowing in suspicion. Ol' Rand Ryan had way too much information.

"They were in the neighborhood and saw the flames." Tomi slipped into the room. "Stopped to make sure no one was injured since they weren't on a call."

Ryan scoffed. "You two always seem to have your stories all worked out. Nice and slick."

"It's easy when it's the truth," Tomi said, folding his arms across his broad chest. "Someone set a fire in our alley with cardboard and booze."

Dax nodded along, smiling pleasantly at the detective. It was the truth. It's just that the "someone" was Tomi. He must have slipped back to make sure Ryan wasn't up to any mischief. Though that left the bar unattended.

Detective Ryan looked back and forth between Tomi and Dax, his eyes narrowed suspiciously. Finally, he let out an exasperated sigh. "It's a good thing nothing worse happened, then. Good day." Though the two words should have been polite, the delivery dripped with disdain and venom. He spun around and stalked out of the tearoom.

Tomi winked at Dax before following the cop in case he decided to question any of the patrons or cause some other trouble. Also, no doubt, someone else needed a drink. Dax slipped out from behind the long table that ran down the center of the room and shut the sliding door.

Settling into his bowl, he scooped in a mouthful of broth. "Damn it. Cold." The fucking detective always managed to ruin lunch when he stopped by. They'd have to poke around and see if the cop left any listening devices. More wasted time and paranoia.

Reaching into his pocket, he reassured himself the disc was still there. He wondered if he'd see the form of the detective again. Tomi hadn't mentioned the disc when he'd handed off the bag. Minh must have slipped it in when she bagged it up for Tomi. Though she wouldn't have expressly been hiding it from him. She knew he knew about the supernatural world. He'd been there with Dax when they'd freed her from a cage in The Collector's menagerie, even though they had no idea what kind of magical being she might be. It didn't matter. She'd showed her gratitude by slipping him discs from their security system when her father refused to.

He'd planned on staying and hanging out with Tomi while he worked, but the disc was burning a hole in his pocket, begging to be watched, and he didn't have anything in the bar that could play it. Perhaps he'd have to visit a secondhand store or a pawn shop and get one of those portable DVD players. There might be a few technological antiques like that kicking around still.

Despite it being colder than he wanted, he finished his pho and cleaned up after himself. Before he left the bar, he made Tomi's pho and covered the bar while he ate it. As Dax departed, he told Tomi to call him when he finished his shift.

"It's important."

TWENTY-EIGHT
DAX

Dax paced across his living room from the door of his bedroom to the front door, grumbling under this breath. His eyes flicked to the paused DVD image on the TV screen, and a burst of fury washed over him. Forcing his eyes away, he concentrated to keep from exploding into reaper form.

Though it might help him slip into a more calm state — sometimes being bones and a robe could almost numb his human emotions — he was afraid of the destruction he could cause if he lost control. He didn't need to level his apartment building.

Turning to find Morty, he finally spotted him tucked into the back corner of the seat of the couch, all four limbs poking into the air. At first, the kitten had found his person's antics amusing, but he quickly grew bored when Dax ignored him.

The silly kitten, with his lack of concerns, momentarily reduced Dax's rage from a rolling boil down to a gentle simmer. Checking his watch, he grunted. Tomi was off his shift and should be there any moment.

Inhaling and exhaling slowly but aggressively, he forced his shoulders down and walked over to the sideboard. His eyes scanned over the selection until he spied what would work best and grabbed a cheap bottle of whiskey. It wasn't bad—he tried not to drink true rotgut—but sometimes he found himself in the mood for something with a rougher kick.

He filled a tumbler almost to the top and took a swig, letting the burn work its way down his throat and into his stomach. He followed it with another and another, then poured in a bit more, refilling it to only halfway this time.

If he didn't want to lose his cool when he rewatched the video with Tomi, he'd need to take his temperature down a few more degrees. Careful not to spill his whiskey, he flopped onto the couch next to Morty and scooped the kitten into his lap.

Morty woke up, barely cracking his eyes, and rolled onto his back, exposing his belly. Dax scratched it gently, enjoying the feel of the kitten's soft, silky fur. Soon, a raspy purr rose from the content kitten.

Dax let his eyes drift closed so he couldn't see the TV while he relaxed with his kitten, taking occasional sips of whiskey while he waited.

By the time Tomi unlocked the door and let himself in, Dax wasn't quite as spitting mad as he'd been earlier. "Grab yourself a drink."

Tomi kicked off his shoes and grabbed a glass of whiskey before plopping down into the recliner. Dax opened his eyes, noticed his glass was almost empty, and moved the kitten from his lap so he could get a refill. As soon as he returned to the couch, he grabbed the remote and rewound the security DVD Minh had slipped into the bag of pho.

Without saying a word or giving any hints to Tomi about what he was about to see, Dax hit play, tossing the remote onto the coffee table where it hit the wood and slid across the surface before falling onto the floor. Morty had followed the path of the remote and bounded off the couch to pounce on it.

The black-and-white image popped into clarity. Dax had rewound it a bit too far, but only by a couple minutes. And since the remote wasn't at hand, he just let it play.

"Exciting stuff," Tomi mumbled.

"Don't worry. It gets positively explosive in a couple minutes."

"Spoilers!" Tomi smirked, lifting his glass to salute Dax.

As they neared the moment, Dax squeezed the glass but stopped himself after a moment so it didn't explode in his hand. He didn't have time to get stitches.

Leaning forward, he rested his elbows on his knees and stared at the screen. A moment later, a shadow moved into the edge of the security camera's view, where it caught the other side of the street and the alley next to Dax's bar.

At this point, he couldn't make out any detail except that the body might be vaguely feminine. It was hard to tell in the baggy clothes, but that was his best guess. They walked into frame casually like they belonged, but to Dax's eye, it looked like they were trying too hard.

Just before they reached the corner at the edge of the alley, they looked over their shoulder, giving a good view of the back of their head. A moment later, they twisted around and looked across the street almost perfectly at the camera.

"Son of a bitch..." Tomi hissed out as he sat forward in the recliner. He shook his head and took a big drink of whiskey. Setting his glass on the coffee table, he stood and stole the remote from the kitten, rewinding the DVD. He paused, missing the moment when the face appeared. He fiddled with it until he was satisfied with the frame choice. "It looks a lot like her, but..."

"Yeah. I thought we could trust her, even after how we met." He downed a swig of whiskey.

"Me too. Damn it. I know she popped you one, but it was a fucked-up situation. I didn't think she'd ever betray you again."

"Me either. I guess I'm going to have to fucking track her down."

"Last I heard, she'd moved out of her apartment in case the bikers came back."

"Yeah. It wouldn't hurt to start there, but I doubt they left a forwarding address. Do you remember the name of that kid she's friends with?" Dax stared at the screen.

"Connor? Colin? Kevin?" Tomi took a drink. "Cory?"

"Cory. That's it. I think I'll give her little friend a look-up and see what he knows. He seems like the kind to squeal easily." He drained the last of his whiskey, setting the glass down heavily on the coffee table.

"I don't know. He seemed pretty loyal to her, and the only reason he talked to us was the bikers kicked the shit out of him and he did it to help his friend."

"Do you remember where you dropped him off?

Tomi nodded, finishing his whiskey. He stood up and grabbed a bottle and filled both their glasses. "Do you want to pay him a little call at home?"

"Maybe not. We don't need his mommy calling the cops on us. But houses are assigned to school districts, aren't they?" He genuinely didn't know. Procuring education for a child had never been anything he'd had to deal with or ever planned on.

"That they are. We just going to scoop him up after school? Do you want to go tomorrow? We're both off. Suzie and Becky are working. And while we're at it, Boudreaux called. He wants you to come down to the morgue tomorrow evening. Winnie will be on the night shift. He said she's working solo, so you'll have the run of the place."

"So we snatch up the kid? Interrogate him, then head to the morgue? That's a full fucking day."

Tomi shrugged. "We can put off talking to the kid…"

"No." He clenched his teeth. "We'll get it done tomorrow. I want to find her."

"So that's the official plan?"

"It's the only plan we have at the moment. Maybe we can motivate him to tell us where to find his little friend Jamie. Then we can ask her why the fuck she blew up my fucking motorcycle!" The flames of his anger burned a radiant blue in his eyes. The glass cracked and shattered. Looking down to survey the damage, he found whiskey dripping from the bones of his fleshless hand. At least he'd avoided cutting himself…

TWENTY-NINE

JAMIE

Jamie, still feeling unclean even after the hot shower, set the filthy, blood-covered clothes in a neat pile by the door to the bathroom. She didn't know where The Rat's laundry facilities were and didn't feel comfortable exploring. It wasn't her home, and she didn't want to annoy the one person lately who didn't want to kill her. Especially as angry as he was about the death and wounding of his rat friends.

She wasn't sure what he was doing. He'd disappeared into one of his cordoned off sections with the wounded rats and dismissed her. Perhaps he had been a veterinarian before...

She didn't know what "the before" might be for a man who spoke to rats. Was he a rat shifter like she was a wolf shifter? Or was he an animal psychic? She sighed, heading for the kitchen. At least she could make herself some food while she waited. But first she walked across to the place where she'd almost had her emotional breakdown to retrieve the book she'd forgot about when The Rat came to fetch her. If it was going to be a while, she might as well bury herself in a book.

It was indeed a while before The Rat reemerged, shoulders slumped, his clothes covered in blood. She was approaching the point of yawning and thoughts of returning to her makeshift bed. It would be another night away from her mom.

It was an odd feeling—missing her mom's presence. They hardly spoke at the best of times, and she'd planned for years to get out of the house and away from her parents. But now that she'd been forcefully chased away from her mom and their temporary living situation, she found she actually wanted to see her mom.

Standing outside the room he'd emerged from, he stared at the ground and sighed. "Tiny chalk outlines…" he mumbled.

Only her enhanced hearing let her pick up his words, and even then, she wasn't sure she'd heard him right. "Um…how did it go?"

He shook his head, collecting himself before looking over at her. "Lost four more. Sad little friends. I think the others will pull through. Time. Time will tell." Blinking his eyes, he looked around. "Shower. Clean clothes. Then food."

Ignoring her, he headed toward the other side of the cavernous room toward the bathroom and his bedroom. While he cleaned up, she returned to the kitchen and made him a sandwich and pulled out a bag of potato chips she'd found when making her food. It seemed like a small gesture, all things considered.

As she set everything on the table, The Rat entered. "Mmm, kind girl. Food appreciated. You should get some sleep. We'll try again tomorrow. My friends are scouting, looking, seeking. I'll know which direction we can try tomorrow."

"OK." She turned and headed to the doorway but stopped before leaving. "Thank you. And I'm sorry about your friends. Good night."

"Night-night, kind girl."

She grabbed the book she'd been reading and headed toward the makeshift bed The Rat had set up for her. Angling her body, she opened the book and tried to forget about the day's horrors by getting lost in her book. Eventually the words worked their magic, focusing her brain, and she drifted off.

THIRTY

DAX

"Dude, I feel like a fucking creep." Tomi's thumbs beat a nervous pattern on the steering wheel.

He wasn't wrong. Sitting outside of a high school waiting for a teen so they could snatch him off the streets was Grade-A creep stuff. They'd mollified themselves with a pep talk before they'd departed.

They weren't going to hurt him…probably. And unless he was intimately involved, they'd release him back in the wild once he gave them what they wanted. Besides—play adult games, win adult prizes.

Dax scanned the crowds emerging from the doors. "I know, Tomi, but I'm tired of people trying to kill me, and she keeps popping up when it happens. He was involved last time."

"I know. And the fact I'm often near you means one of those times could catch me. And I'm not as robust as you. I like you, but I like not being blown up a whole lot more. So that's why I agreed to go along with this terrible plan."

Dax raised an eyebrow as his gaze flicked over to his friend. "Hey, you could have stayed behind."

Tomi barked a laugh. "Who's gonna drive your ass around? You ain't got a car, and your bike is now a deconstructed art project. You going to ride the bus and drag him on before it takes off for its next stop?"

Dax had to laugh at the image of him trying to use the city bus as a kidnapping conveyance. Once his laughter trickled down to a few stray chuckles, he returned to scanning the teens milling about. "Fair point." His eyes narrowed. "Is that him there?" He pointed toward a tall, handsome white kid emerging from a group.

"I think so." Tomi turned on engine and put the car in gear.

As long as the kid headed toward his home, the car was pointed in the correct direction to follow. Dax held his breath while Cory walked toward the gate that connected the school's lot with the sidewalk.

As soon as his foot hit the sidewalk, he turned to the west.

"Good," Tomi said, more to himself than for Dax.

"Aren't you going to go?"

"Dude, if we creep along and pace him as he walks, that's going to seem real fucking creepy. One of those adults, if they're paying attention, will call the cops. And Cory might take off or run back to the school. Just let me do my job."

"Sorry."

Tomi waited until the kid stopped at the nearest stoplight to wait for the walk sign. It gave them the opportunity to drive up to the stoplight and stop like any other normal driver. As soon as the light changed, Tomi zipped through and pulled into the parking lot of a grocery store, turning around so he could stop near the exit to the lot, and waited.

Cory, seemingly in no hurry, strolled along the other side of the street until he finally took a left into the neighborhood across from the grocery store. Tomi, waiting for a car to pass, pulled out and took the left Cory had.

"Want to wait, or are we good enough?" Tomi asked.

"Let's grab him. Park ahead of him and I'll get out. Keep the car running and the doors unlocked. I don't want you fiddling with the locks if we need to hurry."

"Got it." Tomi pulled past Cory and parked at the end of the block about a hundred feet in front of Cory.

Dax climbed out casually, not wanting to draw the teen's attention by acting erratically or frantically, and strolled down the sidewalk toward him. "Good afternoon, Cory."

The kid's eyes grew wider than saucers, and the blood drained from his face. He stood frozen for a moment then he looked around, his eyes flicking all over as he looked for something, possibly an escape route.

Dax held a hand up. "I just want to talk. Are we going to have any trouble?"

The teen blinked hard at him, then licked his lips. "What do you want? I haven't done anything, man."

He wanted to say, *That's what I'm here to determine,* but thought better of it. "I just want to talk. We can do it here if you promise not to run away, or I can invite you to join us in the car."

Cory's eyes narrowed. "OK. What do you want?"

"Where's Jamie?"

"I'm not going to rat my friend out."

Dax's jaw tightened. "What kind of trouble has she gotten herself into?"

"I don't know."

The teen sounded confident about not knowing. But Dax couldn't tell if it was because he didn't know, or he was doubling down on not ratting his friend out.

"Is that the answer you want to stick with?" Dax let a little of the flames slip into his eyes, careful not to overdo it and scare the kid off.

Cory took a step back. "Look, Dax... She's terrified of you. She wouldn't betray you. Not after you spared her the last time. She's not dumb." He narrowed his eyes, staring at Dax for a moment. Swallowing, he slumped slightly, seemingly making a decision. "I don't know where she is. I haven't seen her all week. She ran away from school a few days ago. I haven't seen her since. If she's in trouble, I don't know about it. But... Please, she wouldn't come after you. If she's in trouble, she needs help."

Dax wanted to be angry with the boy. He'd been part of the plot to shoot him, but his words rang true, at least about not having seen Jamie in a while. "What day was this?"

"Monday."

His muscles tightened, and he gripped his fists. The day he'd nearly been blown up. Cory shrank a bit, and the color that had returned to his face blanched away. Apparently, Dax had let too much scary out. He tamped it down.

"How are you not involved in this?" He tried to keep his tone neutral. "Last time, you two were thick as thieves."

The boy drooped, a frown spreading across his face. "My mom won't let me see Jamie anymore. She got rid of my car so I couldn't go very far." He sighed, then lifted his eyes to meet Dax's gaze. "If Jamie's in trouble, I should be there to help her get out of it. It's what we always did. But…"

Dax snorted. "But you bit off too much trouble with me, and mommy got scared?"

Cory nodded sadly. "Yeah."

This kid wasn't capable of this level of subterfuge. Gormless might be a more apt description for him. As much as he wanted… needed…a lead on where the girl was, this kid didn't have it.

Dax nodded at him. "Monday? You're sure?"

"Yeah. She got mad at me, then took off. Told the admin lady that she was taking off to deal with her dead dad."

"What?" He blinked rapidly, trying to process the information. "What happened to her dad?"

"Someone cut his throat. She had to go to the city morgue to identify his body last week."

"Last week?"

"Yeah." He swallowed and took a step back. "You didn't have anything to do with that, did you?"

Gormless or gutsy, but definitely not bright. "No. I haven't seen that wretch since the night you were dumped at my bar."

"Look, man. I'm going to be late, and my mom will come looking for me…"

The boy didn't know where she was. Dax wracked his brain,

trying to see if he missed anything in the kid's words but came up empty.

"Go. If you hear anything from Jamie, tell her I'm looking for her."

Cory nodded and resumed walking, coming toward Dax, his head down and his shoulders slumped. Stepping out of his way, Dax turned and watched him shuffle away before getting back in the car with Tomi.

"Did you hear everything?" Dax buckled his belt, missing the first time as his mind wandered toward the news of the death of Jamie's father.

"Yeah. Do you believe him?" Tomi's eyebrow was raised, but he looked more like his question was about Dax and less about the kid's words.

"I do. His words rang true, and he doesn't have the tools to be that convincing."

Tomi laughed. "No. He does not. The bit about Jamie's dad is interesting."

"I thought so. I'm wondering if the bikers finally collected their debt from him for the last time. And if they did it as a threat to her. Might explain why she got involved again."

"Could be." Tomi didn't sound convinced. "Did the boy say the city morgue?"

"He did."

Tomi chuckled, shaking his head ruefully. "I guess you can ask her old man directly what happened."

"What?"

"Go talk to his ghost. We're going there anyway. Might as well see what he has to say."

It was a thought. Though Dax wasn't sure he'd be able to get much one-on-one time with the ghost if their last visit was any indication. The angry spirits might swarm him and destroy any ability to focus on a single ghost.

"Yeah," he bit out. "I can try to talk to the ghost."

THIRTY-ONE

DAX

Since it didn't take that long to get the information, such as it was, from Cory, they headed toward the morgue, stopping about halfway there to get dinner at an Indian joint. They had the time before they were supposed to meet Boudreaux and Winnie, and Dax didn't want to go in hungry. He'd need all the energy he could get.

The spice cut through the growing bitter taste left on his tongue by the abomination the morgue had become. The psychopomps and their minions were sleeping on the job. Under his watch, it would have never been allowed. The place needed to be cleaned out so the spirits could rest. But he didn't think he had the juice to manage that many entities. And that was assuming sending that many souls through to their next phases didn't attract the kind of attention he'd been trying to avoid by being a meek little human. He wasn't that fond of mortality, but it sure beat the shit out of oblivion.

Grabbing his napkin, he mopped at the perspiration on his brow and grabbed another piece of naan to scoop his vindaloo.

Tomi snorted, shaking his head as he reached for the naan. "I don't know how you can handle that much spice, man. I like a good hot sauce as much as the next brother, but I accidentally grabbed your leftovers out of the fridge once and it nearly blew my fucking face off."

Dax shrugged. "It's a useful sensation."

"What? Reminding yourself you're still a living being? There are less painful ways to do that."

"It tastes good." *Certainly better than the taste of failure and exile,* he thought.

After their leftovers were boxed up, they climbed back into Tomi's car and headed the rest of the way toward the city morgue. Dax had Tomi stop a few blocks from the morgue. He wanted to go in on foot.

"Sure this is a good idea?" Tomi asked. "Being out in the open when someone wants to kill you?"

Dax snorted. "What? Do you think we'll just randomly run into them on the street in a city of this size? Besides, no one has been following us. Their first attack was an ambush."

Tomi shrugged, looking unsure. "It's your ass."

"Don't worry. You can walk a safe distance behind. I won't be offended." He meant it, too. He didn't want his best friend to be collateral damage.

Tomi parked, and they climbed out, meeting on the sidewalk.

"Actually, why don't you hang back a bit anyway. It might be easier for me to pick up something if there's not a human right next to me."

Tomi nodded and stayed put while Dax took his first steps toward the morgue. They'd waited until after the sun was well down. Darkness served two purposes—there were fewer employees for Winnie to move off the schedule, and the veil separating the dead from the living was a bit thinner during the hours when darkness reigned.

Even from a few blocks out, Dax could feel the oppressive anger of tethered spirits. But with the distance, he had enough separation he could actually look around the edges of it and see what was really going on and if he could do anything about it. "Tomi, never mind. I'm going to need you to keep me from wandering out into the street."

"What? But you just said..."

"I know. It's a tradeoff on unknowns, but safety third and all. I mean, I'm not going to intentionally wander into traffic, but I'm not exactly sure what's going to happen. I'm going to try to walk the line between this world and the next. I may not be as aware of the mundane dangers around us as I'd usually be. I just need you to keep an eye on me."

Tomi nodded, looking confused. "OK. I can do that. Do you need me to wake you or something?"

"No. Just keep me from getting hurt. If I'm about to cross a street into an oncoming car, block me with your arm, then release me when it's safe." He sighed and shook his head. "I don't know what's going to happen. I'm being overly cautious and procrastinating."

"Procrastinating? Are you…scared?"

Tomi had never had any trouble admitting when he was afraid. Dax had asked him to participate in any number of weird things, and he'd never failed to show up. Tomi always had his back, no matter how scared he was. Dax appreciated that. He'd learned what friendship was because Tomi was so generous with his. He owed his friend the same sort of candor and loyalty.

Even if he didn't want to admit it. "Yeah. A bit."

"Should I be more scared?"

Dax chuckled, shaking his head. "No. I think you've got the right amount of fear. But you don't need to worry about it. Any tethered spirits will be far more interested in me than a human who can do nothing for them. I'm not saying it won't get weird or scary. But you'll be safe. I won't let anything happen to you."

Tomi nodded nervously several times. "You know I trust you. Don't worry. I'll keep you from joining them."

Dax laughed, smiling at his friend. At this point, there was nothing left to say. "OK. Here we go."

Though his eyes darted around a bit, Tomi gave him a single confident nod.

Reaching out, Dax tried to find the place between the mundane world and the next realm where the dead dominated without stepping too far into their domain. He jolted a step, and a gentle hand nudged his shoulder.

Everything around him seemed desaturated of color. If he stared hard enough, he could see a faint bit of tone like the world was one of those hand tinted sepia-toned black and white photos.

Drawing in a deep breath, he tilted his head up into the distance. Even if he hadn't known where the morgue was, he couldn't miss it. It pulsed with the energy of the dead. He chuckled, though he wasn't sure if the sounds made it to Tomi's ears in the mundane world. The morgue looked as if it was covered in a massive writhing shell of spiritual energy. If it had appeared pink, it would have looked like the art museum in the second Ghostbusters movie.

He wondered if Tomi had ever seen it. He'd discovered it one night on the TV as he flipped through the channels after a closing shift at the pub. The "Ghostbusters" title had captured his attention. The spiritual world had been his domain. What humans could "bust" ghosts? He quickly saw that it was a fictional tale, and quite a humorous one at that. Since he didn't have to work the next day, he'd found the first one after the second one had ended. Then he'd discovered the remake and learned what the world meant by "himbo."

Procrastination. He was delaying the inevitable.

Sinking deeper into the aether and the realm of the untransitioned dead, he tried to find the life threads of those trapped in the morgue. Unfortunately, the pulsing, throbbing energy emanating from the morgue drowned out everything around it.

Dax had no idea how far he'd have to go to find a thread attached to the spirits in the morgue, but it didn't matter. It would likely still be dominated by the power of all the tethered spirits unable to move on to their next steps. Or it would be too weak to provide any information worth obtaining.

His only choice was to go forward. Taking a moment, he moved toward the mundane world to get his bearings, then took a step toward both the morgue and the in-between. Tomi would protect him.

The closer they got to the morgue, the louder the undead energy became, drowning out everything else. He wondered how he hadn't felt it more when he'd last visited. Though, then, he hadn't been looking for it. He'd kept his awareness firmly in the mundane while he was lying in a body bag on their way to the morgue. It hadn't been until he'd shucked his human flesh that he'd started to grasp the depth of what was wrong.

He should have just climbed back into the car and had Tomi drive him directly to the morgue. The trapped spirits had sensed his presence. Now the dome stretched out toward him like a giant dial on a circuit board tuned directly to the entity that could provide them blessed relief.

Unconsciously swatting at something in front of his face, Dax came to a stop. It took a moment to figure out why. One of the morgue's denizens stood in front of him, wispy and translucent. He couldn't tell what it was except for an amorphous blob of spectral energy.

"Imp…"

Dax furrowed his brow, giving his head a little shake. Had it said something?

"Reaper…"

That was clearer.

"Jamie…"

"What?" Dax wasn't sure if he'd said that in the mundane or in the in-between.

"Imp…oster…"

The name of the young woman who'd shot him had been the word most clearly spoken so far.

"Jamie? What about her?"

"Jamie…" The entity solidified slightly into a blurry image of a humanoid. "Danger…"

A gently touch on his shoulder grounded him. Drawing in a bit of his power, he focused it on the spirit trying to address him.

The spirt solidified somewhat, retaining its translucent aura, though it appeared more ragged around the edges than it had before he'd tried to boost its power. He still couldn't pick out any facial features to help him pin a name on the spirit.

"What danger?" Dax asked, injecting a bit of power into the words, hoping they'd link in the ghost's…brain?

"Murder. Betrayal. Beware." The words sounded firmer, though like the raggedness around the edges, they had a note of distortion that wasn't present earlier.

He was mildly impressed with himself that he'd even gotten it to work. Beyond finding and navigating life threads, he'd never tried to manipulate an earthbound spirit. Not since he'd become a human against his will.

The ghost seemed to shift around, dimming on what might be its back, the bright side pointed toward the morgue. "Murderer!" The words were clear, louder. "Imposter! Betrayer!" Then, with a flash of light that forced Dax's eyes closed, the spirit disappeared.

"Fuck." Dax squinted and blinked, trying to get the spots dancing in his eyes to go away.

"What, dude?" Tomi's voice trembled a bit. "Where'd it go?"

"I'm not sure. You saw it?" Dax turned to face his friend.

"Yeah." A shudder ran through his body. "At the end there."

"And the words?"

"Yeah. Heard them too. 'Murder, betrayal, beware.' Not exactly Caspar the friendly ghost, is he?"

Dax narrowed his eyes. "And that's all you heard and saw?"

Tomi nodded. "Just a few seconds. It sounded really pissed at the end."

"Hmm. So only when I gave him a little power," Dax mumbled. "I didn't think I'd given him too much. I couldn't quite see a 'human form,' but it seemed to shift its attention back to the morgue."

"What? When it got mad?" He stared toward the morgue for a moment. "That doesn't sound good."

"No. Mind checking in with Boudreaux and see if anything's going on we should know about before we walk in blithely?"

"On it." Tomi pulled his phone out and started texting.

This was not how he wanted this evening to go. He was already nervous about having to wade into the maelstrom of spiritual chaos. Now he'd been sought out and… Was it a warning? Or was the ghost accusing him of betraying them by not fulfilling his duty as Death?

Tomi shoved his phone in his pocket. "Nothing from Boudreaux. Says he's out in the parking lot. Winnie should be in the morgue."

Dax nodded warily, his eyes narrowing. "I guess I'll just have to be on the lookout. Did you notice anything particular about the ghost?"

Tomi snorted. "It looked like a fucking ghost. All glowy and shit. I don't know. I didn't know I was supposed to card the fucker."

"It mentioned an old friend of ours."

An eyebrow quirked in curiosity, Tomi tilted his head slightly to the side.

"Jamie."

"What trouble did she get herself into?" He held up a hand at the sight of the anger rolling over Dax's face. "I know. If she blew up the motorcycle…" He dragged his thumb across his throat. "But I kind of liked her. She's had a tough life. Thought she might break out of it."

He'd thought the same, and that made the betrayal hurt even more. She seemed like a smart, tough kid.

"But those bikers aren't what you'd call friendly or forgiving. They might have put her up to more murders. Hell. It could be someone she murdered from before. It's not like she filled you in on everything going on in her life between calculus and cheer practice." He folded his arms across his broad chest, a sardonic look on his face. Then he cleared the expression from his face. "I don't know. I'm just rambling."

"I don't know what the ghost meant. Did Jamie betray it? Are they warning us that she's the one who betrayed us? Am I the betrayer for not freeing them?" Dax shrugged. "I won't know more until I talk to the ghost more."

"Why'd it disappear?"

Dax pursed his lips. "I don't know. Whatever drew its attention caused it to flare out and disappear."

"Now what?"

Dax pointed toward the morgue. "We keep walking, and we be careful."

THIRTY-TWO

JAMIE

Jamie had no idea what time it was when she woke up. Being in The Rat's domain felt disconcerting. There was no sun, no night, just darkness or artificial light. The Rat didn't keep a clock around or anything that told time, and her phone was who knew where. Hopefully her mom had picked up her backpack when she led Ivar away from the motel where they'd been staying.

So, it wasn't the sun rising that woke her. As she lay in that in-between place where sleep or wakefulness are equal possibilities, an almost synchronized squeaking pulled her toward the latter option.

She'd grown used to the constant low-level squeaks around her. It was like being in a crowd only half listening to other people hold various conversations. This felt different. Eerily different. It was almost like the rats were chanting in unison. Shivers ran down her spine and the hairs on her arms stood up.

Careful not to move too quickly for fear of being noticed, she stood and dressed as quietly as she could, then poked her head out of her little cordoned off area and found the source of noise.

The Rat stood at one end of the concrete cave and stared out over his army of rats. They almost looked like soldiers in neat little rows, except they weren't as clear in their lines and some still moved around. But they all looked toward the human who seemed to command them, squeaking their weird little chant. The longer she paid attention to it, the more the pattern became apparent. They were indeed chanting and repeating something over and over. She prayed she never ended up on the wrong side of The Rat.

The look in his eyes... She'd seen him angry and sad, but the fury pouring from his eyes was incandescent. The squeaking crescendoed as The Rat raised his arms into the air. When he brought them down with a quick, crisp gesture, silence fell.

The Rat gave one last look over his furry friends then nodded, satisfied. The rats parted for him as he walked through their midst toward her. The earlier fury was gone, replaced by a pleasant grin. "Good morning to my wolf girl guest."

"Um, good morning. Or whatever time it is."

"Wake up time is always morning. You just woke, so morning." He chuckled.

"I guess so..." That answer didn't really help her sense of time-lessness, but it was likely the most accurate answer she'd get from the odd little man.

"Come. Time for breakfast, then we go. Hearty breakfast. Full belly, full heart. Must be ready."

Jamie wasn't sure she actually wanted the answer, but she asked, anyway, "Ready for what?"

"For war. The rats go to war."

THIRTY-THREE

DAX

The ghost who'd tried to warn them didn't reappear before they reached the parking lot at the back of the morgue. Boudreaux was already waiting for them, sitting in a 1965 Black Lincoln Continental. He stepped out, a broad grin on his friendly face.

This was a car that had carried presidents and made *The Matrix* crew look that much cooler. It was a beast of Detroit steel, and parked next to a subcompact car, it made the modern subcompact look like a Hot Wheels toy. This was a vehicle for riding in style, and it was now Dax's.

Boudreaux dangled the keys in the air as he drew closer to them. "Look what I have for you." He reached into his back pocket and pulled out a bent white envelope. "Here are your papers for it. All legal and on the up and up with your name."

Dax nodded, smiling. The sight of his car pushed away the itching the tethered spirits caused in his mind. "Excellent. I'm getting real tired of taking the bus."

"Tired of saving the environment?" Boudreaux asked, a smirk twinkling on his face.

"I have no problem with public transportation, but like everything else in this fucking parody of a city, it's run poorly so those in power can skim off the top. I don't know how many times I've been left standing in the rain when a scheduled bus never showed up." He sighed and shook his head. "Never mind. Can you give me the tour?"

Boudreaux turned and gestured toward the car. "Shiny and black, just like you requested. We tuned up the engine and made some tweaks to add some more power to it. It'll never be a nimble sports car, but it'll haul some ass down a highway if you need to skirt the speed sign…or anyone who's taking an unhealthy interest in you."

"Plates?" Tomi asked.

"The pair on the car? Linked to the registration. And there are a few pairs in the trunk if you want to swap when you're getting up to no good in the neighborhood."

Tomi snickered and nodded appreciatively at his friend.

Dax looked back and forth between Boudreaux and Tomi, his brow furrowing. "What? I don't get it."

"Fresh Prince?" Tomi asked. "Never mind. I'll send you a link."

Boudreaux smirked. "If those spares are compromised, let me know and I'll hook you up with some more."

"They don't rotate with a switch in the dash?" Tomi asked.

"Bruh, what do I look like? Q?"

Tomi snickered. "No missiles behind the headlights?"

"Nope, just a basic black car with a big fucking engine." Boudreaux shifted his attention to Dax. "I hope your bar is making some bucks, because this beast will remind you about its existence at the pump."

The bar wasn't doing well, not after the bombing in the alley. But at least he now had a ride. He'd worry about the gas tank later.

"Anything else I need to know about?" Dax asked.

"Nope. It'll get you where you need to go in a bit of style."

"Excellent. Thanks, Boudreaux." He nodded his head toward the morgue. "We ready to go?"

"Before we get to that, I wanted to update you on what happened with the inspection of your bike's remains."

In all the action since Manman Delphine had told him about it in the clinic, he'd forgotten about it. "Anything useful?"

"We didn't get any prints or anything else like that. Bomb was expertly built and set. Would have turned you into two grease spots—"

"Two?"

Boudreaux cringed. "Yeah. It was set to explode upward from the seat. Would have split you up the middle. But here's the interesting thing. The bomb was remote detonated and pretty short range. Whoever set it was likely within visual range of the alley."

Dax shivered. Luck had been smiling on him that night. "Why not a pressure sensitive one?"

Boudreaux shrugged. "Anything can set them off, if it's heavy enough. Also, it probably would have required more work to actually set it up. With this one, slip into the alley, attach it to the preferred spot, then out again. Less than a minute likely."

That opened a hollow pit in his gut. He wouldn't have recovered from that. The magical bullet had been a precise method but required proper application. A bomb up the ass was mundane overkill, but the kill part would have been assured. He tried to swallow, his mouth suddenly dry. Being a mortal was often confusing and dissatisfying, but he wasn't ready to end it and certainly not that way.

He stopped to take several deep breaths, hoping to get his mind back on the task at hand. "Um... Anything else? Or are we ready to go?"

"Yup. Let me check with Winnie though." He pulled out his phone.

The sight of his new car had distracted Dax, but the news about the bomb had sent his mind tumbling. Maybe he could distract himself from the thoughts of his near death by focusing on the job at hand.

He turned and let the spiritual energy wash over him. It had been teasing at the back of his mind the closer he got to the building, but now that he opened himself to it, it felt like a more muted version of the Ark of the Covenant scene at the end of Raiders of the Lost Ark.

However, he doubted these spirits would melt a Nazi's face. Though, if they'd ended up here in the same manner Jason had, they might like a shot at fucking up some Nazi wolf shifter bikers.

After the first chatty ghost had disappeared, he hadn't seen any others, despite the creeping feeling that the morgue wanted him, needed him to enter its boundaries. Its gravity had pulled at him. He almost felt like sweat would break out at any moment if he continued to resist it. A drop achieved enough mass and rolled down his back. Giving it a little shimmy, he narrowed his eyes and peered through the veil.

Boudreaux cleared his throat to grab Dax's attention. "Winnie gave the all clear. Cameras are down. So what next, Dax?"

"Let me do something out here before we step inside." He took another step closer to the building and stopped.

Drawing in a deep breath, he opened his awareness to the aether a bit wider. Howling shrieks staggered him back half a step.

"Dax?" Tomi's voice sounded nervous.

"Ro-sham-bo to see who the first brother to die in the horror film is?" Boudreaux asked.

"Fuck nah. I'm not tempting fate like that," Tomi replied.

The glowing aura swirling around the building stretched toward Dax.

"Agon…"

"Pain…"

"Release…"

"Terror…"

"Help…"

"Vengen…"

"Murder… Murder… Murder… Murder… Murder…"

Dax shook his head. He couldn't make out a single voice as the spirits assaulted him with their declarations. Each word slapped at his awareness, pleading to be heard.

In the blink of an eye, he could bring out his scythe from the aether and turn the morgue into an inert building with only the spirits housed in their proper living flesh remaining. He could wade through them, sweeping his blade back and forth, harvesting everything around him. But this much energy, this much power shifting would certainly draw attention—attention he was not ready to deal with.

And frankly, he didn't trust that he had the power anymore. Between self-limits and blocks placed on him by the psychopomps via this human shell, he might attempt it and become overwhelmed. Become crushed under the weight of the spiritual distress of this place. Even looking through the veil and allowing some of the pit's essence to seep out staggered him.

There were too many arrayed against him and the loyalties of those who'd backed him or stayed neutral were suspect at best. He wasn't foolhardy enough to bring any of the gods into this equation. His back was still tender from the burns and shrapnel of his murdered motorcycle to take a knife thrust in it.

Tomi set a gentle hand on his shoulder. "Dax? Are you OK?"

He wasn't sure. Closing off the crack he'd opened to the spirits trapped at the morgue, he breathed in a huge gulp of cool night air. A faint breeze teased at the sweat on his forehead and he shivered—partially from the sudden coolness and partially from the raw energy he'd been subjected to.

"I'm not sure."

"What happened?" Tomi asked.

"I opened myself to the spirts." He shivered again. "There's a lot of pain and anger trapped here."

"It's a morgue filled with mostly murdered people," Boudreaux said. "What did you expect?"

"I know that, but there shouldn't be this many. Their spirits should have been harvested and allowed to move on. But they're stuck here, and they're irate about the how they got here and the fact they're still stuck inside their murdered bodies."

He turned and looked at his two friends. "Have you ever been in a situation you didn't want to be where claustrophobia began to take hold?"

They both nodded.

"Now imagine you were powerless to end that situation. Trapped inside a prison of what used to be your living flesh, surrounded by others just like you. You can't help yourself. They can't help you. You can't help them. You're just stuck in a swirling mass of agony and fear."

He held their gazes for a moment. The joviality usually dominating Boudreaux's face had disappeared. Tomi's brows were furrowed, and he'd developed a small quiver in his bottom lip.

"I opened myself up, just a little bit. They sensed something different, someone receptive to their plight, and they all wanted in. They all had something to say. But there was one word they all had in common. One theme to why I'm here."

They waited on bated breath.

Dax looked to each one before speaking. "Murder."

"Hey, you ready?" a woman called from the morgue.

Tomi jumped clutching his chest. "Fuck me…" he mumbled.

Boudreaux waved to the woman. "Hey, Winnie. Let me check with the guest of honor." He turned to Dax. "You ready?"

"Yeah. I guess so. Why don't you two wait here. Things might get weird, and frankly, I don't need the distractions. This is going to be hard enough as is." He didn't wait for the answers, turning and striding toward where Winnie waited, holding the door into the morgue open.

THIRTY-FOUR

JAMIE

Apparently, the scouts had reported back. Their plan to confuse Ivar had worked, though it had effectively blocked those tunnels from their use. He searched through them, following the little scent trails. Then rushed back to another when it dead-ended.

While the plan had been clever, it had been a bit of a double-edged sword on the results side. The exit the coroner with her bombs had claimed as hers was likewise out. The scouts had reported new bombs now that they knew what to look and smell for. They'd watched and listened.

She talked a lot, her only company herself. Plans and bombs. That's what the scouts reported back. With a shrug and sheepish smile, The Rat apologized for the vague information. The rats didn't know that many spoken human words.

But he had another plan.

"Are you sure this is a good idea?" she whispered, per The Rat's instructions, as they neared their destination.

"No ideas in this city are truly good. But she has left the tunnels. Where else would a coroner go?" He waggled his bushy brown eyebrows at her. "To the body house."

"The morgue?" It made sense. But she didn't want to go back there. Not to where her father's body was. And especially not to where her father's ghost was. Out in the open was one thing, but encountering him in the crypt like tunnels? No thank you!

"So, we go to the body house. She invades my home. Kills my friends. Now I return the favor. Invade her home. Though all her friends are already dead." He cackled, then clamped a hand over his own mouth, his eyes twinkling with mirth.

She swallowed and licked her dry lips. "OK…"

She just wanted out of the tunnels. She didn't want to make war. But The Rat was her ticket back above ground. He'd protected her from Ivar and fed and clothed her.

"Don't worry. Stay back. Rats make war. Nice girl can stay safe." He patted her arm. "Now we must be quiet. No laughing at funny jokes. Follow close. Step where The Rat steps or get gross socks. Also, friendly warning. It's about to get stinky."

While they'd eaten breakfast, she'd filled him in on what little she knew about the morgue since she'd been there to identify her father's body.

Her heart rate picked up as they neared the exit. Why else would he want them to be quiet? They had to be near the morgue. She froze for a second. She hoped they wouldn't be emerging *in* the morgue. She just assumed they'd pop out above ground somewhere. Shaking her head, she got her mind back in the game.

They were nearing one of the sections near some leaky sewer lines. She didn't want to get gross socks. She scrunched up her nose. A slight shifting in the air of the tunnel brought with it a strong whiff of sewage. Swallowing the saliva that pooled in her mouth and the acid that burned at the back of her throat, she wished she hadn't stuffed herself as full as the rat suggested.

"Stinky, stinky," The Rat whispered.

"Try having a wolf's nose," she mumbled back. There were times like this that having an extra sensitive nose was not that fun. She was just thankful it wasn't quite as powerful when she was in her human form.

Once they cleared the sewage section, she breathed deeply,

letting the cleaner air into her lungs. It even added a fresh note to the underground mustiness. Swiping back some hair that had fallen in her face, she felt a kiss of breeze cool her damp forehead. She almost detected an aroma of trees or other plants in the air.

She wanted to run forward and claw her way back into the open world. She'd been trapped down here in the dark and claustrophobic tunnels for days now. The thought of fresh air and a night sky nearly caused her to lose control, but she'd made it this far. She could be cool for a little longer. But when she got a free moment, she was going to go find a place where it was quiet, and she could lie on her back and look at the sky.

Her eyes flicked up at the concrete ceiling that seemed to be closing in on her. A quick shake of her head and the ceiling returned to where it belonged.

A grunt escaped her mouth when she bumped into the back of The Rat, who'd stopped in front of her.

He turned around and leaned close to her ear. "It's night outside. Dark. Good for eyes. But watch for headlights or streetlights. Bad for eyes."

She nodded.

"We're almost there. Rats will go first, spread out. Ring of whiskers and fur." His nose twitched like one of his rats. "I'll go out next. Stay low."

She nodded again and gave him a thumbs up.

He turned and moved forward, his feet moving slowly and stepping carefully. His normal nonchalance was replaced by the posture and attitude of an animal on the hunt. She matched his movements and opened up her senses as best she could.

The breeze felt cooler and fresher. Rat nails scrabbling over metal and concrete rose to fill the silence. A faint glow emerged near the top of the tunnel. A wall appeared under it. Tiny little bumps exited through the light, making it look like a river flowing over stones.

She wasn't sure if he'd brought every rat from all of Red City, but it took a while for them all to climb through the exit. Once it was their turn, The Rat climbed up some hidden rungs and pushed up a metal plate. The light of the night and the normal lights of a city at night rained down on them. She looked away quickly despite her desire to bask in it.

"Come, come," The Rat whispered.

Squinting, she looked up and found the rungs. In a moment, The Rat helped her over the edge and guided her toward a bush to hide under. He quietly replaced the metal plate that had covered what looked like a storm drain.

They were in the park near the morgue's parking lot. Yet again, she was impressed by The Rat and his ability to navigate the mind numbingly complex warren of Red City's underworld.

"Ready?" he whispered.

She barely heard it with her enhanced ears. A regular human with listening equipment would likely not have heard a thing. Staying low, The Rat crawled forward. She followed in his wake, aiming for the same set of bushes he had. Around them, his rat friends spread out, most of them forming a wall of fur between them and the morgue's parking lot, though a non-insignificant number brought up the rear to ensure no one snuck up on them.

As they settled under the bush, she heard talking in the distance. Once she tuned in, she picked up a group of men joking with each other. She nearly jumped out of her skin when The Rat tapped her on the shoulder, a broad grin on his face.

"Boudreaux. Friend."

She nodded, assuming he meant one of the men. The name sounded familiar, but at the moment she couldn't place it. It wasn't a terribly common name on this side of the country. But despite the declaration of "friend," The Rat remained where he was, hunched under a bush with his ear pointed toward the parking lot.

What she really wanted was to borrow the burner phone The Rat was "up on" and call her mom to come pick her up. She didn't look forward to walking home in her stocking feet. But that would be entirely too noisy in the present circumstances.

Once she settled in, she tried to distract herself by focusing in on the conversation. At first, they'd talked about a car, then moved onto...a bombing? What all had happened while she was underground?

"Wait… I know that voice," she whispered.

The Rat nodded. "Me too. The scary man. Very scary." He shivered.

She snorted. The Rat was right. Dax was indeed "very scary." What was he doing here? A woman's call interrupted her speculation.

"Her…" The Rat hissed. He stood up, forgetting he was under a bush, and tried to walk forward, getting tangled in the process. "Fucking bush. No bushes in tunnels."

She crawled backward and stood. She tried to disentangle The Rat, but the more he tried to push out, the worse he got. Finally, with a brute grunt, he ripped his way out, taking several limbs with him.

"Stop her!" he yelled. "Murderer!"

She jogged behind him, letting the distance open up.

"What the fuck…" The tall, bald Black man she'd seen after the bar fight turned to face them. "The Rat? What are you doing above ground?"

That's why she recognized the name Boudreaux. He'd been one of the guys with Dax after he set fire to the biker's bar.

"What?" The other guy, Dax's friend…Tomi, looked toward her, his eyes going wide. "I don't believe it. Just the person we were looking for. Dreaux, don't let the girl get away. She's the one who set the bomb."

She slid to a halt. "What? What bomb? I didn't set a bomb…"

THIRTY-FIVE

DAX

Winnie pulled the door shut behind them with an audible click. "I've locked the door so we won't be disturbed."

Dax stopped in the middle of the lobby and turned around. "What if someone needs to make a drop off?"

"There's a bell. And if they need me, they can call my cell." Passing him, she gestured toward the elevator. "Shall we?"

"Feeling a little more comfortable with me being here?" He raised an eyebrow in curiosity.

"Hmm?"

"When you told me about the problem here, you seemed pretty trepidatious."

She shrugged. "I've had some time to think about it. Just needed to rip off the Band-Aid, you know?"

"I guess."

She walked over and pushed the call button for the elevator.

"Let me take a spin around up here before we head down."

"Alright," she said, sounding slightly perturbed. Or perhaps she was anxious about the whole ghost thing and having him in her morgue after all.

Drawing in a slow breath and exhaling it, he closed his eyes and stepped up to the edge of the veil without pushing into it. Instantly, the spiritual turbulence picked up, almost shoving him back.

Trying to find any sense of order or meaning failed. Being on the edge of the veil was like trying to see inside a house through a steam and condensation coated window. Taking another breath, he tried to feel his way around the spiritual mess surrounding him. But that turned out to be a Gordian knot he couldn't figure out from the outside.

Opening his eyes, he realized a noise he'd heard in the background had been the tapping foot of Winnie. Was she being impatient or just nervous?

He gestured toward the elevator. "I guess we'll go down to the body storage."

She gave him a partial smile and a nod, her eyes boring into him as he stepped into the elevator. Once the door closed and it juddered to a start, he developed a slight tremble in his hands. Grasping his fingers together, he watched the light indicating what level they were on. It appeared she was taking him right down to the bottom floor. When the bell binged, announcing their arrival, she stepped aside to let him out first.

The cold blasted through the gap in the door as it opened. He shivered and stepped out, squinting against the bright lights and glare reflected off stainless steel.

As soon as his foot hit the floor, he staggered and was forced to brace himself against the wall. They'd only descended a few floors down, not into the core of the earth, yet the pressure trying to squish him was almost unbearable.

"Are you OK?" Winnie asked, still in the elevator.

He tried to find his center through breathing but was struggling even to get his chest to expand enough to draw in air. Reaching into the aether, he plucked out a bit of power and wrapped it around himself like a body shield. He didn't know if it would last or even work, but he had to do something to create a bit of space for himself.

When he was able to draw in air, he sighed in relief now that he could. Giving himself a few seconds to gather his wits, he straightened up and stepped away from the wall. "I think I will be. Just a bit intense there for a moment."

He wasn't sure what the difference was from the last time he'd been here beyond being in his Grim Reaper form. Something was even more wrong here. He needed to start somewhere.

"Who is your newest body?" He walked around, looking at the drawers and clipboards dangling, and wondered if Jason's body was still here or if he'd been moved somewhere else since his case was still unsolved. Soon it would become a cold case and forgotten. One more victim of Redemption City's lack of justice system.

"Let's see…" Winnie exited the elevator and examined the clipboards on the opposite side of the room.

"Whoa…" His knees trembled.

The pressure in the room shifted, and he began to sweat, bile rising in the back of his throat. Bracing himself against the nearest drawer, he slipped into the in-between and sampled the currents in the room. Anger, fear, vengeance… But it wasn't directed at him.

When he'd experienced the emotions of the tortured and tethered spirits, he'd felt similar feelings, but seeing the contrast helped him evaluate them better. With him, they were mostly explanatory, though some spirits focused their ire on him as the nearest being who could interact with them.

But now… He looked up, focusing on the coroner as she moved from drawer to drawer. The violent emotions were directed at her. That didn't make sense. He'd looked into her thread but couldn't explain why they were so intent on her.

Shaking his head to clear it, he let his eyes drift up toward the junction of the wall and the ceiling. "Did you install more security cameras in here?"

Shit. He probably shouldn't have said that. She didn't know Boudreaux had snuck him in before.

"A few. Had some issues lately. Don't worry. I turned everything off. Though I should probably go check just to be safe." She patted the drawer next to her. "Here's our newest resident. You can take a look while I go double-check the cameras."

Staring at her for a moment, he nodded slowly and stepped away from the wall, glad his knees had decided to cooperate. He crossed the room and grabbed the drawer's handle, pulling it out.

"I'll be back momentarily." Winnie stepped into the elevator and turned around.

Flipping the sheet away from the body's face, he stumbled backward, his eyes widening and jaw dropping. "What the fuck..."

It was the body of Toby Rodriquez. Jamie's father.

He looked up and found Winnie as she reached over and pushed the button. They stared at each for a moment. He couldn't get his brain moving quick enough.

As the door began to close, an evil grin spread across her face. "Oh, by the way, Dax. Ivar and the Black Sun Motorcycle Club send their regards."

Finally, his body let him have control. He darted around the open drawer and aimed for the elevator's call button. He slapped it, but it was too late. "Fuck!"

Winnie had betrayed him. But he didn't have time for that now. He didn't know how much longer he had before whatever "regards" she'd planned was executed.

Yanking out the lowest drawer near the ground, he found a body but shoved it off the shelf and stood on it. Risking it for the sake of having fast knowledge, he yanked one of the cameras from the wall. The cord wasn't attached to anything. He pried open the plastic casing and found what looked like putty attached to wires and some electronics.

"Not another bomb." *No, not another.* He looked around the room, not bothering to count them all. He'd only remembered two or three from his previous visit.

He looked around, frantically trying to come up with a way to get out of this. He couldn't see another exit and there was no way the elevator would be coming back for him. The only thing that had bought him time was a slow elevator and the need for distance before detonating the bombs. As he shifted his weight, the drawer he stood on creaked.

That was not a decision he wanted to make. It was a terrible plan. But it was also the best plan by dint of it being the *only* plan he had.

He tossed the bomb as far away from himself as he could and climbed down into the morgue drawer. Once he was flat, he reached in and placed his palms against the side walls of the drawer and pulled himself inside.

"Come on, come on…" His hands slipped, so he reset them.

It took several inching pulls to get it all the way closed. He just hoped it would be enough. Then, he slipped into his skeleton form and crouched as deeply in the drawer as he could. As a last measure, he grabbed a bit of power and formed a shield of aether around his body, making a thicker wall across the drawer above his head.

The cameras were inside the room, pointing into the space. He just hoped they were shaped and aimed well enough that he'd only get some of the blast. If he believed in such gestures, he'd have knocked on wood for a bit of extra luck, although there was no wood visible in his stainless-steel, refrigerated drawer.

An explosion ripped through the room, and shock waves pummeled his shield and body. Then, nothing.

THIRTY-SIX

JAMIE

The Rat sprinted past Boudreaux and Tomi, a swarm of rats doing their best to keep up with their enraged human. Boudreaux seemed torn between which direction to focus his attention on—the bonkers appearance of The Rat chasing after the coroner or his friend's command to capture the teen girl who'd appeared with The Rat.

Jamie stood there, frozen in place, her mind grinding to a halt at the suggestion that she'd bombed something or someone. It was just too absurd.

"Fuckity!" The Rat screamed, pounding on the door. "Unlock the door!"

Around him, the rats scurried about, agitated, as he banged on the door. Finally, he slumped and stopped pounding on the door.

"Patience. Rats aren't big and mean; rats are cunning. We'll wait for her, my friends."

"What the fuck are you doing, dude?" Boudreaux asked, stopping at the edge of the mass of rats. "My girl didn't murder anyone."

The Rat spun around. "Your girl? *Your* girl?!" He shook his head, disappointed. "Thought Boudreaux was our friend."

"Look, there's got to be some kind of misunderstanding..."

Boudreaux backed up, holding his hands up, palms facing The Rat, in a gesture of peace.

"Hey!" Jamie's brain juddered to a start. "Leave him alone!"

She took a step toward the brewing confrontation. But hands clamped firmly around her upper arms, stopping her.

"You're not going anywhere."

Tomi had used her distraction at focusing on The Rat to sneak around and grab her. She lurched away, but he squeezed harder, hurting her arms. Instead, she plowed backward, hoping to catch him off balance. She hadn't. He pulled her in tighter, releasing her arms, and wrapped his massive arms around her chest, trapping her arms to the side.

"Now, stop it!" he barked.

She stomped down with a foot, only finding packed earth under it. She kicked back, her foot glanced off a shin. He grunted. It probably would have hurt more if she wasn't barefoot.

"Damnit, I don't want to hurt you, now stop it!"

She huffed, breathing heavily, but stopped fighting. He was ready for it. She'd have to play her cards right and wait for him to make a mistake. Looking around for anything that might help her, she saw a rat. Then two. Then twenty. Then a fuck ton.

"Um…" Tomi moved around behind her.

"Let nice girl go." The Rat stopped ten feet in front of her. His rats had pushed Boudreaux away from them, surrounding him in the parking lot with his hands still held in the air. The circling rats reduced their circumference, closing in on them. "I said let her go."

"OK." Tomi released her and took a step back.

A corridor in the rats opened between Jamie and The Rat. Not waiting to be told, she walked through it briskly, finding a spot that put The Rat between her and both Tomi and Boudreaux. The corridor closed.

The Rat fixed his attention on Tomi. "You, funny man, you stay there. Little rat friends, if he moves. Swarm him."

Tomi's eyes flashed wide before his body went rigid.

The Rat turned to Boudreaux. "What misunderstanding?

Coroner woman killed my friends. In my world. In my tunnels. She was not welcome. Made bombs. Made tiny chalk outlines."

Boudreaux perked up. "Dude, bombs? You're not making any sense…"

The Rat nodded, slowly and ominously walking toward the bald Black man.

"Look, man. I don't know what you're talking about. But Winnie hasn't been running around in your tunnels. And I know she hasn't been blowing up your rats with bombs."

The Rat shook his head. "I saw. We smelled. We know."

The rats closed in around Boudreaux.

"I swear! Winnie is a good woman. I've been with her most of the week. She hasn't been in the tunnels."

Jamie had no idea what to think. The coroner had creeped her out when she'd come to identify her father's remains. Her father… Pieces tumbled into place, but she wasn't sure she believed the picture that was forming. Bombs… Imposters. Danger.

She set her hand on The Rat's shoulder and squeezed it gently. "Tomi, right?"

"Yeah. What?" He looked around, keeping his eyes on the rats swirling around him.

"When did you say I set a bomb?"

He snorted, crossing his arms over his broad chest.

"Answer her," The Rat bit out, the rats squeezing in tighter.

"OK, OK! Um, Monday night, maybe midnight." Panic saturated his voice.

"Why are you blaming me?" she asked.

Tomi narrowed his eyes. "We got you on video going into the alley before the bomb was set off."

"Nice girl…" The Rat said lowly.

"Trust me. I think I have an idea what's going on," she said low enough for The Rat to hear.

He nodded, though the anger stayed on his face, nor did his rats retreat any.

"And this was Monday midnight? As in going to Tuesday?"

Tomi nodded.

"Sorry. It wasn't me. I'd come here on Monday. Then some creeps chased me. I hid in an alley over there." She pointed in the direction she'd run. "A homeless person helped me hide. She's probably there right now. We could go find her and ask. Then when I got home, I was chased away by Ivar. By midnight, I was probably lost inside the tunnels." She nodded her head toward The Rat. "He found me. I've been in the tunnels ever since. Until now."

"Is what she said true?" Boudreaux asked.

Before she could answer, the coroner sprinted out of the door, saw them and the rats, and turned, dashing away in a different direction.

"Get her!" The Rat screamed.

"Winnie, stop!" Boudreaux called after her.

But before the rats could respond, the ground shook and thunder rumbled...from under them. The rats squealed painfully, tossing their heads about and trying to cover their ears with their little paws.

"What the..." Tomi said.

Smoke started to roll out the door she'd left open in her flight. Jamie looked around. In the chaos, the coroner had disappeared.

"Fuck. Where's Dax?" Tomi took a step but stopped when the rats turned their attention back to him.

"Look, I don't care about the girl right now. My boy Dax is in that building."

The Rat stared at him for a moment, his brow furrowed, then nodded. The rats moved away from Tomi and Boudreaux. As soon as the way was clear, the two Black men darted toward the building. They reemerged a minute later, holding their shirts over their noses and coughing.

"What's going on?" Jamie asked.

"Bad. Something bad."

Boudreaux and Tomi stopped in front of them, both bending over and placing their hands on their knees as they tried to clear their lungs. After about a minute of coughing and heavy breathing, Boudreaux stood up.

"I don't know what happened. But it's on fire. I think the embalming fluids are burning. The stairwell down to the morgue levels is collapsed. The elevator is fucked as well. It looks like a bomb went off."

"Bomb coroner blows up morgue." The Rat spat on the ground in disgust.

Tomi fixed a worried look on his face as he shifted his gaze to Jamie. "I'm inclined to believe your story. But I don't know why the video would show your face."

She shrugged. "I don't know either."

Boudreaux finally spoke up. "There's a lot of magic in the world. We need the manbo. She might know." He turned to The Rat. "I know that wasn't my Winnie. She's a kind woman. She wouldn't hurt a person or an animal."

Jamie doubted that was entirely true, even if that wasn't "his Winnie," most humans put out traps and poisons to kill what they considered vermin. In truth, a few days ago, she would have been one of them. But she'd grown strangely fond of the little animals.

"I don't know. If they impersonated me, maybe they can impersonate the coroner…"

"Yeah, great, whatever. What are we going to do to get to Dax?" Tomi said, looking back frantically at the morgue.

The Rat narrowed his eyes. "If we can't go down, maybe up or through?"

"What?" Tomi asked.

A knowing smile of understanding spread across Boudreaux's face. "He's The Rat. King of the tunnels. I bet you know a way that'll get us near the underground side of the morgue, don't ya?"

The Rat grinned, his eyes a little bright. "The Rat knows."

Tomi's eyes narrowed. "I know you and your rats are resourceful, but I doubt they can dig us a hole big enough to find Dax. And we don't even know what level he's on. There were several when I was here."

"It'll be the bottom," Boudreaux said. "Bury him deep where it's the hardest to access. Let gravity and time kill him, even if he survived…" He caught the stricken look on Tomi's face. "Oh, I'm sorry, brother. I'm sure he's alive. Or…you know. He's…" He rolled his hand, looking for the right words.

"The fucking Grim Reaper?" Jamie provided.

Off in the distance, sirens broke the relative silence of the night.

"Gang, we're going to have to continue this debate somewhere else," Boudreaux said, looking off in the distance for the lights. "Rat, you still got my number memorized?"

"Yup." He pulled a cheap cellphone out of his pocket. "No more payphones!"

Jamie tipped her head toward him. "He's up on burners."

Boudreaux laughed. "Let's scatter. Tomi, you're with me. There's a spare set of keys in the Lincoln. Call me in ten minutes."

The Rat tapped her shoulder, gesturing away from the morgue and through the park. "Time for ratters to scatters!"

The rats had already received their orders and were sweeping across the park or dropping into the storm drain. The little man took off, running at a good clip. A chuckle fell from her lips as she took off after him. She'd traded running with a wolf for running with The Rat.

THIRTY-SEVEN

DAX

Cracks, crashing, and vibrations called to Dax. It took him a moment, but as he put out a hand, it clacked against stainless steel. He'd survived the blast, finishing his preparations just in time.

Pushing out with his awareness, he found his shields intact, though a bit battered and torn. He reached out and braced against the side of the drawer and pushed, but his bony fingers slipped against the slick stainless steel. He'd need flesh and skin to grip the sides.

Letting his skeleton form go, his flesh snapped back into place. The sound immediately intensified. His first inhale brought with it fumes and smoke. Wracking coughs shook his body. Grabbing his T-shirt, he shoved it over his mouth and tried to calm his coughing. Once he managed to stop it, he clamped his lips shut and held his breath.

He braced himself against the walls with his hands and pushed, but they slipped with a squeak. Too sweaty. Wiping them against his jeans, he tried again, pushing as hard as he could. The drawer moved only a fraction of an inch. Just enough to let in more smoke. Before his body forced him to open his mouth and draw in the tainted air, he pulled with all his might, resealing the drawer. His skeleton form was the only safe option right now.

Relief washed through him as he slipped off the organs of his mortal body. At least the smoke wouldn't torment him for the moment. Though he had no idea how long he could stay in this form. It had been a form of convenience when needed. Now it was a matter of life and death.

But a new sensation descended on him. As the room cracked and burned around him, the ghosts refocused their attention on him. Soon their agonized howling drowned out the flames and the room breaking around him.

"Pain..."

"Fear..."

"Help..."

"Anger...

"Vengeance..."

"Freedom..."

"Peace..."

"Hatred..."

He couldn't tell which thought was coming from where. They swirled around him like he was standing in the eye of a spiritual hurricane.

A creak and the sound of twisting steel shook him in his cadaver drawer. The irony wasn't lost on him. Like the bodies and souls trapped here, he was about to join them if the wall collapsed completely. He'd be buried here. Though he wasn't sure if he'd survive in this form or if a building falling on him would be too much for even this.

Pulling in more power, he reestablished his shields, pushing them out to fill the drawer. He hoped it would reinforce the structure a bit and keep it from squeezing him like a submarine imploding after going too deep. The howling of the dead receded, though they didn't go away entirely. But it was a good side benefit of putting up the shielding.

He'd been curious what the effect of long-term tethering to a dead body would do to a spirit, wondering how additional damage to the body would affect the trapped spirits. This was not how he wanted to get that information. What would it do to him?

He pushed that thought away and concentrated on maintaining the shields around himself. If he wandered down the obscure paths of death, he might lose his control and slip into panic. And panic was a sure way to end up dead.

Control. He must maintain control.

THIRTY-EIGHT

JAMIE

After they'd scattered, Jamie and The Rat ended up in an empty alley, a rarity in Red City. The homeless tended to prefer to stay out of sight to avoid cops and anyone who wanted to harass them. The reason for this alley's emptiness was apparent as soon as the wind shifted. It smelled like eight kinds of ass.

The Rat pulled out his phone and turned it on before slowly punching each number in, his tongue sticking out in concentration. Satisfied that he had Boudreaux's number inputted correctly, he held it up to his ear. Nothing happened. Looking confused, he looked at the screen.

"Um, you need to hit the send button."

"Yes. Send button. The Rat is up on burners. Burners, burners, burners!" He hit the send button, then launched into a quick debate with Boudreaux on the best place to meet up that would be close enough to the tunnels The Rat wanted and far enough away for Boudreaux and his crew to enter them without attracting the attention of anyone dealing with the fire at the morgue.

After all the activity, her stomach growled. Even in the stench of the alley, her body was telling her she needed more food. She was young and a wolf shifter. The Rat had been more than generous, but she didn't want to dig too deep into his stores. She had no idea how easy it would be for him to replace.

"Jamie is hungry. So is The Rat." He winked at her. "Hmmm." He dialed the number again, this time hitting send after. "The Rat needs some munchies, Boudreaux. Hamburger?"

Jamie nodded.

"OK. Four hamburgers, fries, and two colas. The Rat out!" He hung up before she could hear a response.

Boudreaux had at least fifty pounds, all of it muscle, on The Rat. Tomi was a big dude too, yet The Rat knew exactly where his source of power came from and used it.

"Don't worry. Boudreaux is a friend. We'll sort out this mystery. Until then, hamburgers!" He looked around. "Now, let's get out of this alley. Stanky!"

She nodded vigorously. The Rat jogged out and headed north, sticking to the shadows, alleys, and the dark spots. He was a pro at evasion, his footsteps silent and sure. She was no slouch either. Cory and she had played sneaking and hunting games in the woods; she could move silently. But she still learned a lot about stealth and decision making when it came to navigating quickly through the dark of the city.

She doubted anyone but maybe a homeless person or two saw them pass, two ninjas in the night. Cory… She was still mad as fuck at him. But all the same, she missed the big idiot. He'd kept her morale up and provided sanctuary in the chaotic world that was her life. Now she was almost completely adrift, trailing along behind the weirdest being she'd ever met. But he'd looked out for her without a thought to asking for anything in return.

After a while, The Rat found a service hole cover and pried it up, gesturing for her to head down. She did, and he quickly followed, dragging the heavy cover back into place.

Once they descended to the pipe filled tunnel, The Rat slowed down. "Eyes need time."

He was right. It had been nighttime above, but streetlights and neon signs had messed up the night vision she'd developed in the days spent underground with him. After what felt like a half-hour, he picked up the pace as they wound their way through more service tunnels. Once, he popped up a series of rungs, moved aside the cover, and peeked around.

He laughed sheepishly. "Wrong one. Close though."

They backtracked until he found the cross-tunnel he wanted and headed down it. Soon they'd found the place he wanted. He popped out first, then poked his he'd back in.

"Safe for kind girls. Also, burgers! Well, not safe for burgers." He pantomimed eating a burger.

The moment of levity relieved the bit of tension of the last hour. She climbed out, moving out of the way so The Rat could replace the cover.

"Here." Boudreaux tossed her a bottle of hand sanitizer. "Figured you might want a little something to clean up with before eating hand food."

"Thanks." When she was finished, she passed the bottle to The Rat and accepted a greasy bag from the tall Black man.

"We're just waiting on my crew to get all the equipment we're going to need. Not sure what we'll run into down there."

She nodded, her mouth full of food.

Boudreaux picked up his phone again and looked at the screen, his brow furrowing before he set it down again. He grabbed his soda cup and drank from the straw, only getting the sad sucking sound of an empty cup.

When his phone rang, he dropped the cup to the ground and snatched up the phone. "Delphine?"

"I'm here now. She's on the floor, unconscious. Her pulse is too low. And her breath is shallow. I don't like it."

Boudreaux's face sank. "What's wrong with her?"

"I don't know," the woman on the phone replied. "I'm putting in a call to Dr. Ofori. We'll get her looked at. I've got Adele here with me. She'll stay and watch over her. I'll be there shortly."

"Right." Boudreaux sighed. "Thanks for going over. I'm glad you found her."

"I need to go. I have to grab a few things from the shop before I meet you."

Boudreaux set the phone down.

"What did the manbo have to say?" Tomi asked.

"She found Winnie unconscious in her house on the floor. I'm relieved it wasn't actually her, but Delphine is calling the doctor."

The Rat swallowed a mouthful of food. "What's going on?"

"I knew it wasn't Winnie. I had Manman Delphine go check on her. I was right. Whoever is impersonating her must have done something to keep her from showing up or calling me." He didn't look relieved, probably more worried about her well-being than anything.

"Why wouldn't the assassin just kill her?" Tomi asked.

Boudreaux shrugged.

"Hmm." The Rat nibbled on a fry, biting off little pieces from the end using his front teeth. "Connections?"

"What do you mean?" Jamie asked.

"Perhaps the assassin needs the person to be alive. Magic connections. No victim, no imposter."

Boudreaux pulled out a bag and grabbed a burger from it. "Maybe. I just hope whatever it is doesn't cause any permanent damage."

"So…" Jamie cleared her throat. "This assassin probably impersonated me to blow up something." She turned to Tomi. "What was I supposed to have blown up?"

"Um, Dax and his motorcycle. Fortunately, the bomb only sort of blew up Dax. His motorcycle didn't make it."

Jamie felt a sheen of sweat break out on her face, the cool night breeze chilling it. "I hope your friend will be reasonable and give us a chance to explain before he goes…all primal horror."

Boudreaux shivered, looking at Tomi. "Yeah, that is some scary shit. Still gives me nightmares. And he was only kind of mad. Being blown up twice might make him a might testy."

Tomi shrugged. "I'll do the best I can, but it's probably best if Jamie isn't the first one he sees when we drag him out."

"Yeah. I agree. No pissed off Grim Reaper for me. No thank you." Jamie shook her head vigorously.

After they finished their food, they waited as Boudreaux's friends joined them in ones and twos until six had showed up, each unloading bags as well as a few sledgehammers.

It had been nervous waiting. She didn't want to return to the underground tunnels, and certainly not to venture into an area compromised by explosions. But those considerations only caused her some anxiety. At this point, anxiety was like an old friend. Missed when it was absent.

No. It was the possibility of being close to Dax if he lost his cool and tried to kill her summarily without giving everyone time to explain. That didn't make her nervous. That terrified her.

"Y'all ready?" Boudreaux asked after distributing the equipment. Jamie had taken a sledgehammer before anyone could say anything.

After collecting nods from his friends, he turned to The Rat and Jamie.

"Not really," Jamie said. "But I figure I owe him for saving my life. And I'll be able to help."

She didn't want to elaborate on what kind of help. In her wolf form, her nose was highly sensitive. And the extra strength would make swinging the hammer a much easier task than it otherwise would be for a body of her type. But she guessed most of them were humans like Tomi and Boudreaux.

"The Rat is ready. Gathered in his furry masses." He grinned widely.

"Are you forgetting something?" A rich voice said from behind her.

Jamie, her nerves frayed to the last thread, spun around, ready to fight or run. A tall, Black woman in a colorful dress stepped out of the darkness.

"We were in a bit of a hurry, Delphine," Boudreaux replied.

She shook her head. "Fool of a man. Don't worry, I won't be going down into those tunnels with you. But I can provide some protection." She looked around the gathering, her head bobbing as she appeared to tally their numbers. "I'm glad I brought extras."

Reaching into a bag, she pulled out a handful of red flannel bags on a leather thong. A bead was tied into the string closing the bag. She handed one to everyone in their party except Boudreaux, whose hand patted a lump under his T-shirt when she offered him one.

"It's a protection gris-gris. Hold it in both hands, concentrate on feeling safe and protected, then blow onto the bag. It'll activate it. You'll need to keep it around your neck for it work. It'll work against a lot of things, but especially spirits."

Tomi was the first to close their eyes and follow her directions, followed by Boudreaux's friends.

The Rat stood up and joined in, stringing it around his neck when he was done. "Great gift from great lady." He bowed deeply. "Many thanks. Much cherishing."

Seeing as she was the last one, Jamie closed her eyes and thought of feeling protected. It was a hard feeling to find and felt foreign. She couldn't remember the last time in her life she'd felt truly protected and safe. Poverty, arguments, neglect—those had displaced any chance of feeling safe and protected in her home. But she had an imagination and had escaped into it many times. There she could create places where she'd have stability and safety. So, it was to those memories and fantasies that she searched for the needed feelings.

Even then, she wasn't sure she believed a gris-gris bag would do anything. Despite being a wolf shifter, she'd been raised in a world where magic wasn't considered real. Except the kind of magic that made her a wolf shifter. That kind of magic was considered heretical or satanic. The only acceptable *magic* came from big "G" god. Though those who believed in miracles didn't really consider them magic, which if they had happened would be the highest forms of magic. But it couldn't hurt. She was standing next to a man who talked to and commanded rats. She could turn into a wolf. She'd met the Grim Reaper. Why would the manbo's magic be any less real?

She brought the bag up to her lips and exhaled onto it slowly until her last breath left her lungs. She put the leather thong and bag over her head and adjusted her hair over the string. She didn't feel anything different, but she didn't know how the magic worked. Reaching up, she wrapped her fingers around it.

Even if it was nothing but a red baggie filled with things she didn't want to know about, someone had given her something with good intent, and she could appreciate the gift in that spirit. "Thank you, Manman Delphine."

"You are welcome, child. Listen to Boudreaux and The Rat. They'll see you through this." She turned to Boudreaux and pulled him into a hug. "I'll go check on Winnie and send you an update from the clinic."

"Thank you," he replied.

"Manman, tell Mama I'll text her as soon as we're out." Tomi dropped his gris-gris inside the collar of his shirt.

Manman Delphine looked at each one of them, a confident smile on her face. "Bon chans!"

Jamie mumbled her thanks along with everyone else. Hopefully, the manbo's wish of good luck would stand them in good stead, because they were sure going to need it.

THIRTY-NINE

DAX

If Dax was in his human form, he'd probably be sweating buckets. Or more likely dead. He could feel the heat on his shields, the metal drawer warming around him. Fortunately, there probably weren't a lot of things to burn in the stainless-steel morgue, or he'd really be in hot water. As is, he wasn't sure how much longer he could maintain his shields.

Even through his skeleton form, the dull throb of pain niggled at the back of his mind. If he made it out, he was going to need a bucket of ibuprofen to tamp the results of being in an explosion. And he'd need a week of vacation to recover from the mental strain of tying into the aether and siphoning power into his limited shield. Then there was the experience of being blown up. Twice. And being trapped in a morgue drawer.

A tendril of heat pushed through his shield. He snapped back to attention, smoothing out the edges. Help had to be coming. Tomi and Boudreaux were right there. He couldn't think about being buried alive. It would only sap his concentration and let panic take hold.

Panic meant death.

But...

He didn't know how much longer he could keep this up. If it

were possible to have spiritual or magical muscles, they'd be cramping up like at the end of a marathon.

His drawer shuddered.

"What now?"

The destruction hadn't been all at once. Whatever damage the bombs had done inside the morgue had created a chain reaction of cracking, crashing, and shaking. But this one felt different. For one, it felt like it originated near his feet. And second, it was rhythmic.

A spark of hope blossomed in his chest. Were they coming for him? Another tongue of heat lashed him. Concentrate. Focus.

He still had to maintain his shields and stay in his skeleton form. Hope could be as dangerous to him as panic at the moment. Patience. He could be patient. He'd watched eons pass and seen galaxies move through the universe. A few more minutes would be less than the blink of an eye to him.

Though the pep talk sounded logical, he found his focus drifting from the task at hand to the steady pounding at his feet. Each time he had to smooth his shield, it was a little more difficult than the previous time. He thought he might be reaching the end of his endurance. This was a race he didn't want to be a part of. There wouldn't be a prize for second place. They'd just drag his body out of the morgue with the rest after they got down here.

When something pounded into the drawer, it rang like a gong and he let out a short scream. He flashed in from the other side. Clenching his teeth, he concentrated with everything he had left to fix his shields. If they tore that badly again, he didn't think he'd get them back up.

A moment later, a steady vibration and the sound of metal grinding on metal filled the drawer. A tiny stream of cooler air poked in after the grinding stopped.

"Hello?" A distorted voice said. "Anyone home?"

"Yes. But not for long if you don't hurry," he gritted out through clenched teeth.

"Shit. He's alive. Dax, it's me, Boudreaux. Me and the boys will bust you out. It's going to get noisy. And keep your feet away from the end. We'll be careful, but we're moving fast."

"OK. Get to it. I can't hold out for much longer." Relief threatened to wash over him, but he shoved it aside and focused on keeping his protection up.

Boudreaux was right; it was noisy. They pounded with sledgehammers to break the concrete wall that backed the drawer. Then they used some sort of metal saw to cut the end of the drawer away. Once it was yanked out, blessedly cool air filled part of his drawer, doing battle with the heat of fire heated metal.

"Holy fuck. Warn me next time, bro." Boudreaux panted. "About gave me a fucking heart attack."

If Dax had the energy, he'd laugh. Boudreaux probably looked in and saw the white bones of his feet.

"Is it OK if we grab you by the ankles and pull you out? You won't fall apart, will you?" There was a note of humor in Boudreaux's voice.

How fucking humiliating. "No. I won't fall apart. Just hurry."

"Alright, we'll do our best to keep your robe between you and the sharp edges we cut. Try to stay rigid."

He grunted, hoping they heard it. Two hands hovered over his ankles as if hesitating. Whatever the delay, they finally grabbed them and gently pulled, shuffling the robe under him.

"He's heavier than I thought," someone said, sounding strained.

As he emerged, he found four people holding him. He recognized Boudreaux's and Tomi's bodies but couldn't determine who the other two were since he couldn't see their faces. He found out why their voices sounded distorted. They were all wearing gas masks.

He laughed, the hollow sound hitting a couple different spooky harmonics. Four men in gas masks holding up the Grim Reaper like pallbearers as they pulled him from a morgue drawer. It would make one hell of a spooky, goth painting.

"Can you stay in this form? The fumes from the flames are pretty bad right here. We're going to lower your feet so you can stand," Boudreaux said.

"I'm not sure how well I'll be able to stand."

They lowered his legs and set him down, tipping him all the way up. Tomi slipped under his shoulder to help him stay upright. "Dax, we need to walk you away from here so we can get you masked."

"Good. I don't know how much longer I can keep the heat from pouring out." He'd kept his shield in place, morphing it to form more of a plug. "Why is the floor moving?"

"Little friends scurrying about, even though I tell them to stay away. Bad air, bad hot. But they ignore." The Rat stepped into a view. "No tiny little gas masks."

"We can do the heartfelt reunion some other time. Let's go," said one of the guys Dax didn't recognize.

Dax let Tomi bear some of his weight as they crawled through a rough tunnel away from the basement of the morgue, which had almost become his tomb. Once he felt they were far enough away, he let go of his shield, his body sagging in relief. He felt like a threadbare bar rag that had been rung out too many times.

Dax staggered as human flesh encased his bones, and he turned to plain old Dax. "Fuck. I need a month's worth of good sleeps."

"Too tired for vengeance?" The Rat said, his voice high, peeling off his gasmask. "I know where the bad lady is." He said it with a sing-songy lilt.

"Really?" That did give Dax a bit more energy, though he didn't know if he could sustain it.

Seeing that Dax and The Rat seemed to be OK, everyone else peeled off their gas masks and wiped away the sweat that had formed underneath, a few sighing in relief.

"At least I know where she was," The Rat added, rocking forward and backward on his heels. "My little friends will see. Beady little eyes. Spying in the dark. Beady little eyes filled with hate. Oh, they'll find her."

"What do you think, Dax?" Tomi asked, letting the wall take some of Dax's weight so he could take a break. "I know you're tired, and normally I'd be the voice of reason. But this assassin has come after you twice, and the second time destroyed a building and nearly crushed you under it. Do you want to give her a third opportunity? You don't want to be her third time is a charm."

Dax exhaled loudly. He wanted to crawl into bed and not get up.

But Tomi was right on both counts. He was Dax's voice of reason, and they needed to eliminate the assassin before they could try again.

He smacked his lips, his mouth dry. "I'm going to need something to eat and drink, or I won't be good for anything. But Tomi's right. We need to take our shot. The next time might be my last."

As they stood there collecting their breaths and making decisions, a silvery-gray wolf walked up and sat down on its haunches. No one seemed alarmed by it, and if they weren't going to expend the energy, he wouldn't waste what he didn't have.

"I guess while we're taking a breather, we should update you on who the assassin is," Boudreaux stood up, stretching out his back.

"I'm pretty sure your girlfriend is, *buddy*." Anger rose in his chest, setting the fire to burning in his eyes, and he took a step toward Boudreaux. "When she told me she had a gift from Ivar and blew me up, that was a pretty good fucking clue."

Tomi grabbed Dax's shoulder. "Just fucking cool it, Dax. I ain't got the energy for more fighting if we're going to hunt down the assassin tonight. Swinging sledges through concrete is hard fucking work. It's not Winnie. She's with the manbo at the clinic. Whatever the assassin used to knock her out nearly killed her."

Boudreaux held up his phone. A woman that looked like Winnie lay on a hardwood floor. "The manbo sent a picture. She figured it would be useful since you can be a bit paranoid." After Dax had inspected it, Boudreaux put the phone away. "Not that you don't have good reason to be," he added quickly.

"We think that whoever this assassin is, she can change her appearance. Not like makeup, but really for real." Tomi twisted his torso slowly, working out some kinks.

"So…" His brain was feeling mushy after the working to keep his shields in place. But he trusted Tomi explicitly. If he and the manbo, backed by photo evidence, believed Winnie—the real one—was innocent, he'd have to go along with it. "Can they do multiple forms?"

The Rat had slid around so that he stood between the group and the wolf. "Turn around. Close eyes. Wolfy changes." To demonstrate, he put his hands over his eyes. His back was already to the wolf.

They did as they were told. Dax was the last to comply because he was obviously behind on the times compared to the rest of the group. He sighed, turning and closing his eyes. "Fine"

A minute later, The Rat said, "All clear, all clothed."

He turned around, and the flames burst into life in his eyes as he took a step toward Jamie. Tomi grabbed his left arm, and Boudreaux grabbed the right. The Rat maintained his place in front of the girl. Rats had flooded into the tunnel, forming a deep ring around their master and the teen.

Tomi leaned up and spoke into Dax's ear. "She saved your life."

"Kind girl is friend. You will *not* hurt her." The Rat folded his arms over his chest and accented it with a firm nod.

Jamie coughed, then coughed again. "Sorry. The fumes are still getting to me." Her voice sounded raw and a rough. She coughed again.

"She volunteered to sniff you out," Boudreaux said, keeping a firm grip on Dax's upper arm. "Which meant going without a gas mask. And it was nasty down there."

"How did she find me?" The fires in his eyes cooled a bit.

"Dogs can smell things through several feet of concrete. And the walls down there weren't that thick," she rasped out. "Wolf's nose is just as good."

"How do you know my scent?"

She snorted, coughing a couple times after. "Scents form powerful memories. And yours are linked to some pretty scary moments in my recent life. Your scent wasn't the problem." She coughed again. "Finding it with all the fumes was."

"So, you're saying you were impersonated as well?"

She nodded. "I even know when she did it. I came to identify my father's body. She was posing as the coroner. Winnie."

Boudreaux pulled a water bottle out of his bag and handed it to The Rat to hand to Jamie. "That was the missing day Winnie told you about. The assassin had knocked her out and came into work pretending to be Winnie. At least that's what the information we're putting together says."

"She's probably the one that killed Jamie's father. To get her there. If Ivar sent the assassin, he probably gave her all the information about what happened," Tomi added.

"Yeah. It makes sense." She sighed. "Then on Monday—the night I was supposed to have blown up your motorcycle—I saw my father's ghost. He warned me about an imposter and murder. Then Ivar chased me into the tunnels. I wasn't anywhere near your bar."

"Yes, yes. My tunnels. The Rat made a new friend."

Dax let the fire in his eyes go and relaxed his muscles. "So, you're innocent? The assassin impersonated the coroner to get to you as a misdirect, then used her again since she knew where she could trap and kill me." He ran a hand through his sweat-drenched hair. "Fuck. I think it was your father's ghost that tried to warn me before I went into the morgue. Shit." He turned to Tomi. "Where's my car?"

"It's parked safely. Didn't want the cops getting ahold of it when they showed up to put out the fires and investigate the explosion at the morgue. Detective Ryan would drag you in for sure."

"Detective Randall Ryan?" Jamie shivered.

"Yeah?" Dax said.

"That guy is a fucking creep. Grossed me out."

Dax chuckled. "On that we can agree."

He looked at the faces of Jamie, The Rat, Boudreaux, and Tomi. It all made sense. The pieces fit.

Sighing, he straightened his spine and made eye contact with Jamie. "I'm sorry I misjudged you. And thank you for helping to save my life."

"I appreciate the apology. If I'd seen video of me planting a bomb, I might have blamed me, too. Helping out is the least I can do, after…you know."

"Good, good. All friends now," The Rat said happily then clapped a few times. "Now we go clean out my tunnels. The Rat has a plan. Then my rats want words with the bad one."

The last words held none of the previous good cheer and landed ominously. He didn't know what the assassin had done to The Rat and his rat friends, but they didn't seem in the forgiving mood. And neither was he.

FORTY

JAMIE

Jamie drifted to the back of their little group as they made their way through the tunnels. She just couldn't seem to escape them. But at least this time she had a heavily armed group of people around her, especially after they'd made a quick stop to pick up the weapons cache they'd brought down and left before finding Dax and freeing him.

Without knowing it, she'd made her way on to his shit list again. Though this time, she'd made it off pretty easily, all things considered. She shivered as the image of his baleful eyes flashed through her mind.

If she wasn't so damned tired and just done with everything, she might have broken and run. But having The Rat stand in her defense, as well as Boudreaux and Tomi, had done more to strengthen her will than just about anything. Having people stand up and defend her? It felt good. She didn't get that at home, and she'd lost it when Cory's mom had forcibly removed her son from Jamie's life.

She gripped the gris-gris Manman Delphine had given her. She wasn't sure how she really ended up here, stalking through a warren of underground tunnels. Red City's toxic corruption had reared its ugly head and destroyed her life, such as it was, and jumbled her in with this weirdest mix of humans and supernaturals. They were far from what people would call the pillars of society, but they seemed like genuinely good people. And that might have been the strangest thing of all.

Red City had set her adrift, and she'd washed up with others similarly touched. They weren't her friends, but still, they'd looked out for her and she'd been able to do the same for a few of them.

"Time to be stopping," The Rat said, keeping his voice low. "Rats have reported in."

She'd stopped paying attention to the little critters. She'd spent so much time with them over the last few days, they were a part of her background now. They seemed to be in constant motion, moving in and out of the group at will. The groups he'd sent ahead to scout must have returned.

"She is there, but busy. Busy, busy, busy. Packing. We must hurry. I'll send some rats to lead the other group to your point. They know her bombs. Pay attention."

"Latrell, you go with the girl," Boudreaux said. "Take TJ with you. Watch the rats, and don't get blown up."

"You don't survive this long being a bomb guy by being dumb. If you say trust the rats, I'll trust them if means not getting blown up." Latrell, a short, stocky Black man, ran a weapons check then cocked his assault rifle. "TJ, you bring up the rear. Jamie. You stick between us. You hear or smell something, you let us know ASAP. Don't be afraid to speak up. You know how to shoot?"

Dax snorted, crossing his arms over his chest.

"Yeah. A little." She smirked slightly unable to keep her face straight but kept it minimal to not annoy Dax.

Latrell dug into the bag where they'd carried the guns and pulled out a semi-automatic pistol. "Pull the slide to chamber a round. Here's the safety. Safety on. Safety off."

She cataloged everything he showed her. It was a little bit different than the revolver, but close enough.

"And make sure you know where you're pointing it before you squeeze one off. I don't want to accidentally take one in the back." He handed her the pistol. "The safety is engaged. You ready?"

She nodded, stashing the gun in her pocket. She hoped she didn't have to use it. A group of rats broke off from the larger group and headed down their tunnel, stopping a ways down before moving out of sight. Latrell followed them. TJ nodded at her and gestured with his head to follow. She moved in behind Latrell.

The weight of the gun in her pocket felt far heavier than its couple of pounds. In part, it felt nice to have a way to defend herself. However, the last time she'd used a gun, she'd put a bullet into the chest of an innocent man. But if all went to plan, she wouldn't be called on to use it.

The rats proved good leaders, taking them through the tunnels, never wavering on their choice of turns. The further they went, the closer they got to being done with this. She couldn't say she hoped Dax didn't kill the assassin. The assassin had killed her father and used it to get close to her. If she decided to tie up loose ends, Jamie was one of those loose ends.

But she'd seen enough death. Dax had brutally and efficiently killed every biker that had stood against him. She hoped that would be the last time she saw people being killed.

"Stop," Latrell said, holding a fist in the air. The rats had stopped moving, forming a line in front of him.

He handed his assault rifle back, and she took it without thinking. The cold metal and heavy weight felt ominous and full of deadly potential. Pulling out a small flashlight, Latrell squatted, running the beam along the floor.

"Ah. Trip wire." He ran the beam up the wall, stopping it about head height. Stepping closer but being careful not to get too close to the trip wire, he inspected the bomb.

If it was set at head height, the assassin wasn't interested in wounding. That would have killed them instantly. After seeing the results of one that nearly killed Dax, she couldn't look away from it. Her heart pounded, and her palms dampened with nervous sweat.

Latrell reached into a pocket on his belt and pulled out wire clippers. First, he clipped the trip wire, then he pulled down the bomb, opening up the casing. He moved the flashlight to his mouth, holding it with his lips as he inspected the explosive device. A couple more quick clips and he stuffed the device in a pocket, then holstered the wire clippers.

"You're just going to put that in your pocket?" She raised an eyebrow.

He shrugged. "It's deactivated. Plus I'm not going to leave it around where it can be used to hurt somebody." Then he grinned. "Also, free explosives. Always handy to have around."

She snorted and shook her head. Behind her, TJ chuckled.

"Well, thanks to our little furry friends, we can keep going." Latrell took back his gun and turned around.

The rats helped them find three more booby traps. Despite the fact that the rats had kept them safe and Latrell had easily diffused the bombs, it made her more and more anxious with each one they found. If there were this many, it seemed like they might miss one. She didn't know how Latrell could be this comfortable around the explosives, especially with a pocketful of them.

After the second one, they reverted to hand signals only so as not to make any more noise than they had to. She quickly picked up on what the signals meant, obeying his commands quickly.

On the last one, Latrell left his flashlight in its pocket. They could hear the rustling and banging of someone packing up. The same mumbling she'd heard when she and The Rat had found her the last time drifted to them, bouncing around on the hard concrete of the tunnels.

Latrell inched along the ground until he found the wire with his hands and cut it. She wondered if the assassin had changed the tension on her booby traps after the rats set off the other ones. If she had, it probably made the traps less sensitive to gentle touches like Latrell's experienced hands.

Now that they were near the chamber where the assassin had set up, they held back, keeping hidden around the corner and out of the entrance's line of sight. Except for Latrell. With the rats circling around him, he army-crawled forward inch by inch, feeling his way gently with his hands. He wasn't going to rely on the dim light spilling out of the chamber.

Their eyes were well adjusted to the almost dark conditions after spending what felt like hours underground, creeping their way to their rendezvous with revenge. The low-level flashlights had felt pitifully underpowered but had helped them without ruining their night vision or giving themselves away. The chamber would feel positively bright in comparison.

She heard the faint clip and twang of a wire being cut. So many bombs… She didn't want to go into that chamber. Her stomach gurgled. She wasn't hungry. She just didn't want to see her nerves round trip that burger and fries.

A couple minutes later, Latrell crawled around the bend until he was out of sight of the chamber, then stood up and walked back to them, taking a minute to stretch out his neck and back. "Nervous work," he whispered.

She hoped he'd gotten them all. She didn't want to be blown up, even a little bit. Looking back and forth to the clearly capable men who looked like they knew their way around their guns, she made a decision. She was probably more of a liability with the gun than an asset. Pulling it out of her pocket, she handed it to TJ since he was nearest. Then she held up a finger to indicate they should wait a minute.

Turning, she walked back a ways until she was out of their sight, then stripped down, neatly folding her clothes before changing into her wolf. She'd be an asset in a fight now—agile feet, strong muscles, and sharp teeth.

When she returned, both men nodded at her as they spread out the weapons and made sure they had the right ammunition. Once they were ready, Latrell returned to the ground and crawled forward. They gave him a couple minutes before following along, sticking close to the wall. Once they saw him, they stopped. They'd be able to see his signal.

Her jaw dropped open and her tongue lolled out as she panted nervously. She had chosen to do this. She was taking control of her situation. Willingly participating. Hoping it would calm her and stiffen her spine, she repeated the litany on a loop.

A couple quick flashes of low-level light from near Latrell's thigh caught her attention.

TJ leaned down near her head. "It's time."

FORTY-ONE

DAX

The Rat led them through the tunnels quickly until they had to slow down to disassemble the assassin's booby traps. The rats, who'd apparently seen their action firsthand, sniffed them out with extreme prejudice, letting Boudreaux's friend Sonny clear them. Once they reached the end of their journey, they waited in silence.

The Rat took point. He said he'd be able to tell when the rats who'd gone with Jamie, Latrell, and TJ were in place. In the meantime, the swarm of rats who'd come with them seethed around them. Dax had never seen them this agitated. Not even when The Rat had passed out and they'd blocked him from helping. Then, they'd been protective and cautious. Now, he'd say they were more angry and eager to do something about it. If such emotions could be found in a rat. Perhaps they were just reflecting their master's emotional state. All the normal silliness—he wasn't sure he had a better term for the man's general being—had evaporated after they'd split from the other team. He had a job to do and was all business.

After what seemed like forever, The Rat stood up and turned around, giving them an evil grin and a pair of thumbs up. That was

Dax's cue. Brushing off any lingering dust and debris from his clothing, he stood tall, ditching the usual slight stoop he had, and stepped into the middle of the tunnel and into the chamber where the assassin busily prepared to depart.

"Going somewhere?" He cast his voice loud enough so that it'd echo against the concrete. He allowed a bit of the otherworldly harmonics to enter his voice.

The assassin spun around. The face of Jamie stared back at him, though the eyes gave it away. For one so young, Jamie's eyes held a lot of world weariness, but it was still mixed with a bit of innocence and naivete. After the shock cleared, calculating annoyance dominated in the assassin. There was none of the youthful innocence Jamie possessed.

Dax casually strolled forward, his hands behind his back. "You can get rid of the facade. I know it's fake."

Her eyes flicked to the opposite side of the chamber, maybe hoping to beat a hasty retreat and draw him into foolishly pursuing her through her booby traps. A wolf stepped out of the dark entrance to the other tunnel. Her hackles raised as an ominous growl rolled out of her mouth, lips pulled back in an aggressive snarl.

"She doesn't appreciate you stealing her form," Dax said.

The assassin snatched a machine gun from where she was working, spinning toward the wolf. A second later, Latrell and TJ stepped from the tunnel, flanking Jamie on either side. Latrell sprayed a few rounds into the ceiling above the assassin, sending concrete dust showering onto her. Boudreaux and Sonny stepped out, also leveling their guns at her.

She took one of her hands away from the gun and slowly bent over, setting the gun down. "I hear bullets don't work on you, whatever you are." She stood up slowly, her hands visible. "Apparently bombs don't work either," she muttered.

He wasn't bulletproof. But Ivar must have passed that information along when he'd hired her for the job. He'd been shot multiple times—once in the chest—with magical bullets and lived. Ivar's brothers had sprayed bullets at Dax, and he'd had come out alive.

Having a false reputation for being immune to bullets might be useful.

It also made him wary. Boudreaux and his crew just wanted to burst in and fill her so full of lead they'd be able to use her as a pencil. "Nice and easy, lemon squeezy," The Rat had declared. Dax wasn't so sure. She was some kind of unknown supernatural. Who knew what her natural immunities were? She might need to be killed with silver. Or sanctified weapons. Or a magic spell.

All they knew was that she could assume the likenesses of other people, likely only by touch. And she left the victims alive. She might need the victim to be breathing to maintain the image and maybe the personality. But it was all speculation. None of them knew for sure — save for the assassin.

"It does seem to be that way." He stopped, his stance wide and his hands still behind his back.

"So, are you just going to have your goons fill me full of bullets?" Her eyes flicked around, assessing the situation.

Dax shook his head slowly. "No. I thought I might take a more personal approach."

"Hand to hand? You're a fool if you think bombs are my only skill. You don't get to be as experienced and well paid as I am by being a one-trick pony."

"Not going to try to bribe me? Offer me some of the money?"

She scoffed. "It's my money, and I earn it. Or I will in a few more minutes."

"No offers to sell out your employer? Brave woman."

A faint shrug shifted one shoulder. "Brave? Coward? I was paid to do a job, and I don't fail after I've accepted a contract."

"How much is my life worth? I hope you got a good fee, because I'm not exactly an easy bounty. The last people who tried to collect died quickly."

A smug smile spread over her face as she stared at him out of hooded eyes. "The money was good enough. So…are we going to do this? I mean, you've delivered yourself to me. Convenient. Thanks."

"Hand to hand. Choose your weapon. No guns or bombs. That'll just annoy me."

Narrowing her eyes, she slowly reached down behind the case she'd been packing and lifted something long and dark off the ground. Its end gleamed dully. A spear. In this day and age? He wondered if the blade was all steel or if it had anything special mixed in. If she worked for wolf shifters and hunted supernaturals for pay, it might be silver and have some sort of enchantments or divine consecrations on it. He'd have to be careful. He doubted any of those substances would do anything to him, but he couldn't sure about his human body.

She stepped into the middle of the chamber, the spear held casually in her hand.

Dax wasn't ready to reveal exactly what he was. That was an advantage he didn't want to give away quite yet. Reaching into the aether, he wrapped his hand around the smooth, worn wood of his scythe and pulled it into the world. The heavy weight felt reassuring in his hand.

The assassin laughed. "You're going to challenge me with that? I'm not a field of medieval wheat."

Narrowing his eyes, he focused on the spear. He squeezed his hand tightly around the scythe, pouring his intent into it. The two handles—one at the bottom and another in the middle—disappeared, as did the curve of the shaft.

His scythe felt a bit awkward without the bits that contributed to its function. But the straight shaft would allow him more flexibility of motion.

"I don't know if that'll help you," the assassin said, though their voice didn't sound as sure as it had a moment ago.

Whipping out a scythe as your melee weapon was one thing. But changing its physical features with merely a thought spoke to a deeper power the assassin was apparently not expecting. She spun the spear in her hand, adding her other hand to the shaft. She stalked forward, angling toward Dax's side.

Dax moved forward, shifting the other way. Keeping a passive face and his eyes focused on the assassin, he strolled casually, letting the now straight-handled scythe dangle casually from his hand, the butt of the shaft dragging along the concrete floor. He doubted he'd fool her into thinking he wasn't prepared, but maybe she was under-estimating his ability to fight with a polearm. He hoped he hadn't forgotten much. It had been a long time.

Dax stared down the assassin as he circled. "I hope they paid you enough to murder me. Doesn't seem you assessed the risks of the job offered. Can't spend money when you're dead. No matter how hard humans have tried to take their wealth with them, they move on and it stays."

"From what I've seen, you have very little to worry about taking to the next life."

While they did their pre battle banter and dance, he set aside a small piece of his awareness and let it reach out to see if there was anyone else nearing their location he had to worry about. All he found was the assassin's life thread, his associates, and his own, which, thanks to the circumstances, were closer than he'd like. The chamber was sizable compared to the tunnels, but this would be an interesting fight with long weapons.

He chuckled, pitching the hollow, spooky harmonics into it. "Pauper or prince, they all will be reaped. And it appears your time is about due."

"I'll give you marks for bravado and education. You're certainly one of the smarter sounding of my recent marks." Now that they were closer, no more than about fifteen feet apart, he noticed some of the other subtle and not-so-subtle differences between Jamie and the assassin, including body movements that spoke of skill, training, and experience. The young, inexperienced Jamie could claim none of those things.

She wore tight fitting dark attire—having ditched the clothes she'd stolen from Winnie—that helped her blend into the shadows of the dark cavern, though he wasn't sure what the material was since most such clothes tended toward shiny materials.

It was the slightest shift in her stance that warned him as she sprung at him faster than any human had a right to. Without so much as a grunt, she spun her spear around, bringing the bladed end along the ground and upward toward his body.

Shifting his feet, he arched his scythe around and knocked her spear high from the bottom, wood knocking into metal. Not deterred, she shifted to the left, bringing the spear back down at this head.

With a quick step to the right, he deflected it so it whiffed by his left side but didn't counter. Dropping onto her haunches, she whipped the blade horizontally at shin height. He took another side-step, and since it was the closest side to the ground, brought the head and curved blade of his scythe down.

The steel blade of her spear skittered across the cutting edge of his scythe, but instead of the rasp of steel on steel, the contact set up an otherworldly screech like the wail of a tortured soul.

She shuddered and danced back, bringing the bladed end of her spear up between them.

"You're not too bad," she said, resuming her earlier circling. "You might actually make me earn the money."

He chuckled, letting a bit of the hollow harmonics enter his voice. "I thought I was already doing that. You've already tried to kill me twice and failed."

"There's no accounting for luck." She shivered and gave a quick shrug. "I guess the third time will be the charm."

"You clearly didn't demand enough information from your employer about why they brought you in."

"He gave me enough, though he didn't elaborate on how you burned down their clubhouse. But then again, there's nothing much flammable around here." She shifted her stance and how she gripped her spear, reversing her circling.

This time, he laughed harder, letting his voice slip fully into that other form with its hollow raspiness and discordant harmonics. "The fire was an accident."

"Did you bring a whole crew with you?"

"I had a crew, but they stayed outside. I didn't need them for little thugs like those bikers."

She laughed. "I like your braggadocio. So, you want me to believe that you just walked in there and then walked out again, alive?"

"I kicked the shit out of and killed most of them first. But yeah, that's what happened." He gestured with the shaft of his scythe. "Are you tired of talking? Or are you not ready?"

"For what?"

"For me to collect your soul."

FORTY-TWO

DAX

The assassin started to laugh, but Dax cut her off, taking a step forward and spinning around. In mid-spin, he shucked off his human skin and slipped into his skeleton and robe. The lower half of his robe flared out around him as he spun, catching the air. Behind it, the blade of his scythe arced around at waist height.

Caught off guard, the assassin dropped to the ground on her belly and rolled into his attack, sliding under his blade. She kept on rolling until she was once again outside of his reach.

Continuing his spin, he stopped once he reacquired her in his vision. He barked out a laugh, and a shudder ran through her whole body. It had been a long time since he'd enjoyed the contest. Resting the shaft on his shoulder, he reached out his open hand, palm up. "I will make you an offer. Lead me to Ivar, and I'll make your death quick."

She stared at him, then slowly shook her head, pushing herself off the ground into a standing position. "No. I've been paid to do a job. If I quit before it's done, especially for this fee, no one will ever hire me again, and that's assuming they don't come looking for me.

And I never betray an employer. Thank you for the offer, but go fuck yourself."

He chuckled, bringing the scythe down to take a two-handed grip across his body, and ignited the fire in his eye sockets. "So be it."

He stalked forward, all business, and spun his scythe in a lazy circle. She dusted herself off with one hand, leaving swipes of grime across her black outfit.

This time, he didn't wait and take the defensive. One second, his scythe spun in its lazy circle like an idling plane's propeller. The next, he lunged forward, bringing the flat of the blade down in a hard, flat line toward her head.

Shoving her blade up, she ducked her head like a turtle and barely nudged the shaft aside in time to prevent being brained. She flicked the blade of her spear toward his face, but it was more a move to back him up.

He let the momentum of his weapon carry it around as he bent at the back to move out of range of her quick counter. Rotating with the weight of the heavy blade of his scythe, he took a step and swung the blade at shoulder height.

She squeaked and threw herself backward, landing on her back. Taking another step, he spun again and changed the trajectory of the blade so it rotated away from her then up before the arc hit its apogee and he could bring it down.

The blade sank into the concrete, narrowly missing her as she rolled away. He left the scythe's blade stuck in the floor and dropped and spun a low kick toward her legs. He wanted to catch her before she flipped back up, but narrowly missed. His momentum carried him away from her, so he rolled forward onto his shoulder to pop up out of range of the assassin and her weapon. But it also put him out of reach of his own as well.

She huffed, breathing heavily. "You appear to have lost your weapon." She moved forward menacingly.

Instead of saying something pithy, he just extended his arm and opened his hand. The scythe faded out and reappeared in his grip. With the scythe held vertically in his hand, he brought his hand across his body, swiping her lunged stab out of the way.

But instead of resetting to attack with his weapon, he turned into her spear, following his hand and scythe so he blocked the spear with his body. Another pivoting step brought him around along with the cocked fist wrapped around the shaft of his scythe as he smashed it into the side of her head. Bones cracked.

Groaning, she fell forward, stumbling. She planted the butt of her spear on the ground and used it to pull herself along and out of the way. With a grimace, he shook his hand. The hit had dislocated a finger. Reaching over with his other hand, he gripped it, careful not to let his scythe drop, and grunted as it snapped back into place. Wiggling his fingers, he set his feet and brought the scythe up. A bit unsteady on her feet, she shook her head, raising her spear in both hands to bring the blade to bear.

Her eyes looked a bit unsteady as they failed to track him properly.

"This isn't going the way you wanted, is it?"

"No." A bit of her early confidence had dropped out of her voice.

Bringing a foot around to draw a line in the concrete, he dropped low into a balanced combat stance, his scythe held behind him, ready to swing. Extending his free hand, he curled his fingers, wanting her to engage.

A quick shake of her head, and she lunged forward, a growl tripping out of her throat. Instead of bringing the shaft of the scythe around to block her, he pivoted backward until he was behind his weapon. With a flick of his wrist, he sent her spear sliding past him. She pushed through, ducking under the blade of the scythe, and emerged behind him.

Skidding to a stop, she whipped the spear around in a horizontal arc at chest level. He brought the blade of his scythe around in a vertical spin, catching the spear's shaft before it could pierce his chest. Following through, she spun around into him, choking up on the shaft of the spear and brought it around again, but a last-minute shift in her grip brought it down across the front of his left shin.

He hissed, pushing off his right leg to hop one-legged away from her, and propped himself up with the wooden shaft and his good leg. Instead of backing up to reassess, she dove onto her shoulder and rolled over it, coming up in a crouch. With a quick extension of her arms, she sent the tip of the spear shooting toward his unwounded right leg.

Before he could take a second wound or think about the consequences of his reaction, he kicked out with the wounded left leg and caught the metal shaft of her spear just behind the blade right across the wound she'd just inflicted.

He grunted as he followed through with the kick, and pain exploded up his leg. The unexpected move threw her off balance. So instead of trying to keep up the attack, she righted herself and slipped away from him.

Narrowing his vision, he stepped backward, inhaling sharply as his left leg took some of his weight.

"So, you can be wounded," she said, panting.

"This isn't the first time you succeeded at doing that." He took another step backward, his left leg nearly buckling.

"I don't suppose you'd fall on my spear so we can get this over with?"

He shook his head, the hood of his robe twitching from side to side. "No."

She exhaled, wiping sweat from her forehead. "Then we continue."

Only letting his left bear a small amount of his weight, he balanced on his right leg and brought his weapon around into a defensive position. He just needed to buy himself some time. While he could be wounded, he also healed a more quickly than the average human. Already he could feel some of the pain diminish, though not as quickly as it normally would. The wound and the slower than normal recovery highlighted his waning energy. After hours buried alive and shielding himself, he was nearing the point of running on empty.

But she might have assumed he'd have some extra abilities and attacked. Instead of trying to sneak attacks through his defense, she shifted to a more brutal strategy, raining down hard slashes at his head, middle, and lower extremities. She drove him black, wobbly step after step.

Thwack. Grunt. Yelp.

Dax's responses were silent as he did his best to knock aside her attacks or shift his body away from the business end of her spear. Finally, she overextended herself.

He pivoted on his good foot, bringing the shaft around in a blurring spin, and knocked the spear aside. He landed a hard hit with the butt of the shaft into the meaty part of her left shoulder. She yelped and staggered out of the way of his follow-up strike with the blade.

Shifting around, he slid his body into a ready pose reminiscent of kung fu. A low growl fell from the assassin's lips as she reset. He didn't have to wait long to see which strategy she'd take—finesse or muscle or perhaps some other one she'd not deployed yet.

She adjusted her grip so one hand was at the very end of the shaft away from the blade with the other not far above the other hand. Her stance put the maximum amount of spear between her and her target as she brought it around in a sweeping rainbow at his head.

It was a style he'd seen many times, though it would work better if the shaft were made from bendy bamboo instead of the rigid metal composite it was constructed of. Flowing like water, he eased his position backward, waiting for the inevitable change of direction the style favored.

Fortunately, he'd slid into a flexible stance that would allow him to move into the several counters. Block. Shift forward. Pivot away from and upward strike. Wait. Nudge the spear along with the blunt side of his blade.

There.

He moved into the offensive. Grinding his teeth against the pain of his wounded shin, he worked through a series of moves that kept his body moving into a variety of position, making his attacks with his heavy-bladed scythe more unpredictable. With each attack she blocked, he pushed her further back, each of her counters coming just barely in time and nearly out of position.

On his next move, he planted on his left leg but it gave out, and the swipe with his blade clumsily fell out of position, allowing the assassin to regain the offensive.

She brought the blade around hard in a slash at his head. He bent backward and squatted, hoping his legs held him. Raising his blade, he caught her shaft along the wood of his scythe, yanking his hand out of the way as the metal dragged along the wood.

But as her spear neared the crook of this blade, he let the scythe blade shift back into the aether and reappear. Except instead of being attached at its normal ninety-degree angle, it had shifted to the top of the shaft like a hooked bill polearm.

She'd expected her spear to catch at the crook and had planned accordingly, but without the blade there, her momentum carried it and her off balance.

Dropping the blade of his scythe, he yanked it through in a brutal slash at her midsection. It caught, dragging through cloth and flesh. She screamed. With a last flick, he finished his cut and pivoted away from her on his good right leg.

She'd fallen to her knees, her spear forgotten next to her as she tried to hold her intestines in. She gasped in ragged pants, her white face glistening in sweat and tears. She'd paled so much that she nearly glowed in the dim light of the chamber. The false face, Jamie's face, fell from her and her features shifted to that of a white woman who'd blend into any crowd, unnoticed.

At some point, her knit cap had come off. She had short brown hair in a pixie cut.

"P-pl-please make it quick," she panted out.

"I will." He readied his weapon. "But answer me this first—"

"I—" she interrupted.

"I know you won't reveal your employer's whereabouts. I won't ask. But how many of the murder victims in that morgue you blew up did you put in there?"

She looked down, a stream of spittle falling from her lips. "More than I can easily count.

"Do you know what those bullets would do to their victims?"

She nodded faintly.

Gritting his teeth, the flames in his eyes flared brighter, his anger finding new depths to plumb. So much pain and misery. Souls trapped. Subject to unending terror and agony. A complete disruption of the natural order of life and death. He raised the scythe.

"Wait." She looked up at him, fear in her eyes. "Where will you send my soul?"

"I won't send your soul anywhere. Someone else will be along to collect it." He scoffed. "Maybe."

She nodded weakly, her head drooping onto her chest. "Where did you learn to fight like that?"

"I've reaped some of the finest warriors this world has produced." He took the flat of his scythe's blade and placed it under her chin, lifting it up so he could stare her in the eyes. "Not all of them wanted to come quietly."

He lowered the blunt edge of the blade just enough to rest against her clavicles and pushed. A gurgling scream erupted from her mouth as she flopped over backward. He turned around and limped away. Death was a mercy. But some didn't deserve easy mercies.

"Mr. The Rat. She's all yours."

"Wait…" She let go of a weak, gurgling cough. "You said it… would be quick."

"It will be. On a universal time scale, it'll be infinitesimal."

The Rat cackled his high-pitched laugh. "Go, my pretties! Vengeance is yours."

As Dax walked toward the exit to the chamber, hundreds and thousands of rats streamed by him, squeaking enthusiastically. A moment later, bloody screams reverberated off the concrete.

FORTY-THREE

JAMIE

Jamie watched in horror as Dax walked away, leaving the woman grievously wounded. Rats scurried around her legs to join with the mob flooding in from the other side. Her eyes wide and mouth open in horror, she backed away, bumping into rats as they ran by and under her. As soon as the way was clear, she spun around and dashed into the safety of the tunnel so she didn't have to watch.

But she couldn't escape the screams.

She stopped as her stomach rebelled against her. As soon as she finished, she ran to her clothes and shifted back to her human form. Human ears, even wolf enhanced, weren't as good as her wolf ones. As the screams faded, she'd hear even less of them. Desperately, she pulled her clothes on and then dashed away.

"Jamie, stop! You'll get lost," called one of the men. She couldn't tell which one through the echoes and unfamiliarity. But her body forced her to stop as she bent over and dry heaved.

A few moments later, TJ and Latrell stopped a ways from her, their flashlights sweeping over the tunnel while avoiding her. She appreciated the thoughtfulness of not highlighting her loss of control.

"Fuck. We can't go anywhere. We should have marked our trail. All the rats are…busy," Latrell said.

As if to counter his statement, one large rat bumped into her foot and squeaked at her. The screaming had stopped. He put his front paws on her leg and squeaked again.

Sonny chuckled, though it sounded forced. "Looks like you have a friend there."

The rat returned all its feet to the ground and walked away, stopping to look back at them.

"I guess we follow." Latrell moved to follow the rat.

Once he and TJ passed, she tucked in behind. Her mouth tasted like of bile and acid. "Can I have some water, please?"

"Sure. Should have thought of that myself." TJ pulled off his backpack and grabbed a plastic bottle of water for her.

She opened it and rinsed her mouth out, being careful not to guzzle it. She didn't want to throw it up, too. Taking a cue from her, they pulled out their own bottles. Once they were ready, they followed their guide toward the split where they met up with the rest of their friends.

Dax had returned to his human form, though it was no less intimidating at this point. There was no amount of money or pain someone could promise and threaten that would ever make her go after him or challenge him. Her life was hard, but she didn't want to end that way. She shivered, her stomach gurgling again.

She forced the thoughts out of her head, though she couldn't quite get the screams out of her ears. Even though the woman was no doubt dead, Jamie could still hear the fear and pain in her agony filled yelps.

The group formed up in silence. There wasn't enough gallows humor in the world to mitigate what she'd just seen. She should have just gone home when they suggested it. They didn't need her, but she'd gone out of a sense of duty and for the need to make her own decisions and fight back. Now she'd have to live with that.

Through the lack of conversation, only the occasional scuffs of their feet raised a noise. The few rats who'd come with them as escorts didn't even squeak. The silence felt oppressive and slowed the journey back, at least in her head.

She sighed in relief. Ahead, the light of day announced their departure from The Rat's domain. Boudreaux's friends proceeded toward the light, saying their goodbyes as they walked away. Boudreaux wanted to check on his girlfriend. The rats opened a corridor for them to leave through.

She twitched when the weight of something tugged on her pants as it crawled up her leg and then her back, finally settling on her shoulder. It snuffled her hair away from her ear then started squeaking at her. She wasn't sure what to do, so she stood still.

The Rat chuckled. "No, my little friend, she doesn't speak ratty rat talk." He paused as it shifted its attention to him. "No. No lessons for rat talk. Public schools are in decline." He shook his head, laughing.

In spite of herself, a smile spread across her face, tugging at muscles she usually didn't use. Reaching up, she scratched its ears and around its neck. It leaned into her fingers.

"Magic fingers. Happy rat. Friend rat." The Rat stepped forward and carefully removed the rat from her shoulder, holding it up so he looked it directly in the face. It was the same rat that had led them back to their meeting point.

Dax held out his hand to The Rat. "Thank you for your help. I appreciate it."

The Rat bowed his head respectfully. "You found your assassin. I cleaned out my tunnels. Revenge for lost friends for my rats. Justice." He sounded subdued compared to his normal tone and cadence.

"Justice?" Tomi scoffed.

"She received more justice than she deserved." Dax turned to his friend. "Her spirit will go somewhere. It won't be tethered to a body to go insane like all the victims she put in that morgue for money. You don't know because you're young. You're all youth and life. Speak to Manman Delphine about what happens to spirits who aren't allowed to move on."

Tomi nodded thoughtfully. "I'm tired. I just want to crawl into bed."

"As am I, my friend." Dax ran a hand through his sweaty hair. "Can someone give Jamie a phone? Mine's fucked. Her mom can pick her up at the bar."

She didn't know if Dax's explanation made sense to her, but the woman had done something more than just kill people, apparently. It didn't make Dax any less scary. His justice was too rich for her blood. If she could work it, she'd never see him again once she got home.

She dialed her mom's cell number. "Hi, mom. I'm alive. Come pick me up at that bar. Dax's bar. The one from last time."

She handed the phone back to The Rat and stepped into his arms, hugging him. He froze, then patted her back awkwardly.

"Thank you for saving me." He'd treated her with genuine kindness. She wished she could do more than say thanks, but she didn't even own the clothes on her back.

"Kind girl. Friend of mine. Friend of rats. Always welcome." He stepped back, the dim light revealing bright pink cheeks.

Dax reached out his hand and shook The Rat's. "I'll let Boudreaux coordinate it, but I'll have a proper gift basket sent for you and your little friends. I owe you."

"No, no, no." The Rat waved his hands horizontally, palms pointing down. "No debts. Paid back. No debts."

She couldn't blame him. Dax was not an entity you wanted to owe anything to. Too scary. Too comic horror.

"Alright, I'm still sending gifts," Dax replied.

"Tasty gifts?"

"The tastiest."

FORTY-FOUR

DAX

Jamie's mother hadn't even really said much when she picked her daughter up. At least that they could hear through the sobbing. It didn't take long for her to usher her daughter back to the car. After that, Dax drove his new car home, parked it in the garage, and passed out in his bed despite the kitten bouncing all over him. He and Tomi would celebrate surviving another day.

After waking up and feeling much better, he rolled down to the bar to hang out with the crew.

"Are you sure you should be in here tonight, boss?" Tomi asked, swinging around on his stool with a can of Pabst in his hand. "I mean. You know, everything?"

Shrugging, Dax pulled up a barstool near the wall and sat next to his friend. "I'm feeling fine, and I want to drink with my friend."

"Hey, Dax." Geoffrey, in his usual suit, raised his dram of whiskey in greeting.

"What you drinking tonight, Geoffrey?"

"A little Dickel Bottled in Bond."

"Suzie, I got Geoffrey's next one." He was feeling generous, and Geoffrey had proven to be a loyal new customer, spending a good amount of money on their higher end whiskey collection—especially after all the trouble lately.

Suzie nodded, giving him a sarcastic salute. "You got it, Dax."

"Thanks, man!" Geoffrey smiled and nodded.

"Thanks for coming in after…" Dax gestured around.

Geoffrey gave a one-shouldered shrug. "It's my watering hole, and it'll take more than a little noise to drive me off."

Suzie snorted. "Noise?"

"I've heard worse." Geoffrey returned to his whiskey, sliding the empty glass across to Suzie for a refill.

Dax swung around at the sound of the front door opening. Minh stopped, letting the door swing shut behind her. Tomi waved her over, gesturing toward the empty stool on the other side of him.

"Hey, Tomi. Dax." She sounded subdued as she stood next to the stool.

"What brings you in tonight?" Tomi asked. "Not sure I've seen you come in for a drink."

She shrugged. "Just thought I'd stop in and officially thank you both. For… You know."

Tomi nodded, the corner of his mouth quirking up. Tomi and Dax had busted her out of the cage she'd been kept in at The Collector's. Neither of them had any idea what kind of supernatural she might be. She and her father Thuc mostly kept to themselves, except when there were neighborhood business functions.

"Minh"—Tomi gestured toward the bartender—"this is my cousin Little Suzie. First round is on me."

"Gin and tonic?" Minh said, pulling herself up onto the barstool next to Tomi.

Suzie raised a skeptical eyebrow. "Well gin?"

"I wouldn't recommend it the well gin. It's rotgut. Order one of the good brands," Tomi said quietly.

"Sapphire, if that's OK?" Minh said hesitantly.

Tomi nodded to confirm the order with Suzie.

After Suzie set down Mihn's drink, she rested her elbows on her side of the bar across from Dax. "What about you? A Rainier?" She gave the beer's name a silly French pronunciation—rahn-ee-air.

Dax snorted and nodded. He liked Tomi's cousin. She'd been a great addition to the team. Her winning personality and skills behind the bar had gone a long way to bringing the customers back in after the various incidents had driven off some of their business. Next to him, Tomi slipped into charming mode as he chatted up Minh.

When he lifted his beer to his lips but found it empty, he shoved it across the bar. The crack of the tab on a fresh can alerted him to the replacement Suzie already had for him. She pushed it across the bar, but stopped halfway, her hand still wrapped around it. "Holy fuck…"

A moment later, the Scorpions's "Still Lovin' You" came on over the jukebox.

"What the fuck?" Tomi said, swiveling around on his stool to face the jukebox. "We don't have the Scorpions in our juke… Damn…"

"Right?" Suzie said.

Curious what had his friends' attention and about the random appearance of a CD he and Tomi had intentionally not put in the jukebox, he pushed around from the bar. A shorter woman with wild black curly hair that would look at home on the lead singer of a hair metal band stood facing the jukebox, scrolling through the other selections. She had a short black leather jacket that rode up over the waist band of her black leather pants to reveal pale white skin.

The leather pants hugged the generous curves of her hips and ass —hips and ass that looked familiar to him for some reason. He let his eyes drift down to her shapely calves and the short black ankle boots she wore.

"That's a lot of well-fitting black leather," Suzie said quietly.

Geoffrey, who nothing seemed to bother, finally swung around to see what all the fuss was about. He nodded his head, making an appreciative expression and downing the last of his whiskey before swinging back to order another round.

Minh cleared her throat, and Tomi turned around.

"Another G&T?"

"Sure," Minh replied.

Tomi waved to catch Suzie's attention.

Dax, wracking his brain, tried to figure out why the woman

looked vaguely familiar. She didn't look like any of the regulars. He hated that the human flesh he'd had to take to escape the wrath of the psychopomps who'd teamed up against him had so many limits. A lot of his previous experiences and memories just wouldn't fit in the human brain. Though, he could access the full memories of the brain in his body and what the man whose soul he'd pushed out of it had stored there. Maybe she was one of his acquaintances.

A bit of adrenaline seeped into his veins. If she were one of his acquaintances, that could mean trouble. Was she here to take another shot at him? Scouting him out for the biker gang? But why the Scorpions…

Careful to split his attention between keeping an eye on her as she browsed the jukebox and looking into his human brain to see if she was one of his memories, he braced his feet on the metal hoop running around the legs of the barstool in case he had to leap into action. But he couldn't find her in the old memories.

Furrowing his brow and narrowing his eyes, he stared at her, wondering why he couldn't scratch the itch of recognition.

"Dax," Suzie hissed quietly, "you're staring."

He swallowed and gave his head a little shake. Swinging around to face Suzie, he grabbed the beer that was still clasped in her hand. "Thanks."

Suzie nodded, her eyes flicking back to the woman at the jukebox before she too forced her eyes away. She shook her head, a dreamy smirk spreading across her face. "Not that I wasn't doin' the same."

She'd said it so quietly that he wasn't sure if he was supposed to have heard it. Chuckling, he winked at her. She rolled her eyes at herself and looked a bit embarrassed that she'd been overheard.

Dax brought his beer to his lips and took a drink, trying to keep from turning around to see if he could figure out who she was. Coughing at the liquid going down the wrong pipe, he wiped at his chin as a bit of beer dribbled down his chin.

With laughter in her eyes, Suzie handed him a bar towel. "Better keep your mind on your beer, or you'll take care of yourself for your" —her eyes flicked to Geoffrey—"unwanted friends."

"Right," Dax said, lifting the can and giving it a little shake before taking a sip. "See. I can drink without issues."

"Just lookin' out for you, Dax."

"Well"—Geoffrey put down the last of his whiskey and pushed it toward Suzie—"I think I'm going to head home. See ya later, Suzie, Dax, Tomi."

"Later, Geoffrey." Suzie cleared the empty glass.

Dax waved to Geoffrey as he slid off his stool and headed to the exit. Tomi gave a brief wave of his own but didn't take his focus off Minh.

Dax looked around at the whiskey bottles, his eyes settling on a one that was mostly full. "I'll take a glass of the new Scotch we just got in. I'm feeling like celebrating. Tomi?"

"Hell yeah. I'll take one of those, too, Suz."

"Sure thing." Suzie grabbed a couple of drams.

"So, Dax, is it?" said a warm, sultry voice with just a hint of a rasp that only served to add character to the voice. He thought he heard a bit of Irish lilt in it as well.

He turned his head to see the woman in black leather had taken the seat Geoffrey'd vacated. She faced toward the backbar, so he couldn't really see her face around the wild thatch of teased curls.

"Wha-what will you have?" Suzie's voice squeaked before she caught herself.

"Whiskey."

Suzie gestured toward the shelves loaded with bottles of whiskey. "Which one? We have a fine selection of Bourbons, Irish whiskeys, Scotch, Japan—"

"Irish, your finest," she barked out. "Dax here will pay for it."

He perked up, spinning around to face the woman, and lifted an eyebrow in curious annoyance. "He will, will he?"

"He will." She turned on the stool.

The blood drained from his face. "You…"

FORTY-FIVE

DAX

At the sound of venom in Dax's voice, Tomi swiveled around on his stool. "What's going on, Dax?"

The lights flickered, and the bottles rattled on the shelves.

"Earthquake?" someone sitting at one of the tables asked.

A lightbulb burst, spraying glass and sparks.

A hand settled on his shoulder from behind.

"Dax, you doing this?" Tomi whispered. "If so, turn it off." He squeezed harder. "Before we chase off the regulars again. Now, dude."

Dax inhaled a shuddering breath and forced his shoulders down, letting go of the power he'd unconsciously grabbed hold of. He remembered where he knew the essence of those hips from. The music and the choice of faces brought it all into focus. "What are you doing in my bar?"

"Getting a whiskey." She flicked an annoyed glance toward Suzie. "If your barmaid will ever get around to it."

"Dax?" Suzie asked uncertainly. She'd pushed away from the bar and had her back pressed up against the back counter.

Not taking his eyes off the woman in front of him, Dax gave a curt nod. The tinkle of broken glass was followed by Suzie cursing. A minute later, a glass of whiskey was slid across the bar toward the woman.

"Your whiskey, ma'am." Suzie backed away.

"Thank you," the woman rasped, a hint of creepy harmonics entering her voice.

"Dax, I think you're going to need to take this to the back room," Tomi hissed into his ear. "We just got out of trouble. We don't need to look for more."

Clenching his jaw, Dax grabbed his Scotch and gestured roughly toward the back of the bar with his head. "Follow me."

He didn't wait for acknowledgement before he slid off his barstool and stalked toward the back. Fortunately, the door to the tearoom was unlocked, or he might have yanked the lock out of the jamb. As is, the door slid open violently, slamming hard into the end of its track before bouncing and rolling back out a few inches. A moment later, someone slid it shut. He had no idea if she'd followed him or if it was Tomi coming to check on him or referee.

"You've done well for yourself," she said.

He spun around. "I'll repeat. What are you doing in my fucking bar, Morrigan?"

"Is that the way to greet an old friend?" She quirked up an eyebrow flirtatiously. "Or an old lover?"

His chest clenched, tightening and forcing his breath to shallow. "It's more greeting than a betrayer deserves."

She shook her head, a bit of red light slipping into her eyes, but she quickly got it under control. After his exile, he'd done a lot to forget all the times they'd spent together. The human brain had helped. He'd once found her pale face beautiful and her low, slightly raspy voice sultry. Now, he had to do everything to keep from slipping into his other form and pulling out his scythe from the aether.

Breaking eye contact with him, her face returned to a neutral mask as she looked around the room. "You always were fond of tea. It's why you always wanted to go reaping in Asia."

His eyebrows flashed up slightly before quickly returning to his hurt and enraged furrow. Tea had always been a lovely human ritual, one he thought he'd picked up to fit in and feel linked to the human experience. It must have been one of things he forced out of his mind or the human brain had taken from him.

"You still haven't answered my question," Dax said, his voice curt and the words clipped.

She sighed. "Can't I visit an old friend?"

"We aren't friends, not anymore. Not after what you did to me."

"Are you going to just stare daggers at me, or can we at least be civilized and share a whiskey together? Or a whisky, in your case." She slipped into a Scottish accent for the last line.

Stalking forward, he hooked one leg of the bench with his foot and pulled it out roughly. The wood groaned and squealed as it skittered over the concrete of the floor. Sinking onto the bench, he gestured to the other side of the long table.

Morrigan strolled across the room from where she'd stopped just inside the door, her hips swaying with the slow walk. Each strike of her heel and sole sounding soft and sharp in the small space. Without bending over to move it, the bench moved away from the table without making a noise.

Gracefully, she lifted one leg over the bench, then the other, as she settled onto it across from him. "I'd ask for you to make me a pot of tea if I didn't think you'd give me the dregs of your collection."

The corner of his lip lifted in a half sneer. "There are no dregs in my collection." He grinned maliciously. "I'll make you a pot of coffee though."

"Ha! At least you have some fire in your belly." She lifted her dram of Irish whiskey and ran it under her nose. Her eyebrows lifted, and she hummed appreciatively. "Your bar wench poured me something worthy." She took a deep drink, sighing happily after she swallowed.

"She's not a bar wench. They're called bartenders."

Morrigan shrugged. "She's a woman who tends bar. Bar wench."

"Bartender," Dax gritted out between clenched teeth.

She huffed. "Fine. Bartender."

He relaxed almost imperceptibly. A little part of him wanted to chuckle, but he kept it tightly under wraps. Suzie would have probably gotten a kick out of letting the beautiful, leather-clad woman call her a bar wench, though she'd have curb-stomped him or just about anyone else who tried it.

"Would it help if I said I was sorry for the way things went down?" Her voice had softened and the otherworldly harmonics had disappeared.

He shook his head slowly. "No. It won't help."

"Well, I am." She sighed, taking another sip of her whiskey.

"What am I supposed to do with your sorry?" He set his glass of Scotch on the table and gestured around him with both arms. "This is where it got me. I run a dive bar that's barely making ends meet. I have a shitty apartment in a cinderblock building." His voice began to rise again. "And someone is fucking trying to kill me. I've been blown up twice this week alone." He thrust two fingers at her. "And they almost succeeded. This is where your betrayal led me."

Shaking her head, her curls exaggerating the gesture, she huffed and raised her glass to her lips but stopped short. "You're alive. You have a friend. Maybe more."

"I'm surviving."

"Yes, you are," she said firmly. She lifted the glass the last couple of inches to her lips. "You have good whiskey. That's new."

"Even old entities can learn new tricks." He leaned back, rolling his head on his neck to try to loosen it up. "You still haven't answered my question."

"I came to warn you. Your actions here aren't going unnoticed."

"Do you think I don't know that? You're not the first... psychopomp to warn me."

"Oh?" A thick black eyebrow lifted slowly. "Who?"

Dax snorted. "Do you think I'm so naïve as to trust you with any information after you fucking betrayed me!"

She stood up violently, the bench shooting out behind her and tipping over with a loud thump. "I didn't..." She clenched her fists on the table as she leaned over. "Damnit. I didn't betray you."

The bench shot out from under him as he lurched to his feet. Placing his hands on the table, the glasses rattled but didn't tip. "You sold me out to those who'd conspired to steal my power. To steal my essence. What else would you call it? A favor for a friend? I won't make the mistake of trusting you again. Not after what you did to me. Not after you betrayed all the trust I had in you."

"Fuck you." She pushed off the table and turned her back to him.

"That's all you have to say?" He leaned further over the table. "Traitor."

She spun around faster than his unprepared human eyes could track and delivered a brutal backhanded slap right across his cheek. He pulled back, his legs tangling in the bench. Flailing his arms, he tipped over backward, landing on his butt, his head hitting the front wall of the bar. Stars exploded in his vision briefly. Groaning, he shook his head and tried to clear it.

The door slid open and Tomi poked his head in. "What the fuck? You OK, Dax?"

Growling, Dax disentangled himself from the bench and rolled onto his hands and knees to push himself up. "I'm fine."

Tomi glanced toward Morrigan. She stood, her arms crossed, an amused smirk on her face.

"Do you, uh, need some help?"

"No, Tomi. There's nothing you can do. But thank you."

"OK…" Tomi reached over to pull the door closed.

Dax held up a hand. "Wait. Open the jukebox when you go back to the bar and destroy the Scorpions CD."

A grin spread across Tomi's face. "With pleasure." He pulled the door shut, a faint chuckle fading into the distance the only sign he'd been there.

Brushing off his hands, he bent over and righted the bench. "I think you've overstayed your welcome."

"If this is how you make someone welcome, I think you could use a refresher on the rules of hospitality." She unfolded her hands and squeezed the bridge of her nose, shaking her head. "Damn you… Dax? What kind of name is that anyway? Never mind. It doesn't matter." She paused, exhaling some tension. "I didn't betray you. Not in the way you think."

Dax sneered, his mouth opening to counter the point.

"Damnit, let me finish what I'm saying, then I'll go. I didn't betray you to take your power. I did it to save you from being obliterated." She let go of her nose and paced the length of the table. "That's what they wanted. Complete and total destruction. No exile. Just nothingness. I did what I had to do to prevent that from happening."

"Why should I believe anything from you? Huh?" He sighed heavily, his shoulders slumping. "I trusted you, and you sold me to my enemies, whatever your motives were. That's the result."

Morrigan stopped pacing, angry red filling her dark eyes. But they contrasted with the soft, sad expression he'd never seen before. Not on the Battle Crow's face. She nodded curtly once. "Stop messing around at the morgue. Your little escape the other day is drawing angry attention from those who wanted your oblivion. Hate me or not. I don't care. Just knock it off. I don't want to see your destruction."

He stared blankly at her, the muscles in his cheek flexing as he clenched his jaw. He didn't trust himself to open his mouth. Instead, he opted for a low boil kept under a lid.

Her shoulders slumped and a frown spread across her face. "Well, I've delivered my warning. Do with it what you will."

She held his gaze for a moment, then melted in midair, turning into a big black crow, the red of her eyes still burning bright. The sliding door opened harshly as she flew out. A moment later, the side door leading to the alley slammed open, banging into the wall. He cringed. She'd broken the hinge that kept the door from opening that far.

He wasn't sure how long he stared out the door, but his jaw was growing tired from the clenching and grinding. Letting out a long, rough sigh, he grabbed the Scotch off the table and slammed it down, wincing at the peaty smoke and burn of cask strength alcohol.

He'd just set the water behind the bar to boil when Tomi slipped into the room, closing the door behind him.

"I'll fix the door tomorrow. It still closes and locks."

Dax scoffed. "We're lucky she left it in the frame."

"What did you do to piss her off so hard?" Tomi picked up the bench Morrigan had tipped over, then sat on it. "She left most of her whiskey." He picked it up and tossed it back. "Damn. That's a shame. It's good stuff."

Dax nodded. "We got a bit distracted."

"We heard."

He hung his head. "Do we have any customers left?"

"I turned up the jukebox. You could only hear if you were sitting at the bar, and it was just me and Suz."

"Minh head out?"

Tomi nodded. "Yeah. Finished her drink and bid me farewell." He had a slight smile on his face. "So, who the fuck was that?"

Dax shook his head.

"You called her what? Morgan? She was hot as fuck, but a bit scary. A bit off, too. I thought Suzie was going to faint or break out into giggles. I could almost see her blushing. And that's a neat trick with dark skin like we have."

Dax snorted, appreciating his friend's attempt to bring some levity to the situation. "I'd rather not talk about it."

"Ah. Ex?"

Dax drew in a deep breath through his nose and released it out through his nostrils with a bit of a groan added in. "Something like that."

"Damn, dude. I didn't think you had that in you. I mean"—he rolled his hand to convey some silent meaning—"you know. You are who you are."

Dax nodded. He did know who he was. And that was someone who'd stepped outside his normal role and daily routine to extend a deeper level of trust to someone who'd taken that trust—and all that he'd attached to it—and betrayed him, selling him out to those who'd sought his downfall.

He was used to being feared. But his neutrality and steadfast attention to his duty had left him untouched.

Until it didn't.

And she'd directly contributed to his exile when she'd professed to be his most steadfast of allies and…companions. And now because of her, the dead weren't receiving the succor they deserved. If Winnie's morgue was inundated with the spirits of the dead, how many others were suffering a similar problem? What about the battlefields of the world?

Though the earth was experiencing more peace than it ever had in its history, there were still hot spots generating plenty of dead. Were they too spectral wastelands? The psychopomps had wanted to harvest the dead for their own purposes. But he wondered why they weren't.

He tried to push those thoughts away. The dysfunctions of the gods the humans had created in their need for explanations and order weren't his to worry about anymore. They'd made that more than clear when they'd forced him to take the body of a human if he wanted to continue to exist.

"Where'd you go, boss?"

Dax's brow furrowed. "What?"

"I know that look. You were doing a deep dive in your psyche. Or wherever it is you go when you're thinking about your past."

"You know what, Tomi. I think I'd rather you didn't call me 'boss' anymore."

It was Tomi's turn to furrow his brow and look confused. "Why? I always have."

"That's when I was the guy with the briefcase full of money and a surprisingly robust fake ID. We own this building fifty-fifty. Your mama's about to open a business we all own and are equal partners in. I'm not exactly your boss anymore."

"Business partners?" Tomi raised an eyebrow.

"Friends."

"Friends?"

Dax nodded once. "Friends.

"Alright, Dax. Though it's habit at this point, but I'll do my best to drop it. For what it's worth, I never really meant it in a boss-employee sort of way." He shrugged.

"I know, but I think the word has worn out its usefulness between us. We've gone beyond it, my friend."

Tomi smiled goofily. "We have."

Dax sighed, looking at his watch. "I'm going to go home. If I stay here, I'll get blackout drunk, and neither of us needs that. We'll celebrate soon."

Tomi leaned an elbow to the table. "Dax. If we're friends, you can tell me about that woman and what happened. Bending ears is what friends are for."

"And I will, but not today. I need to let the scab harden first. Then we'll talk."

"Until then, Dax. See you tomorrow."

EPILOGUE

DAX

The bar smelled like the spice and aromas of New Orleans cuisine. Today had been the grand opening of Mama Adele's. Tomi's mother had been doing takeaway business while they waited for the last of their licenses so they could do dine-in service, and they'd finally come.

Dax, who could sling booze, had volunteered to cover the bar while Suzie and Tomi waited tables around the corner. They were helping out until Adele could hire some of her own people. He just wasn't qualified for that task, though Mama Adele promised to train him up on the less busy days so he could chip in when needed. The full tables and the steady stream of food coming into the bar hinted at a bright future for the little restaurant. It had certainly helped bring back some regulars to the bar who wanted food with their booze but didn't want to bother going to a restaurant first.

All in all, things were looking up.

Though he couldn't shake the funk of having seen the Morrigan again for the first time in a while. Not since he'd been exiled to live as a human, thanks in part to her actions.

After the raw pain and anger of seeing her transformed into a dull ache, he was finally able to give her words some thought.

Maybe she had saved him from a worse fate. And if her words could be trusted, that fate might still be hanging out there if he wasn't careful. But he'd have to mull it over some more, maybe talk it over with Tomi. He needed an opinion of someone he could trust, and he'd kept his friend at arm's length on the topic for too long.

"Hey, Dax!" Becky's chipper voice always felt out of place, even though she'd fit in almost instantly with the crew and the customers. She just seemed too damned preppy for a punk and metal dive bar, though she had gotten into the spirit, mixing more black into her wardrobe.

He pushed himself off the backbar. "Hey, Becky. What you got there?"

"What do mean?"

He pointed to something shiny on her forearm.

"Oh! Got my new tattoo." She lifted her arm and showed him what looked the start of a sleeve. "Still got a few sessions to go to get the rest of the line work done and then the color. But finally got it!"

He nodded, giving her a closed-mouth smile. "Congratulations. I can't wait to see it when it's finished. You ready to go?"

"Yup, just let me throw my stuff in the office."

He nodded, grabbing a bottle of whiskey off the shelf, and poured another round for Geoffrey. Once Becky was behind the bar, he grabbed an unopened bottle off the shelf along with four of the dram glasses, and left the bar, heading up to the roof of the building that housed the restaurant and the bar. The late spring heat had cooled off, leaving the roof a perfect temperature.

He poured himself a glass of whiskey and kicked back, waiting for Tomi, Suzie, and Adele. The restaurant was closed for the night, and they should be up any time. He'd finished his first glass when the sound of laughing announced their presence.

Setting down his glass, he filled the other three and stood, handing them out as they sat. He remained standing and lifted his glass. "Adele, congratulations on your first full day!"

She reached over and patted her son's knee. "Thanks to you boys."

"It's the least I could do after all you and Tomi have done for me.

You looked out for me and provided me with a family when I had none. I know I'm not the most loquacious person, but I don't know where I'd be if I hadn't met you all those years ago. I guess what I'm trying to say is thank you."

Adele stood up and pulled him into a hug. "Family looks out for each other, honey."

Dax swallowed, the corner of his eyes burning. The simple familial gesture of a hug nearly overwhelming him. When he stepped back, he dashed the heel of his palm across his cheeks. "Thank you, Mama Adele, for making me part of the family."

Tomi held up his glass. "To family!"

Taking his seat, he brushed his glass against the other three, and they all drank.

Adele turned to her niece. "Suzie, you look out for Dax, and he'll look out for you. He's good people."

He had to laugh at the thought of being considered "good people." Most days, he barely thought of himself as a person. But he appreciated Adele's endorsement.

Suzie smiled brightly at her aunt. "Don't worry, Auntie Adele. I think I got Dax figured out. I'm glad to be part of the family."

After that, they listened to Adele reminisce about some of the restaurants she'd worked at in New Orleans, regaling them with stories of the kooky and wild line cooks she'd met over the years. After her second glass of whiskey, she bid them goodbye. Suzie followed her out to head down to the bar to keep Becky company.

"Man, you're going to have to pry me off this roof for my shifts." Tomi filled his glass again. "This is the life."

Dax smirked. "Until the sun starts beating down on you and there's no shade."

"Don't trouble me with realities." Tomi stretched out and stared up into the night sky. "Even a few stars out."

The view wasn't bad, not bad at all. He took a sip of whiskey and watched a shooting star streak across the sky. He'd seen the stars from space with no atmosphere to interfere, a million points of creation and destruction forming their universal symphony. Scenes so magnificent they'd melt an artist's brain.

But right now, there were no vengeful psychopomps or bikers. There were no worries about bills or tomorrow. Those were all problems for another day, probably a day very soon. But for the space of an evening, he'd found contentment in his situation and his world.

At the moment, on this rough roof top patio with a bottle of whiskey and his best friend… He wasn't sure he could top this. This moment of family and friendship and just being human.

The Red City Reaper will ride again in **Death With A Twist!**
Keep reading for a brief sample.

THE RED CITY REAPER RIDES AGAIN IN

DEATH WITH A TWIST

Dax pulled up to the roadhouse dive thirty minutes outside Red City. The wood of the building had been weathered by rain, snow, and time, making it look like a prairie derelict, except it was still fully standing, and the disrepair appeared more intentionally cosmetic than poor maintenance.

The parking lot was filled with pickups, cars of all varieties, and a fair few motorcycles gathered in small packs. Neon beer signs for domestic brands belched their light from shadow boxes spread about the covered porch that ran down the entire front of the place. A few smokers sat at the two top tables running down the length of the porch as a pretty server in a tight shirt and short shorts fuzzed about dropping beers and collecting more orders. Old-school "outlaw" country, dulled a bit by the walls, drifted into the night.

As he drove around the parking lot, he looked for anything suspicious, but it was hard to tell if anything was out of place since he'd never been out here to The Honky Tonk Woman. He'd always been curious about the bar named after the famous Rolling Stones song—though he didn't know if it was in fact named after it—but it was a long drive to drink cheap beer and listen to country music.

Pulling around the lot, he slid into a spot that pointed out to the road where he couldn't be blocked in from the front if he needed to make a quick exit. He normally didn't like to live his life planning to be…bushwhacked—as the denizens of a country bar might say—but with the bikers back in town potentially looking for trouble and the new meeting place, he let caution dictate his actions.

Taking one more look around his mirrors, he decided everything looked like a dive bar having a busy night.

Stepping out, he shut the door and shoved his hands into the pockets of his black leather jacket. With a glance back at his black 1965 Lincoln Continental, he decided he'd have to get it washed tomorrow to knock off the dust of the road and the parking lot.

As he approached the door, a thick, tall bouncer stood by set of double doors, his muscular arms folded menacingly over his bulging chest. With a shaved head and a scruffy medium length beard, a black T-shirt, and black leather vest, he looked the part. The mean mug he gave as people walked in served as punctuation.

Walking in like he belonged, Dax nodded politely to the door guy as he passed. When he pushed through the doors, the wall of sound nearly knocked him back out the door. They had the juke box cranked up tonight.

He stepped out of the way of the door and looked around until he saw the thatch of red hair and beard that belonged to Ragnar Gunnarsson. He sat in a booth in the left front corner of the bar. As he strode toward the booth, eyes swung his way, checking out the new guy.

"Ragnar," Dax said, stopping at the edge of the table.

Ragnar gestured to the open booth seat opposite him. "Dax."

As soon as his butt hit the vinyl of the booth's seat, a server in a tight T-shirt and short shorts sauntered up to the table. "What can I get for ya, hon?"

He caught the can of PBR sitting in front of Ragnar out of the corner of his eye. "I'll take a Pabst tallboy and one for my friend if he wants one."

Ragnar nodded, and the server smiled at him and departed.

"Thanks for the beer, Dax." Ragnar leaned back, stretching an arm down the back of the booth top. "And thank you for driving out here to meet me."

"It's a bit out of my range, but I was curious. After what happened at Delphine's, I figured I wouldn't see either you or your father, though I figured the same when last your father's path crossed mine."

"The bullet?"

Dax nodded. Ragnar seemed a man of few words, which might make this difficult since Dax was too. But instead of pressing, he decided on patience. Ragnar had made the effort to invite him out; he'd get to the point eventually. And if he invited Dax just to scope him out, it still would be worth it. In the present circumstances, a relationship with a man with knowledge of Nordic runes who'd be willing to share that information would be worth cultivating.

He'd hoped Ragnar's father would be that man, but he, like so many people in Red City, was afraid to get involved. Dax wasn't interested in getting involved either, but for different reasons.

Gunnar had a community to protect, which Dax assumed included Ragnar. He'd considered refusing the meeting to honor Gunnar's wishes to not involve him any deeper than he could control, but Ragnar was a grown man who could make his own decisions.

He looked around the bar, then fixed his gaze on Dax, lifting a coppery eyebrow. "So, what do you think of the Woman?"

"The Woman"? Oh, he must mean the bar. "I like it so far. Definitely gives classic roadhouse from the outside and doesn't disappoint when you walk in."

Ragnar quirked the corner of a lip up and nodded. Apparently, that was all he acknowledgment he was going to give Dax. When the server returned, he gave her a ten-dollar bill and put the change back in his wallet, save for two bucks for the tip. Pabst wasn't his favorite cheap beer, but he didn't know if they had Rainier here, and he didn't want to make a fuss over which cheap beer to order.

Taking his cue from Ragnar, he relaxed into the back of the booth with his can of beer, taking a sip. Some old Kris Kristofferson song blared over the radio. Dax had always enjoyed the bit of outlaw country he'd heard. He felt it was the flip side of the coin to punk. Both were antiauthoritarian and made by outsiders for outsiders. He didn't get much of a chance to listen to it since Tomi wasn't a fan, preferring hip-hop and rap when they weren't listening to punk or metal.

He caught himself bobbing his head along after a couple songs. The only thing that tipped him off was the appreciative smile on Ragnar's face.

"Didn't think you'd be into country-western. Dad said you owned a punk and metal bar." Though Ragnar didn't speak loudly, his smooth voice carried over the music just enough to land in Dax's ears.

"It's good." Dax smirked. "It's just punk with a steel slide guitar and slowed down a bit."

Ragnar narrowed his eyes and leaned forward, staring at Dax. At first he snorted, then shook his head as a chuckle bubbled into a laugh. "That's a good point." He lifted his can of PBR, tipping the top slightly toward Dax. "Fuck the man."

Dax raised his can. "Fuck the man."

Leaning forward, Ragnar adjusted his seat, resting his elbows on the table in front of him. "How much do you know about…the magic community in Red City?"

Tapping his forefinger on his can, he tried to order a list in his head. "Not much really. I've lived here for a few years, but until recently, I've minded my own business and kept to myself. I assumed there were some, but beyond myself, I didn't know of anyone else, nor did I go looking."

"Nor?" Ragnar smirked.

Giving half a shrug and eye roll, Dax continued, "But beyond Delphine and I guess your father and you, I only know The Rat and a few wolf shifters, besides the white supremacist bikers that is."

Nodding, Ragnar slid his fingers into his beard and scratched his jaw before smoothing it out. "I'll sketch some basics in for you. My grandparents immigrated from Norway before my father was born. They thought Redemption City sounded like a good place, mostly based the name."

He snorted derisively, shaking his head. "That was a mistake, but by the time they figured it out, they were here and too broke to move anywhere else. Having my father kind of cemented their fate. It wouldn't have been so bad if they could have found a community. Sure, they stayed in the neighborhoods where other Scandinavian immigrants tended to gather, but what they were looking for was a new wolf pack to join."

He paused and raised an eyebrow, and Dax gave him a slight nod to acknowledge that he understood the information he was being given. Apparently, he knew at least two more wolf shifters. He'd just assumed Ragnar and his father were rune mages of some sort.

Ragnar continued. "When he couldn't find one, even though there were other wolf shifters in town, he tried to form one, in spite of being warned not to by some of his new friends. Though he never could get a firm answer from them.

"However, he did get an answer when a group of men showed up at his door. They were Norse like my grandfather, but they informed him that only one pack was allowed to exist and only those of pure

Scandinavian heritage could join. They offered to let my grandfather and his family join under the condition he quit associating with shifters of other cultures."

Dax lowered his surprised eyebrows. "I'm guessing these fine gentlemen who accosted your grandfather were the same bikers I'm stuck dealing with now?"

Ragnar nodded but didn't continue his story. A moment later, the reason why sidled up to the table to see if they needed another round. Ragnar ordered them another round, putting it on his tab. He kept silent until after the server returned and dropped off their next round of tallboy cans.

"Back to your question. You are correct. One and the same. Anyway, my grandfather told them to go fuck themselves, though probably in a more polite tone. But he didn't quit. Behind the scenes, he tried to bring together the disparate wolf shifters of Red City. But every time he tried, the Norse gang would intimidate those who might throw in with my grandfather."

"Why didn't they get tougher with your grandfather?" Dax asked.

"I think they were still hoping to get him to join. People liked him and he'd gotten further than anyone else, so they thought he'd be a good asset. But the old man wasn't into that racist bullshit. Once they realized he wouldn't join, they did get more aggressive with him." Ragnar looked down, his shoulders tightening. "They eventually murdered him."

"Let me guess. The police couldn't find a suspect, and no one was arrested?"

Ragnar tapped his nose. "Yup. Even back then, the cops and bikers were in bed together. They make for cheap hired muscle when you need dirty work done that you don't want laid on your doorstep. I guess it's officially a cold case, like a lot of other murders the cops either did or sanctioned through one of their cronies."

Dax had assumed a link between the cops and the bikers, but having it confirmed, even if it was still opinion and conjecture, helped him solidify some fuzzy lines in the chart of suspects he had running in his head. "Is that why your father is into keeping a lower profile?"

"Yeah. Don't get me wrong. I love and respect my dad, but losing his father that way scarred him. He's a good leader and looks out for the unaffiliated wolf shifters of Red City, as quietly as he can. But without being able to form a real pack, he's limited to community organizing like any other activist. He's a smart man and keeps it on the down-low."

Dax narrowed his eyes. "But you don't exactly agree with his methods?"

"I'm sure our little argument spelled out some of the differences. But—"

A short brown man wearing a black cowboy hat with the sides folded up sharply and a rattlesnake head on the front of the band stopped by their table. "Ragnar, it's time for soundcheck. You ready? Or are you going to flap your gums all night?"

"Yeah. I'll be up shortly."

Seeing Dax, the man lifted his hat slightly and tipped his head down. "Sorry for interrupting."

"No problem," Dax replied.

"Well, I have to go onstage for a bit. I figured we'd be done talking before they called soundcheck." Ragnar slid out of the booth and strolled across the busy barroom floor toward the stage. On his way to centerstage, he picked up a guitar, plugging it in once he stood at the front of the stage behind the mic.

The Red City Reaper will ride again in **Death With A Twist**!

GLOSSARY

Adyeu - Goodbye
Bon chans - Good luck
Bonswa - Good afternoon/evening
Bourré - A popular card game played in the New Orleans region of Louisiana
Byenveni lakay, zanmi m - Welcome home, my friend
Cher - dear (a term of endearment)
Lwas - spirit, god, saints
Manbo - female voodoo priest
Manman - mother (a term of respect)
Misye Lanmò - Mr. Death
Mwen, oswa chat ou? - Me or your cat?

NEWSLETTER

The Centurion Immortal is a Luke Irontree prequel novella and is exclusive to the Dispatches from C. Thomas Lafollette newsletter. Please sign up for your free copy and you'll also receive a twice-monthly newsletter with news, book updates, recipes, drinks tips, and other fun stuff. Your email will never be given out, rented, or sold.

CThomasLafollette.com/newsletter/

ABOUT THE AUTHOR

C. Thomas Lafollette is a student of history and a world traveler. He's dined with a Prime Minister, read poetry with Yevgeny Yevtushenko, and drank beer with monks. He's the author of the action-adventure urban fantasy series Luke Irontree & The Last Vampire War and the forthcoming Red City Reaper series. Besides reading and writing, he loves a good action movie, be it a Hollywood blockbuster or a classic Samurai flick, as well as the occasional rom-com. He lives in Portland with his partner – the devastatingly talented author Amy Cissell – his stepdaughter, and their two jerk-face cats.

ALSO BY C. THOMAS LAFOLLETTE

Luke Irontree & The Last Vampire War

Book 0 - The Centurion Immortal

Book 1 - Dark Fangs Rising - March 22, 2022

Book 2 - Dark Fangs Raging - April 19, 2022

Book 3 - Dark Fangs Descending - May 17, 2022

Book 4 - Blood Empire Reborn - August 23, 2022

Book 5 - Blood Empire Avenged - September 20, 2022

Book 6 - Blood Empire Infiltrated - October 18, 2022

Book 7 - Blood Empire Burning - November 15, 2022

Book 8 - Ancient Sword Falling - March 21, 2023

Book 9 - Ancient Sword Unyielding - August 22, 2023

Book 10 - Ancient Sword Shattering - January 4, 2023

The Luke Irontree Historical Adventures

Rise of the Centurio Immortalis - April 5, 2022

Fall of the Centurio Immortalis - May 31, 2022

The Moonlight Centurion*

The Highway Centurion*

Red City Reaper - A Dark Urban Fantasy Adventure

Book 0 - Dead in Red City*

Book 1 - A Shot For Death - March 26, 2024

Book 1.5 - Death Uncaged - March 21, 2024

Book 2 - Death Orders a Double - July 23, 2024

Book 3 - Death With A Twist* - October 8, 2024

Book 4 - Death On The Rocks*

Book 5 - A Fifth Of Death*

Book 6 - A Dash Of Death*

Book 7 - A Chaser of Death*

Book 8 - A Nightcap of Death *

Red City Runesmith - A Wolf Shifter Urban Fantasy*

Titles To Be Determined

*Forthcoming

Titles and release dates may be subject to change.

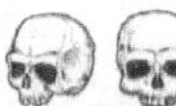